Miss Read, or in real life Dora Saint, was a teacher by profession who started writing after the Second World War, beginning with light essays written for *Punch* and other journals. She then wrote on educational and country matters and worked as a scriptwriter for the BBC. Miss Read was married to a schoolmaster for sixty-four years until his death in 2004, and they have one daughter.

In the 1998 New Year Honours list Miss Read was awarded an MBE for her services to literature. She is the author of many immensely popular books, including two autobiographical works, but it is for her novels of English rural life for which she is best known. The first of these, *Village School*, was published in 1955, and Miss Read continued to write about the fictitious villages of Fairacre and Thrush Green until her retirement in 1996. She lives in Berkshire.

By Miss Read

Village School

Village Diary

Miss Read

Illustrated by J.S. Goodall

Village School
First published in Great Britain
by Michael Joseph Ltd in 1955

Village Diary
First published in Great Britain
by Michael Joseph in 1957

This omnibus edition published in 2007
by Orion Books Ltd
Orion House, 5 Upper St Martin's Lane
London WC2H 9EA

A CIP catalogue record for this book is available
from the British Library.

ISBN 978-1-4072-1106-0

Printed in Great Britain by
Clays Ltd, St Ives plc

The Orion Publishing Group's policy is to use papers that
are natural, renewable and recyclable products and
made from wood grown in sustainable forests. The logging
and manufacturing processes are expected to conform to
the environmental regulations of the country of origin.

Village School

Miss Read

CONTENTS

* * *

PART THREE

Summer Term

PART ONE
Christmas Term

* * * *

1. EARLY MORNING

The first day of term has a flavour that is all its own; a whiff of lazy days behind and a foretaste of the busy future. The essential thing, for a village schoolmistress on such a day, is to get up early.

I told myself this on a fine September morning, ten minutes after switching off the alarm clock. The sun streamed into the bedroom, sparking little rainbows from the mirror's edge; and outside the rooks cawed noisily from the tops of the elm trees in the churchyard. From their high look-out the rooks had a view of the whole village of Fairacre clustered below them; the village which had been my home now for five years.

I had enjoyed those five years – the children, the little school, the pleasure of running my own school-house and of taking a part in village life. True, at first, I had had to walk as warily as Agag; many a slip of the tongue caused me, even now, to go hot and cold at the mere memory, but at last, I believed, I was accepted, if not as a proper native, at least as 'Miss Read up the School,' and not as 'that new woman pushing herself forward!'

I wondered if the rooks, whose clamour was increasing with the warmth of the sun, could see as far as Tyler's Row at the end of the village. Here lived Jimmy Waites and Joseph Coggs, two little boys who were to enter school today. Another new child was also coming, and this thought prodded me finally out of bed and down the narrow stairs.

I filled the kettle from the pump at the sink and switched it on. The new school year had begun.

Tyler's Row consists of four thatched cottages and very pretty they look. Visitors always exclaim when they see them, sighing ecstatically and saying how much they would like to live there. As

5

a realist I am always constrained to point out the disadvantages that lurk behind the honeysuckle.

The thatch is in a bad way, and though no rain has yet dripped through into the dark bedrooms below, it most certainly will before long. There is no doubt about a rat or two running along the ridge, as spry as you please, reconnoitring probably for a future home; and the starlings and sparrows find it a perfect resting-place.

'They ought to do something for us,' Mrs Waites told me, but as 'They,' meaning the landlord, is an old soldier living with his sister in the next village on a small pension and the three shillings he gets a week from each cottage (when he is lucky), it is hardly surprising that the roof is as it is.

There is no drainage of any sort and no damp-course. The brick floors sweat and clothes left hanging near a wall produce a splendid crop of prussian blue mildew in no time.

Washing-up water, soap-suds and so on are either emptied into a deep hole by the hedge or flung broadcast over the garden. The plants flourish on this treatment, particularly the rows of Madonna lilies which are the envy of the village. The night-cart, now a tanker-lorry, elects to call in the heat of the day, usually between twelve and one o'clock, once a week. The sewerage is carried through the only living-room and out into the road, for the edification of the school-children who are making their way home to dinner, most probably after a hygiene lesson on the importance of cleanliness.

In the second cottage Jimmy Waites was being washed. He stood on a chair by the shallow stone sink, submitting meekly to his mother's ministrations. She had twisted the corner of the face-flannel into a formidable radish and was turning it remorselessly round and round inside his left ear. He wore new corduroy trousers, dazzling braces and a woollen vest. Hanging on a line which was slung across the front of the mantelpiece, was a bright blue-and-red-checked shirt, American style. His mother intended that her Jimmy should do her credit on his first day at school.

She was a blonde, lively woman married to a farm-worker as fair as herself. 'I always had plenty of spirit,' she said once, 'Why, even during the war when I was alone I kept cheerful!' She did, too, from all accounts told by her more puritanical neighbours;

and certainly none of us is so silly as to ask questions about Cathy, the only dark child of the six, born during her husband's absence in 1944.

Cathy, while her brother was being scrubbed, was feeding the hens at the end of the garden. She threw out handfuls of mixed wheat and oats which she had helped to glean nearly a year ago. This was a treat for the chickens and they squawked and screeched as they fought for their breakfast.

Their noise brought one of the children who lived next door to a gap in the hedge that divided the gardens. Joseph was about five, of gipsy stock, with eyes as dark and pathetic as a monkey's. Cathy had promised to take him with her and Jimmy on this his first school morning. This was a great concession on the part of Mrs Waites as the raggle-taggle family next door was normally ignored.

'Don't you play with them dirty kids,' she warned her own children, 'or you'll get Nurse coming down the school to look at you special!' And this dark threat was enough.

But today Cathy looked at Joseph with a critical eye and spoke first.

'You ready?'

The child nodded in reply.

'You don't look like it,' responded his guardian roundly. 'You wants to wash the jam off of your mouth. Got a hanky?'

'No,' said Joe, bewildered.

'Well, you best get one. Bit of rag'll do, but Miss Read lets off awful if you forgets your hanky. Where's your mum?'

'Feeding baby.'

'Tell her about the rag,' ordered Cathy, 'and buck up. Me and Jim's nearly ready.' And swinging the empty tin dipper she skipped back into her house.

Meanwhile, the third new child was being prepared. Linda was eight years old, fat and phlegmatic, and the pride of her fond mother's heart. She was busy buttoning her new red shoes while her mother packed a piece of chocolate for her elevenses at playtime.

The Moffats had only lived in Fairacre for three weeks, but we had watched their bungalow being built for the last six months.

'Bathroom and everything!' I had been told, 'and one of those hatchers to put the dishes through to save your legs. Real lovely!'

The eagle eye of the village was upon the owners whenever they came over from Caxley, our nearest market-town, to see the progress of their house. Mrs Moffat had been seen measuring the windows for curtains and holding patterns of material against the distempered walls.

'Thinks herself someone, you know!' I was told later. 'Never so much as spoke to me in the road!'

'Perhaps she was shy.'

'Humph!'

'Or deaf, even.'

'None so deaf as those that won't hear,' was the tart rejoinder. Mrs Moffat, alas! was already suspected of that heinous village crime known as 'putting on side.'

One evening, during the holidays, she had brought the child to see me. I was gardening and they both looked askance at my bare legs and dirty hands. It was obvious that she tended to cosset her rather smug daughter and that appearances meant a lot to her, but I liked her and guessed that the child was intelligent and would work well. That her finery would also excite adverse comment among the other children I also surmised. Mrs Moffat's aloofness was really only part of her town upbringing, and once she realized the necessity for exchanging greetings with every living soul in the village, no matter how pressing or distracting one's own business, she would soon be accepted by the other women.

Linda would come into my class. She would be in the youngest group, among those just sent up from the infants' room where they had spent three years under Miss Clare's benign rule. Joseph and Jimmy would naturally go straight into her charge.

At twenty to nine I hung up the tea towel, closed the back door of the school-house and stepped across the playground to the school.

Above me the rooks still chattered. Far below they could see, converging upon the school lane, little knots of children from all quarters of the village. Cathy had Jimmy firmly by the hand: Joseph's grimy paw she disdained to hold, and he trailed behind her, his dark eyes apprehensive.

Linda Moffat, immaculate in starched pink gingham, walked primly beside her mother; while behind and before, running, dawdling, shouting or whistling, ran her future school fellows.

Through the sunny air another sound challenged the rooks' chorus. The school bell began to ring out its morning greeting.

2. OUR SCHOOL

The school at Fairacre was built in 1880, and as it is a church school it is strongly ecclesiastical in appearance. The walls are made of local stone, a warm grey in colour, reflecting summer light with honeyed mellowness, but appearing dull and dejected when the weather is wet. The roof is high and steeply-pitched and the stubby bell-tower thrusts its little Gothic nose skywards, emulating the soaring spire of St Patrick's, the parish church, which stands next door.

The windows are high and narrow, with pointed tops. Children were not encouraged, in those days, to spend their working time in gazing out at the world, and, sitting stiffly in the well of the room, wearing sailor suits or stout zephyr and serge frocks, their only view was of the sky, the elm trees and St Patrick's spire. Today their grandchildren and great-grandchildren have exactly the same view; just this lofty glimpse of surrounding loveliness.

The building consists of two rooms divided by a partition of glass and wood. One room houses the infants, aged five, six and seven years of age, under Miss Clare's benevolent eye. The other room is my classroom where the older children of junior age stay until they are eleven when they pass on to a secondary school, either at Caxley, six miles away, or in the neighbouring village of Beech Green, where the children stay until they are fifteen.

A long lobby runs behind these two rooms, the length of the building; it is furnished with pegs for coats, a low stone sink for the children to wash in, and a high new one for washing-up the dinner things. An electric copper is a recent acquisition, and very handsome it is; but although we have electricity installed here there is no water laid on to the school.

This is, of course, an appalling problem, for there is no water to drink – and children get horribly thirsty – no water for washing hands, faces, cleansing cuts and grazes, for painting, for mixing paste or watering plants or filling flower vases; and, of course, no water for lavatories.

We overcome this problem in two ways. A large galvanized iron tank on wheels is filled with rainwater collected from the roof, and this, when we have skimmed off the leaves and twigs and rescued the occasional frog, serves most of our needs. The electric copper is filled in the morning from this source and switched on after morning playtime to be ready for washing not only the crockery and cutlery after dinner but also the stone floor of the lobby.

I bring two buckets of drinking water across the playground from the school-house where there is an excellent well, but we must do our own heating, so that a venerable black kettle stands on my stove throughout the winter months, purring in a pleasantly domestic fashion, ready for emergencies. The electric kettle, in my own kitchen, serves us at other times.

The building is solid structurally and kept in repair by the church authorities whose property it is. One defect, however, it seems impossible to overcome. A skylight, strategically placed over the headmistress's desk, lets in not only light, but rain. Generations of local builders have clambered over the roof and sworn and sawn and patched and pulled at our skylight – but in vain. The gods have willed otherwise, and year after year Pluvius drops his pennies into a bucket placed below for the purpose, the clanging muffled by a dishcloth folded to fit the bottom.

The school stands at right angles to the road and faces across the churchyard to the church. A low dry-stone wall runs along by the road dividing it from the churchyard, school playground and the school-house garden. Behind this the country slopes away, falling slightly at first, then rising, in swelling folds, up into the full majesty of the downs which sweep across these southern counties for mile upon mile. The air is always bracing, and in the winter the wind is a bitter foe, and that quality of pure light, which is peculiar to downland country, is here very noticeable.

The children are hardy and though, quite naturally, they take their surroundings for granted, I think that they are aware of the fine views around them. The girls particularly are fond of flowers, birds, insects and all the minutiae of natural life, guarding jealously any rare plant against outsiders' prying eyes, and having a real knowledge of the whereabouts and uses of many plants and herbs.

The boys like to dismiss such things as 'girls' stuff,' but they too can find the first mushrooms, sloes or blackberries for their mothers or for me; and most of the birds' nests are known as soon as they are built. Luckily, stealing eggs and rifling nests seem to be on the wane, though occasional culprits are brought to stern judgment at my desk. They suffer, I think, more from the tongues of the girls in the playground in matters like this, for there is no doubt about it that the girls are more sympathetic to living things and pour scorn and contumely on any young male tyrants.

In one corner of the small, square playground is the inevitable pile of coke for the two slow combustion stoves. These coke piles seem to be a natural feature of all country schools. This is considered by the children, a valuable adjunct to playtime activities. A favourite game is to run scrunchily up the pile and then to slither down in gritty exhilaration. Throwing it at each other, or at a noisy object such as the rainwater tank, is also much enjoyed, hands being wiped perfunctorily down the fronts of jackets or on the seats of trousers before the beginning of writing lessons. All these joys are strictly forbidden, of course, which adds to the fearful delight.

Furthest from the wall by the road at the other side of the playground grows a clump of elm trees, and their gnarled roots, which add to the hazards of the playground's surface, are a favourite place to play.

The recesses are rooms, larders, cupboards or gardens, and the ivy leaves from the wall are used for plates and provisions, and twigs for knives and forks. Sometimes they play shops among the roots, paying each other leaves and bearing away conkers, acorns and handfuls of gravel as their purchases. I like to hear the change in their voices as they become shopkeepers or customers. They affect a high dictatorial tone of voice when they assume adult status, quite unlike the warm burr of their everyday conversations.

The fields lie two or three feet below the level of the playground and a scrubby hedge of hazel and hawthorn marks this boundary. The sloping bank down is scored by dozens of little bare paths, worn by generations of sturdy boots and corduroy breeches.

Altogether our playground is a good one – full of possibilities for resourceful children and big enough to allow shopkeepers, mothers and fathers, cowboys and spacemen to carry on their urgent affairs very happily together.

On this first morning of term Miss Clare had already arrived when I walked over at a quarter to nine. Her bicycle, as upright and as ancient as its owner, was propped just inside the lobby door.

The school had that indefinable first-morning smell compounded of yellow soap, scrubbed floorboards and black-lead. The tortoise stove gleamed like an ebony monster; even the vent-pipe which soared aloft towards the pitch-pine roof was blackened as far as Mrs Pringle, the school cleaner, could reach. Clean newspaper covered the freshly-hearthstoned surroundings of the stove – which officially remained unlit until October – and the guard, just as glossy, was neatly placed round the edges of the outspread *News of the World*.

My desk had that bare tidy look that it only wears for an hour
or so on this particular morning of term; and the inkstand, an
imposing affair of mahogany and brass, shone in splendour. I
wondered as I walked through to Miss Clare's room just how
quickly its shelf would remain unencumbered by the chalk,
beads, raincoat buttons, paper clips, raffia needles and drawing
pins that were its normal burden.

Miss Clare was taking a coat-hanger out of her big canvas
hold-all. She is very careful of her clothes, and is grieved to see the
casual way in which the children sling their coats, haphazard, on
to the pegs in the lobby. Her own coat is always smoothed
methodically over its hanger and hung on the back of the classroom door. The children watch, fascinated, when she removes
her gloves, for she blows into them several times before folding
them neatly together. Her sensible felt hat has a shelf to itself
inside the needlework cupboard.

Miss Clare has taught here for nearly forty years, with only one
break, when she nursed her mother through her last illness twelve
years ago. She started here as a monitress at the age of thirteen,
and was known officially, until recently, as 'A Supplementary
Uncertificated Teacher.' Her knowledge of local family history is
far-reaching and of inestimable value to the teaching of our
present pupils. I like to hear the older people talk of her.
'Always a stickler for tidiness,' the butcher told me,
'the only time I was smacked in the babies' class was
when Miss Clare found me kicking another boy's cap
round the floor.'

Miss Clare is of commanding appearance, tall
and thin, with beautiful white hair, which is kept
in place with an invisible hair-net. Even on the
wildest day, when the wind shrieks across the
downs, Miss Clare walks round the playground looking immaculate. She is now
over sixty, and her teaching methods have of
late been looked upon by some visiting
inspectors with a slightly pitying eye. They
are, they say, too formal; the children should
have more activity, and the classroom is unnaturally quiet for children of that age. This may be,

but for all that, or perhaps because of that, Miss Clare is a very valuable teacher, for in the first place the children are happy, they are fond of Miss Clare, and she creates for them an atmosphere of serenity and quiet which means that they can work well and cheerfully, really laying the foundations of elementary knowledge on which I can build so much more quickly when they come up into my class.

Her home is two miles away, on the outskirts of the next village of Beech Green. She has lived there ever since she was six, a solemn little girl in high-buttoned boots and ringlets, in the cottage which her father thatched himself. He was a thatcher by trade, and many of the cottages in the surrounding villages are decorated with the ornate criss-crossing and plaiting which he loved to do. He was much in demand at harvest time for thatching ricks, and Miss Clare often makes 'rick-dollies' of straw for the children like the ones her father used to put on top of the newly-thatched stacks.

In the corner of the room John Burton was pulling lustily at the bell-rope. He stopped as I came in.

'Five minutes' rest,' I said, 'then another pull or two to tell the others that it's time to get into lines in the playground.'

Miss Clare and I exchanged holiday news while she unlocked her desk and took out her new register, carefully shrouded in fresh brown paper. She had covered mine for me too, at the end of last term, and written in the names of our new classes in her sloping copper-plate hand.

We should have forty children altogether this term; eighteen in the infants' room and twenty-two in mine; and though our numbers might seem small, compared with the monstrous regiments of forty and fifty to a class in town schools, the age range, of course, would be a considerable handicap.

I should have five children in my lowest group who would be nearly eight years old and these would still have difficulty in reading fluently and with complete understanding. At the other end of the classroom would be my top group, consisting of three children, including Cathy Waites, who would be taking the examination which would decide their future schooling at eleven. These children would need particular care in being shown how to tackle arithmetical problems, how to understand written questions and, more important still, how to set out their answers and express themselves generally, in clear and straightforward language.

Miss Clare's youngest group would consist of the two new little boys, Jimmy Waites and Joseph Coggs, as well as the twins, Diana and Helen, who had entered late last term owing to measles and had learnt very little. Miss Clare was of the opinion, knowing something of their family history, that they might well be in her bottom group for years.

'What can you expect,' she said, looking at the hieroglyphics that passed for writing on their blackboards, 'their grandfather never stuck at one job for more than a week and the boy took after him. Added to that he married a girl with as much sense as himself, and these two are the result.'

'I'll get the doctor to look at them specially, when she comes,' I comforted her, 'I think if they had their adenoids removed they might be much brighter.'

Miss Clare's snort showed what good she thought this would do two of the biggest duffers who had ever come into her hands.

Her aim with the top group in her class will be, first, to see that they can read, and also write legibly, know their multiplication tables up to six times at least, and be able to do the four rules of addition, subtraction, multiplication and division, working with tens and units and shillings and pence. They should also have a working knowledge of the simple forms of money, weight and length, and be able to tell the time.

John, who had had his gaze fixed on the ancient wall-clock, now gave six gigantic tugs on the rope, for it said five minutes to nine, and then, leaping up on to the corner desk, looped it up, out of temptation's way, on to a hook high on the wall.

Outside, we could hear the scuffle of feet and cries of excited children. Together Miss Clare and I walked out into the sunshine to meet our classes.

3. The Pattern of the Morning

My desk was being besieged by children, all eager to tell me of their holiday adventures.

'Miss, us went to Southsea with the Mothers' Union last week, and I've brought you back a stick of rock,' announced Anne.

Eric flapped a long rubbery piece of seaweed like a flail.

'It's for us to tell the weather by,' he explained earnestly. 'You hangs it up – out the lobby'l' do – and if it's wet it's going to rain – or is it if it's been wet it feels wet? I forgets just which, miss, but anyhow if it's dry it ain't going to rain.'

'Isn't,' I corrected automatically, rummaging in the top drawer of the desk for the dinner book.

'I know where there's mushrooms, miss. I'll bring you some for your tea s'afternoon.'

'They's not mushrooms, miss,' warned Eric. 'They's toadstools – honest, miss! Don't you eat 'em, miss! They's poison!'

I waved them away to their desks. Only the new children stood self-consciously in the front, looking at their shoes or at me for support. Linda Moffat's immaculate pink frock and glossy curls were getting a close scrutiny from the other children, but, unperturbed, she returned their round-eyed stares.

The children sit two in a desk and Anne, a cheerful nine-year-old, seemed Linda's best desk-mate.

'Look after Linda, Anne,' I said, 'she doesn't know anyone yet.'

Holding her diminutive red handbag, Linda settled down beside Anne. They gave each other covert looks under their lashes, and when their glances met exchanged smiles.

The four young ones, just up from Miss Clare's class, settled in two desks at the front. Once sitting in safety their shyness vanished, and they looked cheerfully about, grinning at their friends. They were at that engaging stage of losing their front milk teeth, and their gappy smiles emphasized their tender years. I went over to the piano.

'As we haven't given out the hymn books yet, we'll sing one we know by heart.'

They scrambled to their feet, desk seats clanging up behind

them, and piped 'The King of Love my Shepherd is,' rather sharp with excitement.

Our piano is made of walnut, and is full of years. The front has an intricate fretwork design and through the openings pleated red silk can be seen. The children look upon its venerable beauties with awed admiration. It has a melancholy, plangent tone, and two yellow keys which are obstinately dumb. These keys give a curiously syncopated air to the morning hymns.

Usually the whole school comes into this one classroom for prayers, but on the first morning of term it always seems best to stay in our own rooms and settle in quickly.

After the hymn we had a short prayer. With eyes screwed up tightly and hands solemnly folded beneath their chins the children looked misleadingly angelic. Patrick, the smallest, with head bowed low, was busily sucking his thumb, and I made a mental note that here was a habit to be corrected or otherwise his new second teeth would soon be in need of a brace. As I watched, a shilling fell from his clasped hands and rolled noisily towards me. Patrick opened one eye. It swivelled round like a solitary marble, following the shilling's journey, then, catching my own eye upon it, it shut again with a snap.

After prayers we usually have a scripture lesson, or learn a new hymn or a psalm, until half-past nine, when arithmetic lesson begins; but on this morning we settled to more practical matters and the children came out in turn with their dinner money for the week. This was ninepence a day. Some children had also brought National Savings money, and this was entered in a separate book and stamps handed over to the child, if it possessed a safe place to put them, or put in a special Oxo tin until home time.

All but four children, who went home for their dinners, brought out their dinner money, and as they put it on my desk I looked at their hands. Sometimes they arrive at school so filthy, either through playing with mud on the way, or through sheer neglect in washing, that they are not fit to handle their books, and then out they are sent to the stone sink in the lobby, to wash in rainwater and carbolic soap. In this way too I can keep a watch on the nail-biters, and those culprits who, after a week's self-control, can show a proud sixteenth of an inch, are rewarded with sweets and flattery. Scabies, too, which first shows itself

17

between the fingers, is a thing to watch for, though, happily, it is rare here; but it spreads quickly and is very aggravating to the sufferer.

While I was busy with all this, Miss Clare came through the partition door.

'May I speak to Cathy?' she asked. 'It's about Joseph's dinner money. Does his mother want him to stay?'

'Yes, miss,' said Cathy, looking rather startled, 'but she never gave me no money for him.'

'Didn't give me any money,' said Miss Clare automatically.

'"Didn't-give-me-any-money," I mean,' repeated Cathy, parrot-wise.

'I'll write a note for you to take to Mrs Coggs when you go home,' said Miss Clare, and lowering her voice to a discreet whisper, turned to me. 'May be difficult to get the money regularly from that family – a feckless woman!' And shaking her white head she returned to the infants.

The children were now beginning to get restless, for, normally, when I was busy they would take out a library book, or a notebook of their own making, which we called a 'busy book,' in which they could employ themselves in writing lists of birds, flowers, makes of cars, or any other things which interested them. They could, if they liked, copy down the multiplication tables, or the weekly poem or spelling list which hung upon the wall; but, at the moment, their desks were empty.

'Let me see who would like to come out and play "Left and Right,"' I said.

Peace reigned at once. Chests were flung out and faces assumed a fierce air of responsibility and trustworthiness.

'Patrick!' I called, choosing the smallest new boy, and he flushed a deep pink with pleasure.

'Left and Right' is the simplest and most absorbing game for occasions when a teacher is busy with something else. All that is needed is a small object to hide in one hand, a morsel of chalk, a bead or a halfpenny, any one, in fact, of the small things that litter the inkstand. The child in front, hands behind him, changes the treasure from one to the other; then, fists extended before him, he challenges someone to guess which hand it is in. Here the teacher, with half an eye on the game, one and a half on the business in hand, and her main object peace in which to carry it out, can say, 'Choose someone really quiet, dear. No fussy people; and, of course, no one who asks!' This deals a severe blow to the naughty little boys who are whispering 'Me! Choose me! Or else—!'

'Richard!' called Patrick to his desk-mate.

'Left!'

'No, right!' said Patrick, opening a sticky palm.

'That's left! Miss, that was left!' went up the protesting cry.

Patrick turned round to me indignantly.

'But you're facing the other way now!' I point out, and the age-long problem, which puzzles all children, had to be explained yet again.

At last the game continued its even tenor. Dinner money and savings money were both collected, checked and put in their separate tins. The register was called for the first time, and a neat red stroke in every square showed that we were all present.

The clock on the wall said twenty-past ten when we had finished handing out a pink exercise book each for English, a blue for arithmetic and a green for history and geography. Readers, pens, pencils, rulers and all the other paraphernalia of daily school life were now stored safely, and at the moment tidily, in their owner's possession.

The children collected milk and straws and settled down to refreshment. Luckily this term there were no milk-haters and all twenty-two bottles were soon emptied. When they had finished they went joyfully out to play.

I went across to my own quiet house and switched on the kettle. Two cups and saucers were already set on the tray in the kitchen, and the biscuit tin stood on the dresser. Miss Clare would be over in a minute. We took it in turns to do playground duty, guarding the coke pile from marauders, watching out for any sly teasing, and routing out the indoor-lovers who would prefer to sit in their desks even on the loveliest day. I went back to the playground while the kettle boiled.

Linda was undoing her packet of chocolate and Anne was trying to look unconcerned. Anne was always rather hungry, the child of a mother who went by early morning bus to the atomic research works some miles away, and who had little time to leave such niceties as elevenses for her daughter. There was no shortage of money in this home, but definitely a shortage of supervision. Anne's shoes were good, but dirty; her dinner money was often forgotten, and her socks frequently sported a hole. Her suspense now was shortlived, for Linda broke off a generous piece of her slab, handed it over, and cemented the friendship which had already begun.

'D'you mind being new?' asked Anne squelchily.

'Not now,' answered Linda, 'once all that staring's stopped, I don't mind; and if anyone tries hitting me my mum said I was to tell her.' She eyed the noisy children around her complacently. 'Not that they will, probably – and anyway,' she added, dropping her voice to a sinister whisper, 'I bites horrible!' Anne looked properly impressed.

Cathy, between bites of apple, was encouraging Joseph Coggs and her young brother to visit the boys' lavatory behind its green corrugated iron screen. At the other end of the playground, similarly screened, were two more bucket-type lavatories with well-scrubbed wooden seats, for the girls' use.

Mr Willet is our caretaker, and has the unenviable job of emptying the buckets three times a week; and this he does into deep holes which are dug on a piece of waste ground, some hundred yards away, behind his own cottage. Mrs Pringle, the school cleaner, scrubs seats and floors, and everything is kept as spotless as is possible with this deplorable and primitive type of sanitation.

Above the shouting of the children came the sound of the school gate clanging shut, and across the playground, his black suit glossy in the sunlight, came the vicar. Miss Clare hurried in to fetch another cup and saucer from the dresser and I went to meet him.

The Reverend Gerald Partridge has been vicar of Fairacre, and its adjoining parish of Beech Green, for only four years, and so is looked upon as a foreigner by most of his parishioners. His energetic wife is as brisk and practical as he is gentle and vague. He is chairman of the managers of Fairacre school and comes in every Friday morning to take a scripture lesson with the older children.

On this morning, he carried a list of hymns, which he asked me to teach the children during the term, and I said I would look through them. He sighed at my guarded answer, for he knew as well as I did that not all the hymns would be considered suitable by me for teaching to children. His weakness for the metaphysical poets led him into choosing quite inexplicable hymns about showers and brides, with lines like:

'Rend each man's temple-veil and bid it fall.'

or, worse still, Milton's poems set as hymns, containing such lines as:

'And speckled vanity
Will sicken soon and die,
And leprous sin will melt from earthly mould,'

all of which may be very fine in its way but is quite beyond the comprehension of the pupils here. The vicar smiles and nods his mild old head when I protest.

'Very well, my dear, very well. Just as you think best. Let us leave that hymn until they are older.' And then he meanders away to talk to the children, leaving me feeling a bully and browbeater.

He drank his tea and then started up his car, setting off, very slowly and carefully, down the road to his vicarage.

4. THE PATTERN OF THE AFTERNOON

One of the most difficult things to teach young children is to express themselves in sentences. When you listen to them talking you realize why. There is hardly a complete sentence in the whole conversation.

'Coming up shop?' says one.
'Can't! Mum's bad.'

'What's up with her?'

'Dunno.'

'Doctor come?'

'Us rung up. May come, s'pose,' and so on. There is a sure exchange of thought and some progress in this staccato method, but it does not make for any literary style when it comes to writing a composition.

The children in these parts are not, as a whole, great readers. A neighbouring schoolmaster, Mr Annett, put it succinctly: 'Most parents take the viewpoint of "What the devil are you doing wasting your time with a trashy book, when the carrots want thinning!" Or the beans want picking, or the wood wants chopping, or the snow wants sweeping – any of the urgent outdoor matters which beset a country child more than the town one. So out they are sent, with a clump on the ear to help them, and it almost seems wrong to some of them to read.'

Because of this attitude, and the children's own very understandable desire to help in outside activities in an agricultural area, they do not get accustomed to seeing or hearing thought expressed in plain English. A great number of them have great difficulty in spelling, other than phonetically, for they are not readers by habit and not familiar with the look of words. However, phonetically, they make the most gallant efforts, one of the nicest I ever received being the information that 'Donkeys like ssos' (thistles).

So, after play, we settled down to writing together on the blackboard a composite account of the holidays.

'John, tell me something that you did.'

'Went to the seaside, miss.'

'How?'

'Bus.'

'By yourself?'

'No. Lot of us kids went. Us went with the Mothers' Union, miss.'

'Right. Now put all that into sentences that I can write on the blackboard.'

There was a horrified silence. It was one thing to answer leading questions, but quite another thing to put them into even the simplest English.

'Well, come along. You can start by saying, "During the holidays I went to the seaside." '

John repeated this with some relief, hoping that left to my own devices I would do the whole composition for him. The first sentence was put up.

'What shall we put next?'

'I went in a bus,' said Anne.

I put it up.

'Now what?'

'I went with the Mothers' Union.'

'I went with some others.'

'I went on a Saturday.'

'I went with my sister.'

I pointed out that although these were all good sentences in themselves, it became a little monotonous to start every one with 'I went.' It was while we were wrestling with different wordings of the sentences that footsteps and clankings were heard. Sylvia rushed to the door and revealed Mrs Crossley, or, as the children call her, 'The Dinner Lady.'

She was balancing three tin boxes in an unsteady pile against her cardigan, and willing hands relieved her of them.

'Only two canisters today,' she said, and the children sat rigidly, hoping to be the lucky person chosen to fetch them from the mobile dinner-van at the school gate. Anne and Linda were chosen for this envied task and while they were gone, I signed the daily chit for Mrs Crossley, to say that I had received the number of dinners ordered. Then I gave her the slip showing how many dinners I estimated that I should need for the next day.

Mrs Crossley drives the dinner-van, loaded up about ten in the morning at the depot, and delivers dinners at about a dozen schools on her round of about twenty miles. Each school has a plate-heating oven which is switched on just before the dinners are due, and the tins are put in to keep warm with the plates. The big canisters are heat-retaining and very heavy to handle. Stews, hot potatoes and other vegetables, custard or sauces, are delivered in these and the meals are usually very good indeed. In the summer, salads are frequent, and the children eat most things heartily except fish. This, even when fried, is not relished, and recently it has been struck off the menu as there was so much wasted.

Cathy was sent through to the infants' room to see if the tables were ready. Miss Clare's class had gone out for the last period of the morning to have their physical training lesson, leaving the classroom empty for the arrangement of three trestle-tables for the dinner children. Miss Clare had switched on the oven, which was in her room, and Cathy laid the tables for thirty. Those who went home to dinner were sent off; the others washed their hands and then we all took our places at the tables. It was ten past twelve and we were all hoping for something good in the tins.

Miss Clare and I served out slices of cold meat, mashed potatoes and salad, and Sylvia and Cathy and Anne carried them round. Miss Clare sat at the head of one table and I at another, and when we had finished the first course two big boys, John and Ernest, cleared away. It was followed by plums and custard. Jimmy Waites was still rather awed by his new surroundings and ate very little, but Joseph Coggs, who, I suspected, very seldom had a dinner as well-prepared as this, ate a prodigious amount, coming up for a third helping of plums and custard with the older children.

When we had stacked the dirty crockery and cutlery ready for Mrs Pringle, and cleared the tables of their checked mackintosh tablecloths, the children went out to play and Miss Clare and I went over to the school-house to wash ourselves and tidy up ready for afternoon school.

Mrs Pringle was surrounded by clouds of steam when I returned to the lobby.

'Did you have a good holiday?' I asked her.

'Not much of a holiday for me, scrubbing this whole place out!' was the rejoinder.

'Well, it all looks very nice, anyway.'

'How long for?' said Mrs Pringle acidly. She is one of the happy martyrs of this world, hugging her grudges to her and relishing every insult as a toothsome morsel. Why she carries on the job of school caretaker I can't think, unless its very nature, that of work quickly undone, appeals to her warped spirit. Children she looks upon as conspirators against cleanliness and order; and the idea of any sort of mess of their making being accidental, or, worse still, legitimate, is unbelievable to her.

Her great loves are the two slow-burning tortoise stoves. These two ugly monsters she polishes till they gleam like jet, and it gives her real pain to see them lit, with the ashes dropping untidily round them. The coke cauldrons are a torture to her, for these make more mess, and during the winter months relations are more than usually strained between us.

There is almost a battle when it comes to starting up the stoves at the approach of the cold weather. I refuse to have the children sitting in a cold schoolroom, incapable of work and the prey of any germs at large, when the stoves are there and mountains of coke stand between us and misery.

Mrs Pringle's methods are subtle when I have given firm orders for the stove to be lit. For a day or two she stalls with 'Ran out of matches,' or 'Mr Willet did say he'd bring up the kindling wood, but he ain't done it yet,' but finding that I have lit the fire myself she gives in and continues, most reluctantly, to renew it each day. This does not mean to say that the matter is closed. Far from it; for should she have occasion to enter the room she will fan herself ostentatiously with her hand – often mauve with the cold – and say, 'Phew! How can you stick this heat, I don't know! Makes me come over real faint meself!' Sometimes the attack is on a broader front and the ratepayers are brought in as support.

'Coke's going down pretty smartish. Shouldn't be surprised if we don't get a letter from the Office the way we gets through it. Stands to reason the Office has to keep upsides the ratepayers!'

'The Office' is, of course, the local education office and the only real link between it and Mrs Pringle is the cheque which arrives from it for her services at the end of every month. Mrs Pringle, consequently, looks upon 'The Office' in rather the same way as she looks upon the Almighty, invisible and omnipotent.

This afternoon I beat a retreat into my classroom, but was closely pursued by Mrs Pringle, dripping from the elbows.

'What's more,' she said malevolently, 'we're a spoon short. You been mixing up paste again?'

'No,' I said shortly, 'you'd better count them again.' This is an old feud, dating from five years ago when I once committed the unforgivable crime of borrowing a school spoon because I had mislaid the usual wooden one. Mrs Pringle has never allowed me to forget this deplorable lapse.

At a quarter past one the children came back into their desks, breathless and cheerful, and after we had marked the register we tackled our joint composition again. After a while afternoon somnolence began to descend upon them, and when I thought they had studied the example of fair English, which they had been driven into producing, long enough, I went to the piano and we sang some of the songs which they had learnt the term before.

After play large sheets of paper were given out and the boxes of wax crayons; and the children were asked to illustrate either their day at the seaside or any other particular day that they had enjoyed during the past few weeks.

Industriously they set to work, blue crayons were scrabbled furiously along the bottom of the papers for the sea and yellow suns like daisies flowered on all sides. The room was quiet and happy, the afternoon sun beat in through the Gothic windows and the clock on the wall stepped out its measured tread to home-time at half-past three. As most of the children stay to dinner, and those that do go home live so very near, it seems wiser to have a short break at midday, start afternoon school early and finish early. In the summer this means that the children get a long spell of sunshine outdoors, and in the winter they can be safely home before it becomes dark.

We collected up our pictures and crayons and tidied up the room. The first day at school is always a long one, and the children looked sleepy.

The infants, who had been let out earlier, could be heard calling to each other as they ran up the road.

We stood and sang grace, wished each other 'Good afternoon' and made our way into the lobby. Jimmy and Joseph were standing there, anxiously waiting for Cathy.

'Did you enjoy school?' I asked them. Jimmy nodded.

'What about you, Joseph?'

'I liked the dinner,' he answered diplomatically in his husky gipsy voice. I left it at that.

Miss Clare was wheeling her bicycle across the playground. It struck me suddenly that she was looking old and tired.

She mounted carefully and rode slowly away down the road, upright and steady, but it seemed to me, as I stood watching her progress, that it needed more effort than usual; and this was only the first day of term.

How long, I wondered, would she be able to continue?

I had my tea in the warm sunshine of the garden at the back of my school-house. The schoolmaster who had lived here before me was a great gardener, and had planted currant bushes, black and red, raspberries and gooseberries. These were safely enmeshed in a wire run to keep the birds off, and I bottled the crops or made jelly and jam in the evenings or in the holidays.

I had planted two herbaceous borders, one on each side of the garden, both edged with Mrs Sinkins' pinks which liked the chalky soil. Vegetables I did not bother to plant, not only because of the lack of room, but also because kind neighbours gave me more than I could really cope with, week after week. Broad beans, shallots, peas, carrots, turnips, brussels sprouts, cabbage, they all came in generous supplies to my doorstep. Sometimes the donors were almost too generous, forgetting, I suppose, how relatively little one woman can eat. I have found before now no less than five rotund vegetable marrows, like abandoned babies, on my doorstep in one week.

The difficulty is in handing these over to someone who might like them, without offending the giver. In a village this is doubly difficult as almost all are related, or close neighbours, or know exactly what is going on in the cottages nearby. I have been driven to digging dark, secret holes, under cover of night, and shovelling in many an armful of lettuce or several mammoth parsnips that have beaten my appetite.

I made some jam in the evening with a basket of early black plums which John Pringle, Mrs Pringle's only son, and a near neighbour of mine, had brought me.

The kitchen was very pleasant as I stirred. The window over the stone sink looks out on to the garden. A massive lead pump with a long handle stands by the side of the sink, and it is from this that I fill the buckets for the school's drinking water. When the water supply is laid on through the village, which may be in a few years' time, I have been promised a new deep sink by the managers.

In one corner stands a large brick copper and my predecessors used this to heat water for their baths, lighting a fire each time, but I have an electric copper which saves much time and trouble. The bath is a long zinc one, which hangs in the porch outside the back door, and it is put on the kitchen floor at bath time and filled from the tap at the bottom of the copper and cooled with buckets from the pump. With a bath towel warming over the hot copper and the kitchen well steamed up it is very snug.

The rest of the house downstairs consists of a large dining-room with a brick fireplace, a small hall and a small sitting-room. I rarely use this room as it faces north, but live mainly in the dining-room which is warmer, has a bigger fireplace and is convenient for the kitchen.

Upstairs there are two bedrooms, both fairly large, one over the kitchen and sitting-room, and the other, in which I sleep, directly above the dining-room. Throughout the house the walls are distempered a dove grey and all the paintwork is white. It is a solidly-built house of red brick, with a red-tiled roof, and in its setting of trees it looks most attractive. I am very fond of it indeed, and luckier, I realize, than many country headmistresses.

5. First Impressions

In their adjoining cottages at Tyler's Row the two new pupils at Fairacre School were safely in bed, but not yet asleep.

Jimmy Waites lay on his lumpy flock mattress in a big brass bedstead which had once been his grandmother's. It had been the pride of her heart, and she had slept in it as a bride and until her death. The brass knobs at each corner, and the little ones across the head and the foot of the bed, had been polished so often that they were loose. His grandmother had told Jimmy that when she was a young woman she had tied a fresh blue bow at each bed-post, and the sides had been decently draped in white starched valances reaching to the floor. The edges of these she had crimped with a goffering iron. With a patchwork quilt on top, the bed must have been a thing of great beauty.

These refinements had long since passed away. The remains of the patchwork quilt were still in use as an ironing cloth; but the bows and the valances had vanished. Even so, Jimmy was very proud of the brass bedstead. In one of the loose knobs he kept his treasures: a very old piece of chewing gum, a glass marble, and a number of leather discs which he had cut secretly from the flock mattress. This operation had, in part, contributed to the general lumpiness.

Cathy shared this bed with him on the landing-bedroom. The stairs came straight up from the living-room to this room of theirs, and it was inclined to be draughty. A small window gave what light it could, but an old pear tree growing close against the side of the house spread its branches too near to allow much illumination. In the summer the light filtered through its thick green foliage gave a curiously under-water effect to the room, as the shadows wavered against the walls. In the winter the skinny branches tapped and scraped the glass, like bony questing fingers, and Jimmy buried his head under the clothes to muffle his terror.

His two older sisters slept downstairs, for they had to be up first, and were out of the house and waiting at the top of the road for the first bus to Caxley at seven each morning.

His father and mother slept in the only other bedroom that

opened out from the landing and was situated over the living-room. Until recently Jimmy had slept with them in his cot in the corner, but this he had now outgrown, and so he had been promoted to the brass bedstead. When one of his sisters married, which was to be this summer, the remaining one would probably take his place with Cathy in grandmother's bed, and he instead would have to sleep downstairs on the sofa. He did not like the idea of sleeping in a room of his own and resolutely put this fear from him at nights, determined to enjoy his present comforts.

As he lay there, sucking his thumb, drifting between sleeping and waking, the sights and sounds and smells of his first day at school crowded thick upon him. He saw the orderly rows of desks; some of them, including his own, had a twelve-inch square carved on to the lid, and he had enjoyed rubbing his fat forefinger along the grooves.

He remembered Miss Clare's soft voice; her big handbag and the little bottle of scent which she had taken from it. The top had rolled away towards the door and he had run to pick it up for her. She had dabbed a drop of cold scent into his palm for payment, but its fragrance had soon been lost in the ball of plasticine which he pummelled and rolled into buttons and marbles and, best of all, a long sinuous snake. He remembered the feel of it in his hand, dead, but horribly writhing as he swung it to and fro. Holding his stub of chalk, when he had tried to copy his letters from the blackboard, had not been so pleasurable. His fingers had clenched so tightly that they had ached.

He remembered the clatter of the milk bottles when the children returned them to the steel crate in the corner. He had enjoyed his milk largely because he had drunk it through a straw and this was new to him. It was gratifying to see the milk sink lower and lower in the bottle and to feel the cold liquid trickling down in his stomach.

He sighed, and wriggled down more closely into the lumpy mattress. Yes, he liked school. He'd have milk tomorrow with a straw, and play with plasticine snakes, and perhaps go and see Cathy again in the next room. Cathy . . . he was glad Cathy was there too. School was all very nice but there was nothing quite like home, where everything was old and familiar. Still sucking his thumb, Jimmy fell asleep.

Next door Joseph Coggs lay on a decrepit camp bed and listened to his parents talking downstairs. Their voices carried clearly up the stairs to the landing-bedroom, and he knew that his father was angry.

'Ninepence a day! Lot of nonsense! Pay four bob a week, near enough, for Joe's dinners alone? Not likely! You give 'un a bit o' bread and cheese same as you gives me, my girl.'

Arthur Coggs also went on the early bus to Caxley. He was employed as an unskilled labourer with a building firm, and he spent his days mixing cement, carrying buckets and wheeling barrows. At twelve o'clock he sat down with his mates to eat the bread and cheese, and sometimes a raw onion, which his wife had packed for him. Joseph knew those packed dinners by sight – thick slabs of bread smeared with margarine and an unappetizing hunk of dry cheese – and his spirits drooped at the thought of having to take such victuals to school, and, worse still, of having to eat them within sight and smell of the luscious food such as he had enjoyed that day.

Beside his own bed, so close that he could touch the grey army blanket that covered it, was an iron bedstead containing his two younger sisters. They slept soundly, their matted heads close together on the striped ticking of a dirty pillow which boasted no such effete nonsense as a pillowslip. Their small pink mouths were half open and they snored gently.

Next door, in his parents' bedroom, he could hear the baby whimpering. He was devoted to this youngest child and suffered dreadfully in sympathy when it cried. Its small red fists and bawling mouth affected him deeply and he would do anything to appease its wants. He wished his mother would let him hold it more often, but she was impatient of his offers of help and pushed him out of her way.

'Mind now,' he heard his father shout, 'you do as I say. He can pay for what he's had, but you put him up summat same as me!'

To Joseph, listening aloft, these were sad words, for although he too had dwelt on the new experiences of the day, as had the boy next door, and though the plasticine, milk bottles, desks and children had all made their lasting impression on his young mind, it was the dinner, warm and plentiful, the plums and, most of all, those three swimming platefuls of golden custard, that had meant most to young Joseph Coggs.

Two fat tears coursed down his face as, philosophically, he turned on his creaking bed and settled down to sleep.

Mr and Mrs Moffat were making a rug together, one at each end. It was an intricate pattern of roses in a basket on a black background.

It was designed to lie before the shiny tiled fireplace of the small drawing-room, which was Mrs Moffat's new joy. When they had lived above their shop in Caxley, she had thought long and often about the furnishing of a drawing-room when she should have such a luxury, and she had cut out of the women's magazines, that she loved, many pictures and diagrams of suggested layouts for such rooms, as well as actual photographs of film stars' apartments.

If she had had her real wish she would have had a tiger skin as a hearth-rug, but she realized that her present drawing-room, which was only twelve feet by ten, would be hopelessly dwarfed by this extravagance, and that dream was put away with the others.

As their hooks flashed in and out of the canvas, Mr Moffat inquired about his daughter's debut at the village school.

'She didn't say much,' said Mrs Moffat, 'and she kept her clothes nice and clean. She's sitting by Anne Someone-or-other. Her mother works up the Atomic.'

'I know her dad. Nice chap he is; works for Heath the farmer. I met him at the pub.'

'Well, that's something! I don't want Linda picking up anything. Those ringlets take enough time without anything else.'

'She'll pick up nothing from that family she didn't ought!' replied Mr Moffat shortly. 'Won't hurt her to rough it a bit. You make a sissy of her.'

Mrs Moffat went pink. She realized the rough truth of this remark, but she resented the fact that all her striving and ambition for their only daughter should go unrecognized, and simply be dismissed as feminine vanity. It was more than that, but how to express it was beyond her powers.

She relapsed into hurt silence. If it hadn't been for her efforts they would still have been living over that poky shop, she thought to herself. She wanted Linda to have a better chance than she had had herself. She wanted her daughter to have all the things that she had wanted so dreadfully herself when she was young. A dance frock, with a full skirt and ruched bodice, a handbag to go with each change of clothes; she wanted Linda to join a tennis club, even perhaps go riding in immaculate jodhpurs and a hard hat. What Mrs Moffat's fierce maternal love ignored was the fact that Linda might be very well content without these social trappings that meant so much to her mother.

Mr Moffat sensed that he had upset his wife again. In silence they thrust the wool through the canvas and Mr Moffat thought, not for the first time, what kittle-cattle women were.

Linda, in her new pale-blue bed in the little back bedroom was thinking about her new friend Anne. It was a pity she was so untidy; her mother would mind about that if she invited her to play one Saturday, but nevertheless she would do so. She liked this new school; the children had admired her frock and red shoes and she realized that she could queen it here far more easily than at the little private school which she had attended in Caxley. There had been too many other mothers of the same calibre as Mrs Moffat there, all vying with each other in dressing up their children and exhorting them to speak in refined voices. It had been an effort, Linda realized now, all the time. At the village school, despite her mother's warnings, she knew that she would be able to relax in the other children's company.

The thing that worried Linda most, as she looked back upon her first day at school, was the lavatories. She was appalled at this primitive sanitation. Caxley had had main drainage, and her own new bathroom at the bungalow was fitted with a water-closet. She had never before come across a bucket-type lavatory and the memory of her few minutes there that morning, with her nose firmly pressed into her hands which smelt of lavender soap, made her shudder. She made a mental note that she would sprinkle toilet water on her handkerchief tomorrow against the perils of the day; and while she was debating which of her two minute bottles, lavender or carnation, she would use, she dropped suddenly into sleep.

While Miss Clare and I were enjoying our tea one morning at the school-house, the telephone rang. It was Mr Annett's high-pitched voice that assaulted my ear with a torrent of words. He is the schoolmaster at Beech Green, a quick, impatient man, a widower, living with an old Scotch housekeeper in the school-house there. He had only been married for six months when his young wife was killed in an air-raid at Bristol, near where his London school had been evacuated. Very soon afterwards he had sold most of their possessions and taken the little headship at Beech Green. He spends his life fighting a long, losing battle against the country child's slowness of wits and leisurely tempo of progress. He is also the choirmaster of St Patrick's.

'Look here,' he gabbled, 'it's about the Harvest Festival. Mrs Pratt can't get along to play the organ tonight – one of the children's down with chicken-pox – and I wondered if you could step in. We want to practise the anthem, "The Valleys Stand so Thick with Corn." D'you know it? You must do; we've had it every Harvest Festival since the war ended and still they don't know it!'

There was the sound of a scuffle at the end of the telephone.

'Well, get out of the way, you fool!' shouted Mr Annett exasperated. 'Not you, of course, Miss Read, the cat! Well, can you? At half-past seven? Thanks, I'll see you then.' The telephone dropped with a clatter and I could imagine Mr Annett sprinting on to the next job, quivering with nervous energy.

I finished my tea reviewing the evening's work before me. One thing, I was certain of plenty of amusement.

6. Choir Practice

The heavy church door groaned open, and the chill odour, a mixture of musty hymn-books and brass polish, greeted me as I tiptoed down the shining aisle for choir practice.

Mr Annett was already there, flitting about the chancel from one side to the other, putting out copies of the anthem, for all the world like an agitated wren. His fingers flickered to his mouth, and back to his papers, as he separated them impatiently.

'Good evening, good evening! This is good of you. Anyone in sight? No sense of time, these people! Nearly half-past now! Enough to drive you mad!' His words jerked out as he darted breathlessly about. A leaflet fluttered down to the hideous lozenge-patterned carpet which covers the chancel floor.

As he was scrabbling it up wildly, we heard the sound of country voices at the door, and a little knot of people entered. Mr Willet and his wife were there, two or three of my older pupils, looking sheepish at seeing me in an unusual setting, and Mrs Pringle brought up the rear. Mrs Pringle's booming contralto voice tends to drown the rest of the choir with its peculiarly strong carrying qualities. As her note reading is far from accurate, and she resents any sort of correction, Mrs Pringle is rather more of a liability than an asset to St Patrick's church choir; but her aggressive piety, expressing itself in the deepest genuflections, the most military sharp-turns to the east and the raising of eyes to the chancel roof, is an example to the fidgety choir-boys, and Mr Annett bears with her mannerisms with commendable fortitude.

I went through to the vestry to see if Eric, my organ blower, was at his post. The vestry was warm and homely. The table was covered with a red serge cloth with a fringe of bobbles. On it stood a massive ink bottle containing an inch of ink, which had dried to the consistency of honey. Leaning negligently against the table was Eric, looking unpleasantly grubby, and blowing gum bubbles from his mouth in a placid way.

'For pity's sake, Eric,' I protested, 'not in here, please!'

He turned pink, gobbled, and then, to my consternation, gave an enormous gulp, his eyes bulging.

'Gorn!' he announced with relief.

'I didn't intend you to *swallow* it, Eric—' I began, while dreadful visions of acute internal pains, ambulances, distracted parents and awful recriminations crowded upon me.

'It don't hurt you,' Eric reassured me. 'I often eats it – gives you the hiccups sometimes. That's all!'

Shaken, I returned to the organ and set out the music. Four or five more choir members had arrived and Mr Annett was fidgeting to begin. Snatches of conversation drifted over to me.

'But a *guinea*, mark you, just for killing an old pig!'

'Ah! But you got all the meat and lard and that, look! I knows you has to keep 'un all the year, and a guinea do seem a lot, I'll own up, but still—'

'Well, well!' broke in Mr Annett's staccato voice. 'Shall we make a start?'

'Young Mrs Pickett said to tell you she'd be along presently when she'd got the baby down. He's been a bit poorly—'

This piece of news started a fresh burst of comment, while Mr Annett raised and lowered himself impatiently on his toes.

'Poor little crow! Teeth, I don't wonder!'

'She called in nurse.'

'Funny, that! I see her only this morning up the shop—'

Mr Annett's patience snapped suddenly. He rattled his baton on the reading desk and flashed his eyes.

'Please, please! I'm afraid we must begin without Mrs Pickett. Ready, Miss Read? One, two!' We were off.

Behind me the voices rose and fell, Mrs Pringle's concentrated lowing vying with Mrs Willet's nasal soprano. Mrs Willet clings to her notes so cloyingly that she is usually half a bar behind the rest. Her voice has that penetrating and lugubrious quality found in female singers' renderings of 'Abide With Me' outside public houses on Saturday nights. She has a tendency to over-emphasize the final consonants and draw out the vowels to such excruciating lengths, and all this executed with such devilish shrillness, that every nerve is set jangling.

This evening Mrs Willet's time-lag was even worse than usual. Mr Annett called a halt.

'This,' he pleaded, 'is a cheerful lively piece of music. The valleys, we're told, laugh and sing. Lightly, please, let it trip, let it be merry! Miss Read, could you play it again?'

As trippingly and as nimbly as I could I obliged, watching Mr Annett's black, nodding head in the mirror above the organ. The tuft of his double crown flicked half a beat behind the rest of his head.

'Once more!' he commanded, and obediently the heavy, measured tones dragged forth, Mr Annett's baton beating a brisk but independent rhythm. Suddenly he flung his hands up and gave a slight scream. The choir slowed to a ragged halt and pained glances were exchanged. Mrs Pringle's mouth was buttoned into its most disapproving lines, and even Mr Willet's stolid countenance was faintly perturbed.

'The *time*! The *time*!' shouted Mr Annett, baton pounding on the desk. 'Listen again!' He gesticulated menacingly at my mirror and I played it again. 'You hear it? It goes:

'They *dance*, bong-bong,
    They *sing*, bong-bong,
    They *dance*, BONG and BONG, *sing* BONG-BONG!

It's just as simple as that! Now, with me!'

With his hair on end and his eyes gleaming dangerously, Mr Annett led them once more into action. Gallantly they battled on, Mr Annett straining like an eager puppy at the leash, while the slow voices rolled steadily along behind.

The lights had been put on in the chancel, but the rest of the church was cavernous and shadowy, making an age-old backcloth, aloof and beautiful, for this one hour's rustic comedy.

On the wall of the chancel stood the marble bust of Sir Charles Dagbury, once lord of the manor of this parish, staring with sightless eyes across the scene. On each side of his proud, disdainful face fell symmetrical cascades of curls, and his nostrils were curved as though with distaste for the rude mortals busking below.

The furious tapping of Mr Annett's baton broke the spell.

'David,' he was saying to the smallest choir-boy, 'get up on a hassock, child! Your head's hardly showing.'

'But I'm up on one, sir,' protested David, looking aggrieved.

'Sorry, sorry! Never met such badly-designed choir-stalls in my life,' announced Mr Annett, with the fine disregard of the townsman for the dangers this sort of remark incurs. 'Much too tall, and hideous at that!'

There was a sharp hiss as Mrs Pringle drew an outraged breath.

'My old grandfather,' she began heavily, 'though a trying old gentleman at the last, and should by rights have gone to the infirmary, such a dance as he led his poor wife, was as fine a carpenter as you could wish to meet in a day's march, and these choir-stalls here,' she leant forward menacingly and slapped one of them with a substantial hand – 'these here very choir-stalls was reckoned one of his best bits of work! Ain't that right?' she demanded of her abashed neighbours.

There were awkward mutterings and shufflings. Mr Annett had the grace to flush and look ashamed.

'I do apologize, Mrs Pringle,' he said handsomely. 'I meant no offence to the craftsman who made the choir-stalls. First-class work, obviously. It was the design I was criticizing.'

'My grandfather,' boomed Mrs Pringle, with awful intensity, 'DESIGNED THEM TOO!'

'I can only apologize again,' said Mr Annett, 'and hope that you will forgive my unfortunate remarks.' He coughed nervously. 'Well, to continue! Next Sunday we shall have "Pleasant are Thy Courts Above" and I thought we'd try the descant in the second verse only. All agreeable?'

There was a murmur of assent from all except Mr Willet, who has a somewhat Calvinistic attitude to church affairs.

'I likes to hear a hymn sung straightforward myself,' he said, blowing out his tobacco-stained moustache, 'these fiddle-faddles takes your mind off the words, I reckon.'

'I'm sorry to hear that you think so,' said Mr Annett. 'What's the general feeling?' He looked round at the company, baton stuck through his hair.

Nobody answered, as nobody wanted to fall out with either Mr Willet or Mr Annett. In the silence Eric could be heard creaking about in the vestry. There was suddenly a shattering hiccup.

'Then we'll carry on,' said Mr Annett, jerked back to life by this explosion. 'Descant verse two only. The psalms we've practised and – oh, yes – before I forget! We'll have the seven-fold Amen at the end of the service.'

Mr Willet snorted and muttered heavily under his moustache.

'Well, what now?' snapped Mr Annett irritably. 'What's the objection to the seven-fold Amen?'

'Popish!' said Mr Willet, puffing out the moustache. 'I'm a plain man, Mr Annett, a plain man that's been brought up God-fearing; and to praise the Lord in a bit of respectable music is one thing, but seven-fold Amens is taking it too far, to my way of thinking. And my wife here,' he said, rounding fiercely on the shrinking Mrs Willet, 'agrees with me! Don't you?' he added, thrusting his face belligerently to hers.

'Yes, dear,' said Mrs Willet faintly.

'It's a pity—' began Mr Annett.

'And while we're at it,' continued Mr Willet loudly, brushing aside this interruption, 'what's become of them copies of the hymn-books done in atomic-sulphur?'

Mr Annett looked bewildered, as well he might.

'You know the ones, green covers they had, with the music and atomic-sulphur written just above. I'm used to 'em. We was all taught atomic-sulphur years ago at the village school, when schooling WAS schooling, I may say – and all us folks my age gets on best with it!'

'I believe they are in a box in the vestry,' said Mr Annett, pulling himself together, 'and of course you can use the copies with tonic solfa if you prefer them. They'd become rather shabby, that's why the vicar put them on one side.'

Mr Willet, having had his say, was now prepared to be mollified, and grunted accordingly.

Mr Annett began to shovel music back into his case.

'Thank you, ladies and gentlemen. Next week, at the same time? Good evening, everybody. Yes, I think the anthem will go splendidly on the day – good night, good night.'

They drifted away into the shadows of the church, past the empty pews, the font, and the memorial tablets and tombs of their forefathers. Quietness came flooding back again. I locked the organ and went out to the vestry.

Eric, glistening from his exertions, was still struggling with recalcitrant hiccups, but seemed otherwise in excellent health. Mr Annett was giving him a shilling for his labours.

'And if you buy any more of that horrible gum,' I told him, 'eat it at home. If I see any in school it goes into the waste-paper basket, my boy!'

Grinning cheerfully he clattered off down the vestry steps and we followed him into the soft evening air.

The choir members were gossiping at the church gate, hidden from us by the angle of the wall. Their voices floated clearly across the graveyard.

'I believes in speaking my mind,' Mr Willet was saying firmly, ' "Speak the truth and shame the devil!" There's plenty o' sense in that. That young Annett'd have us daubed with incense, like Ancient Britons, if he had his way!'

''Tis nothing to do with him – incense and that. 'Tis the vicar's job and he's all right,' asserted a woman's voice.

Mrs Pringle had the last word. 'I trounced him proper about my grandpa! What if he was a sore trial at times? He was my own flesh and blood, wasn't he? Fair made me boil to hear him spoke of so low—' The booming voice died away as the footsteps grew fainter and fainter on the flinty road.

7. MISS CLARE FALLS ILL

Term was now several weeks old. Jimmy, Joseph and Linda had settled down and played schools, space-ships and shops in the playground as noisily as the rest.

Mrs Coggs had taken a job at the public house down the lane. Each morning she spent two hours there, washing glasses and scrubbing out the bar parlour, while the baby slept in its pram in the garden where she could keep an eye on it.

This arrangement had happy results for Joseph. For three or four weeks he had brought craggy slices of bread to school for his lunch, with an occasional apple or a few plums to enliven it; and this dreary meal he had eaten sadly, his dark eyes fixed upon the school dinners that his more fortunate fellows were demolishing.

But now, with money of her own in her pocket, Mrs Coggs was able to rebel against her husband's order of 'No school dinner for our Joe!' and to everyone's satisfaction Joseph returned to the dinner table, a broad smile on his face and a three-helping appetite keener than ever.

The weather had been mellow and golden all through September. The harvest had been heavy, the stacks were already being thatched, and housewives were hard at it bottling and jamming a bumper crop of apples, plums and damsons. Even Mrs Pringle admitted that the weather was lovely, and looked with gratification at the two unsullied stoves.

But one morning I awoke to a changed world. A border of scarlet dahlias, as brave as guardsmen the afternoon before, drooped, brown and clammy; and the grass was grey with frost.

The distant downs had vanished behind a white mist and

below the elm trees the yellow leaves were thickening fast into an autumn carpet.

After breakfast I went across to the school to face Mrs Pringle. She was rubbing the desks with a blue-check duster. Her expression was defensive.

'Mrs Pringle,' I began bravely, 'if it is like this tomorrow we must put the stoves on.'

'The *stoves*!' said Mrs Pringle, opening her eyes with amazement. 'Why, miss, we shan't need those for a week or so yet. This 'ere's a heat mist. You'll see – it'll clear to a real hot day!'

'I doubt it,' I replied shortly. 'Get firewood and coke in tonight in case this weather has set in. I'll listen to the forecast this evening and let you know definitely first thing tomorrow morning.'

I returned to the school-house feeling that the preliminary skirmish had gone well. Mrs Pringle I had left, muttering darkly, as she flicked the window-sills.

During the morning a watery sun struggled through, its rays falling across the children's down-bent heads as they struggled with their arithmetic. It was very quiet in the classroom. There was a low buzzing from the infants' side of the partition and the measured ticking of the ancient clock on the wall.

Suddenly, we were all frightened out of our wits by a heavy banging at the door. It was Mr Roberts the farmer, and one of his men, Tom Bates. Each carried a stout sheaf of corn. Behind me, the children chattered excitedly.

'Vicar said you'd be needing this for decorating the church for Harvest Festival on Sunday,' said Mr Roberts in his cheerful bellow. He is one of our more energetic school managers, as well as our near neighbour, so that he comes in to see us very often. He stamped into the room followed by Tom Bates and put the corn down by a long desk which stands at the side of the room. The floor-boards shook with the tremor of their heavy boots and the thud of corn.

The children always like Mr Roberts to come into the schoolroom. He is an enormous man with hands like hams and legs as thick as tree trunks. Once when he visited us he stepped back into the easel, capsizing the blackboard, a pot of catkins and a small boy who had been hovering in the vicinity. The children are always hopeful that this glorious confusion may happen again; and certainly their eyes light up at Mr Roberts' advent.

'If you want any more,' said Mr Roberts, stepping perilously near the milk crate, 'just you let me know. Plenty where that came from!' He skirted the easel adroitly and vanished into the lobby after Tom.

Hubbub broke out; long division, shopping bills, pounds and ounces were all neglected as the children surveyed the riches on the floor.

'Can us do 'em this afternoon, miss?'

'You said us boys could make the bunches this time.'

'The girls done it all last time.'

'Vicar said all us schoolchildren could do the altar rail.'

'No, he never then! The Guides always does the altar rail.'

I interposed. 'Nothing will be done until this afternoon. Get on with your arithmetic.'

Sadly they bent to their task again. Pens scratched in ink-wells, fingers were surreptitiously counted under desks, brows were furrowed and lips moved, as if in prayer, as the work went on again.

It has always been the custom in this parish for the children of Fairacre School to decorate certain parts of the church for Harvest Festival. The pew ends are always in our care and, this year, the altar rail had been given into our charge too. Last year we had been allowed to adorn the font steps, and striped marrows had jostled with mammoth cooking apples for a foothold. The corn is divided up into small bunches to be tied to the pew ends, the rest being left for the other decorators to use in other parts of the church.

Mrs Pringle snorted with disgust as she passed through the room after dinner, on the way to her steaming boiler.

'Fine old mess, that's all's to be said about corn! Fancy bringing that ol' stuff in here all over my clean floor! No more than a pighole this room'll be for two days, I can see! Shan't waste me strength on it till the lot's cleared out.'

She kicked the sheaf contemptuously to one side with her black laced boot to show her disgust of the whole concern.

*

The children squatted among the straw like so many clucking hens, their fingers busily arranging the corn into neat bunches. They chatted to each other as they scratched about the floor.

Next door the infants were employed in the same way. There was always a great surge of happiness in the school as they prepared for Harvest Festival. Tomorrow they would bring their own offerings from home: scrubbed carrots, bronzed onions, cabbages like footballs, and any other fruits of the earth that they could cajole from their parents. These, with our bunches of corn we would carry to the church, and this was the excitement to which they were now looking forward so eagerly.

While they were busily employed the door of the partition opened a crack and a dark eye appeared. I waited to see what would happen.

Gradually the crack widened and Joseph Coggs, finger in mouth, gazed silently at me. I gazed back, amused, wondering if he would come in or scamper away. He did neither. He stood stock-still and then beckoned to me urgently.

'Say!' he called in his husky voice, 'Miss Clare's been and fallen over!'

Panic gripped me as I fled into the infants' room. The chattering of my own class continued unconcernedly behind me as I closed the dividing door.

It was very quiet in Miss Clare's room. The children stood round her chair gaping, while slumped across the table, her white hair lying in a pool of water from an overturned vase, lay their teacher. Her lips were blue and she moaned in a terrifying rhythm.

'Take your bunches,' I said hastily, 'and go into my room.' They moved away slowly as I bent over her. At this moment she gave a little sigh and raised her head. Voices floated through the door.

'Look at all them babies coming in our room!'

'Here, what's up?'

'You git back in your own place!'

'You are all to work together,' I ordered from the door. 'And quietly! Miss Clare's not very well. There will be sweets for people who work best!' This shameless piece of bribery was justified by the occasion, I felt.

I shut the door firmly. Miss Clare looked at me with a wan smile.

'A drink,' she whispered.

The floor of the lobby was still damp from Mrs Pringle's scrubbing brush and the windows covered in steam. I whipped the clean cloth from the top of the drinking bucket and filled a mug.

The colour gradually crept back into Miss Clare's cheeks as she sipped. I sat on the front desk and watched her anxiously.

'Will you be all right for a minute while I go across to fill a hot bottle? Then I will help you over there.'

'There's no need,' protested Miss Clare, flushing pink at the thought of leaving her post in the middle of the afternoon, 'I can manage now. This isn't the first time this has happened; but luckily it's never happened in school.'

'Just sit still for a few minutes and I'll be back,' I told her, and went through to the children, my legs wobbling under me in the most cowardly fashion. It was a relief to enter this normal buzzing atmosphere and to breathe the homely smell of straw.

'Get on quietly,' I said as I tottered through. 'I'll be back soon.'

I switched on the kettle and rang Miss Clare's doctor. By a miracle he was in and promised to come at once. I helped Miss Clare across to the school-house and Dr Martin arrived as I was tucking the rug round her on the sofa. I poured them some tea and returned to school.

It is a funny thing, but faced with a crisis, children always suffer a sea-change for the better. When they might well be resentful at changes of plan and deprivation of their liberty they become instead soft-voiced and unnervingly angelic. Perhaps the sudden removal of adult supervision lessens the tension, and they feel relaxed and happy. I can't account for it, but it has happened to me many times. On the occasions when an accident has befallen one child and I have imagined rioting and mayhem breaking out among the others in my absence, I have always tortured myself unnecessarily, and returned to find as meek a flock of lambs as ever rejoiced a teacher's heart.

This afternoon was no exception, and thankfully I passed round the sweet tin.

Cathy collected the bundles of straw; dozens of them, ranging from sleek beauties to ragged mops; the floor looked like a chicken run, littered with straw and some bright specks of grain which Jimmy Waites was picking up with his fat fingers.

'For me bantam cock,' he explained, 'and if he lays an egg I'll bring it for you, miss.' Cathy gave me a sidelong smile, as one woman to another in the presence of innocent childhood.

As they sang grace I pondered on the best message to send by the children about their early home-coming. It was inevitable that the news of Miss Clare's illness would get about rapidly, but I did not want a succession of visitors during the next hour or so. The majority would, no doubt, be anxious to be of use, but there were one or two whose ghoulish desire for any grisly details would bring them to my door, and these I felt I could not face for a little while.

'Tell your mothers,' I announced, 'that you are home early as Miss Clare is not very well this afternoon. I expect she will be back tomorrow.'

This white lie I hoped would keep the more avid newsmongers at bay.

A spiteful little wind had sprung up, spattering the windows with the flying elm leaves, as the children straggled away. A tiny whirlwind chased the dead leaves rustling round and round by the door-scraper. With a rush they rattled suddenly over the threshold. Winter was forcing its way in.

'Stoves alight tomorrow, Mrs Pringle,' I said aloud.

Dr Martin, I noticed with some annoyance as I entered the kitchen, was drying his hands on my clean tea towel. He was whistling tunelessly to himself.

'How is she?'

'She'll be all right now; but I'd like her to stay here for the night if you can have her.'

'Of course.'

'I'll call in to see her sister on my way back. It might be as well if she stayed with her for a week or two, though I doubt if she will go there. It's a pity they don't hit it off better.'

Dr Martin is now in his seventies and knows the histories of the village families intimately. Twice a week, on Wednesdays and Saturdays, he comes to Fairacre to hold his surgery in the drawing-room of Mr Roberts' farmhouse. His enormous white cupboard, smelling of drugs and ointments, dominates this room, which is set aside for his use.

'Has she needed to call you in before?' I asked. 'She's said nothing to me about these attacks.'

'Had them off and on for two years now, the silly girl,' said Dr Martin, folding the tea-towel into a very small damp square that would never dry and putting it carefully on the window-sill. He faced me across the kitchen table.

'She will have to give this up, you know. Should have done so last year, but she's as obstinate as her father was. Do your best to make her see it. I'll call in tomorrow morning.'

He put his head round the door of the living-room.

'Now, Dolly, stay there and rest. You'll do, my dear, you'll do!'

Outside the back door he checked, and I thought he had some last minute instructions to give me, but he was staring at a climbing rose, that nodded in the wind.

'Now, that's a nice one,' he said intently, and carefully picked a bloom. Tucking it into his buttonhole he trotted briskly across to his car, and I remembered with amusement what I had heard the villagers say about him. 'That ol' Dr Martin – can't never resist a rose, nor a glass of home-made wine. They're his failings, see?'

Dr Martin must have put a match to the fire for its cheerful light was the first thing I noticed in the quiet living-room. Miss Clare was lying back on the sofa with her eyes shut, and I thought that she slept.

'I heard,' she said, without opening her eyes; and for the life of me I could say nothing – nothing of comfort to an old tired woman who was facing the end of more than forty years' service – that would not sound presumptuous or patronizing. For a minute I hated my own boisterous good health that seemed to put up a barrier between us. She must have thought from my silence that I had not heard her, for she sat up and said again: 'I heard what Dr Martin said. He's right, you know. I shall go at Christmas.'

Now, although I could have spoken, I was afraid to do so, lest she should hear from the tremor in my voice how much I was moved. She looked anxiously at me.

'Or do you think I should go at once? Is that what you think? Do you wish I'd gone before? You must have noticed that I was not doing my job as I should.'

This had the effect of loosening my tongue, and I told her how groundless were these thoughts.

'Don't think about plans tonight,' I urged her. 'We'll see what the doctor says about you tomorrow and talk it over then.'

But although she acquiesced with surprising meekness about the postponement of her own arrangements, her mind returned to school affairs.

'Should you phone to the office, do you think, dear? It closes at five, you know, and if you need a supply teacher—'

'I shall manage easily tomorrow on my own,' I assured her, 'we shall go over to the church to get it ready, and I can ring the office when I've seen Dr Martin. Don't worry about a thing.' I got up from the end of the sofa to go upstairs to get the spare room ready for her. She sat very still with her head downbent. There were tears on her cheek, glistening in the light from the fire.

'I always loved Harvest Festival,' she said, in a small shaken voice.

8. HARVEST FESTIVAL

Mrs Pringle greeted me in a resigned way when I went over to the school soon after eight the next morning. She was limping ostentatiously – a bad sign – for it meant that she expected to be 'put upon' and so her leg, as she expresses it, 'had flared up again.' This combustible quality of Mrs Pringle's leg obliges one to be careful of expecting any extra effort – such as lighting the stoves, the present fear.

'I haven't got round to the stoves yet,' breathed Mrs Pringle painfully. She winced as she moved the inkwell on the desk. It was apparent that this morning's 'flare-up' was more than usually fierce.

'Don't bother!' I said, 'I shall have all the children in here today, and in any case we shall spend quite a time over at the church.' At this her face relaxed and there was a marked improvement in the afflicted limb as she walked quite briskly to open a window.

'Sad about Miss Clare,' said Mrs Pringle, arranging her features in a series of down-turned crescents. 'A fit, so Mr Willet understood.'

'No, not a fit—' I said, nettled.

'Can't hardly ever do anything about fits,' Mrs Pringle went on complacently. She folded her arms and settled down for a cosy gossip. 'My sister's boy, what's due to be called up any time, why he's had 'em since a dot. Just after whooping-cough it started; my sister had a terrible time with him over whooping-cough. Tried everything! Dr Martin's stuff never helped – all that did was to take the varnish off the mantelshelf where the bottle stood; and Mrs Willet's old mother – who was a wise old party though she lost her hair terrible towards the end – she recommended a fried mouse, eaten whole if possible, to stop the cough!'

'Surely not!' I exclaimed, feeling that a fried mouse, in my case, would successfully stop respiration altogether, let alone a cough.

'Ain't you ever heard of that? Oh, a good old-fashioned cure, that is – though it never done Perce much good. These 'ere fits come on after that. It's the swallering of the tongue that makes it more trying like.'

I said I was sure it was and beat an ignoble retreat before fresh horrors were thrust upon me.

There were several bunches of flowers for Miss Clare when the children trickled into school and these I took over to her as she lay breakfasting in bed. She seemed better, and awaited Dr Martin's visit with composure.

The work of making straw bunches proceeded briskly. Dust thickened the golden bars of sunshine and every time the door opened a little eddy of chaff would whisper round the floor. The long desk at the side was packed high with apples, marrows, giant parsnips and a fine bright orange pumpkin that Linda Moffat's grandfather had brought for her from his Caxley back-garden. It was much admired, as an exotic bloom from foreign parts.

In the midst of the hubbub a visitor arrived. A tall cadaverous woman, dressed in a fawn overcoat and fawn hat, came round the door and stood gazing down upon the squatting children with an expression of strong distaste.

I hastened to welcome her, noticing that her complexion was as fawn as her attire and wondering, not for the first time, why sallow people are so magnetically drawn to this colour. Even her teeth were a subdued shade of yellow, and had I been capable of seeing her aura I have no doubt that that too would have been in the beige range.

'I am Miss Pitt, the new needlework inspector,' she said, revealing the teeth a little more. 'This doesn't appear to be a very convenient time to call.'

I explained that we were about to go over to the church, but that it was no bother to show her our work.

Ankle deep in straw, I pushed across to the needlework cupboard and returned with girls' bags.

'The bigger ones are making aprons with cross-over straps. That brings in buttonholes,' I enlarged, pulling one or two specimens into view, 'and the small girls are making bibs or hankies.'

I left her to look at them while I broke up a quiet but vicious fight which had started in a corner. Someone's special pile of extra-large-eared corn was being purloined and there were stealthy recriminations going on.

'Oh, dear!' said Miss Pitt, scrutinizing an apron, 'oh, dear! I'm afraid this is very out-of-date.'

'Out-of-date?' I repeated, bewildered. 'But children can always do with pinafores!'

Miss Pitt passed a fawn hand across her brow, as one suffering fools, but not gladly.

'We just don't,' she began wearily, as though addressing a very backward child, 'we just don't expect young children like this to do such fine, close work. Pure Victoriana, this!' she went on, tossing Anne's apron dangerously near an inkwell. 'All this HEMMING and OVERSEWING and BUTTONHOLING – it just isn't done these days. Plenty of thick bright wool, crewel needles, not too small, and coarse crash, or better still, hessian to work on, and THE VERY SIMPLEST stitches! As for these poor babies with their hankies—!' She gave a high affected laugh, 'Canvas mats, or a simple pochette is the sort of thing that they should be attempting. Eyestrain, you know!'

'But not one of them wears glasses,' I protested, 'and they've always been perfectly happy making these things for themselves or their families. And surely they should learn the elementary stitches!'

'No; I'm not criticizing—' I felt I should like to know just what she was doing then, but restrained myself, 'it's all a matter of APPROACH! Have you any hessian in the school?'

'Only a very small amount for the babies,' I replied firmly, 'and as I've used up all our money on this cotton material I'm afraid the aprons and so on will have to go forward.'

'A pity,' said Miss Pitt, sadly. She sighed bravely. 'Ah well! I will call in again some time next term and see if I can give you some more help. We do so want to bring Colour and Life into these rather drab surroundings, don't we?'

I could have suggested that a more colourful wardrobe might help towards this end, but common courtesy forbade it.

'One meets such hardworking people in this job,' she continued smiling graciously at me – she might have been slumming – 'such really worthy fellow-creatures. It's a great privilege to be able to guide them, I find.'

She gave a last look round the room, averting her eyes quickly from the outcast aprons. 'Good-bye, Miss Annett,' she said, consulting a list. 'This is Beech Green School, isn't it?'

'This is Fairacre School,' I pointed out. 'Mr Annett is headmaster at Beech Green School.'

'Then he's next on my list,' replied the imperturbable Miss Pitt, her self-esteem not a bit ruffled. She stepped out into the sunshine.

'Turn right here,' I told her, 'and it's about two or three miles along the Caxley road.' I watched her turn her car and drive off. 'And what Mr Annett will have to say to that fawn fiend I should dearly love to know!' I thought.

The church seemed very tranquil after the bustle of the schoolroom. The children tiptoed in with their treasures and set to work lashing the bunches of corn to the pew heads with strands of raffia. The four biggest children, John, Sylvia, Cathy and Anne were in charge of the altar rail, and, full of importance, they arranged beetroots, marrows and apples in magnificent pyramids, standing back with their heads on one side, every now and again, to admire the effect.

Sir Charles Dagbury looked down as disdainfully as ever upon them, as they enlivened his cold home, while, in the body of the church, more sightless eyes gazed down upon the young children from the church walls.

The troubles and vexations of the last twenty-four hours suddenly seemed less oppressive. It is difficult, I reflected, to take an exaggerated view of any personal upheaval when standing in a building that has witnessed the joys, the hopes, the griefs and all the spiritual tremors of mortal men for centuries.

These walls had watched the parishioners of Fairacre revealing the secrets of their hearts from the time when those kneeling men had worn doublets and hose. Some of the effigies had been here when Cromwell's men had burst in, as the mutilated marble bodies on two magnificent tombs testified. Bewigged papas, and later, crinolined mamas had sat in these pews with rows of nicely-graded children beside them, and these had been followed, in their turn, by their grandchildren and great-grandchildren, some of whom now chattered and scurried up and down the aisle.

In the presence of this ancient, silent witness, it was right that personal cares should assume their own insignificant proportions. They were, after all, as ephemeral as the butterflies that hovered over the Michaelmas daisies on the graves outside. And, hurt as they might do at the moment, they could not endure.

Dr Martin had prescribed at least three weeks' rest for Miss Clare.

'But she's so anxious to clear up her affairs properly at school that I see no reason why she shouldn't have the last two weeks of term here, if she makes the progress I think she will,' he added. 'It will be a wrench for her after all these years – perhaps this break may help the parting a little.'

Her sister came to fetch her after tea. Miss Clare had agreed to stay with her for a week, although it was quite obvious that her independent spirit rebelled against submitting to a younger sister's ministrations.

My problem now was to find a substitute for Miss Clare for the next few weeks, and I rang up the local education office at Caxley to see if there was a supply teacher available.

Supply teachers are a rarity in country districts, but I was in luck.

'Have you come across Mrs Finch-Edwards?' asked Mr Taylor, officially the Divisional Organizer, at the other end of the line.

'No, does she live near here?'

'They live in Springbourne.' This is a hamlet two miles away from Fairacre, further from Caxley. 'Only been there two or three months. She's had experience with infants in London. I'll see if she can be with you on Monday.'

'That's wonderful!' I said thankfully, putting down the receiver.

Mrs Finch-Edwards turned out to be a large, boisterous young woman, with a high colour, a high voice and a high coiffure done in masses of helped-auburn curls. Her hearty efficiency and superb self-confidence made me feel quite timid and anaemic by contrast. All through the few weeks of her sojourn at Fairacre School the partition rattled with the vibrations of her cheerful voice and the innumerable nursery rhymes and jingles, all, it seemed, incorporating deafening hand-clapping at frequent intervals, which the infants learnt eagerly. They all adored her, for she had an energy that matched their own, and her extensive wardrobe, of many colours, intrigued them.

The girls in my class were full of admiration for Mrs Finch-Edwards.

'She's real pretty,' said Anne to Linda as they hung over the fireguard that surrounded the roaring stove. 'Even if she is a bit fat.'

'Didn't ought to wear mauve, though,' said Linda judicially, smoothing her new grey skirt. 'It's too old for her. You have to be very fair or very dark for mauve, my mum says.'

We worked well together, although I missed Miss Clare's tranquil presence sorely. Mrs Finch-Edwards could not resist pointing out the deficiencies of Fairacre School as compared with the palatial palaces she had known, strewn, it would appear, with such luxurious equipment as individual beds for afternoon rest, sliding-chutes, dolls' houses, sand pits, paddling pools and – the acme of civilization – several drinking fountains. She was appalled by the jug-mug-and-drinking-pail apparatus in her outside lobby.

'I should never have *dreamt*—!' she told me, 'when I think of Hazel Avenue Infants' or Upper Eggleton's Nursery School with their own towels, each one appliquéd with each child's motif, you know, a toy soldier, say, or an apple – and when I think of the stock they had – well, it does just *show*, doesn't it? How you struggle on here, year after year, dear, I don't know. It must be truly frustrating for you. Tells on your looks in the end, too,' she added, taking a quick look at herself in the murky background of 'The Angelus' behind my desk. She pinned up a fat curl thoughtfully. 'I thought at one time I might fancy a country headship; that was before I met my hubby, of course. He wouldn't let me do that now.'

She always spoke of 'hubby' as though he were a hulking caveman and she a clinging little wisp dependent on him for everything. This 'trembling-with-fear-at-his-frown' attitude was all the more absurd when one had seen 'hubby,' who stood five-foot-six in his dove-grey socks, had next to no chin and a pronounced lisp. His wife's magnificent physique completely overshadowed his own modest appearance and it was obvious that in any action she dashingly led the way. I bore her comments on the poverty of equipment at Fairacre School, and the poverty of looks of its headmistress with all the humility I could muster.

'We usually give a concert at Christmas,' I told her, 'and I think we could manage one this year. Could you teach the infants two or three songs with actions or perhaps a very short play? Miss Clare could cope with the carols when she comes back, and my class are going to do "Cinderella." What do you think about it?'

Mrs Finch-Edwards was most enthusiastic and bubbled over with suggestions for costumes which she offered to make, with some help. An idea struck me, as I saw Linda Moffat twirling round and round in the playground showing off the two and a half yards of flannel in her new skirt.

'I'll call on Linda's mother. I know she's clever with clothes, and has a machine. She may help too.' I was glad that I had thought of this opportunity of seeing Mrs Moffat again, for I suspected that she was not very happy in the village yet, and despite the beauties of her bungalow, a lonely woman.

'Come with me,' I urged Mrs Finch-Edwards, 'we'll go one evening next week and see what happens.'

I little realized that that evening was going to begin a strong friendship between the two women that would flourish for the rest of their lives.

9. GETTING READY FOR CHRISTMAS

Winter had really come. The milk saucepans, which lived under my kitchen sink for the warm months of the year, were now at school and put on the hot stoves, one in my room and the other in the infants'.

Woolly scarves, thick coats and wellingtons decked the lobby. Gloves were constantly getting lost; children vanished, in the wrong wellingtons, on foggy afternoons, and others had to hobble home in those that were left, or pick their way through the puddles, to their mothers' wrath, in inadequate plimsolls. The classroom resounded to coughs, sniffs and shattering sneezes, and toes were rubbed up and down legs to ease chilblains.

The vicar, on his weekly visits, wore his winter cloak, green with age but dramatic in cut, and a pair of very old leopard-skin gloves, to which he was much attached. They had been left to him, 'more years ago than he cared to remember,' by an old lady who had embroidered no less than seven altar-fronts for him. His voice became so soft, and his eye so liquid, when he spoke of his departed friend, that it was impossible not to suspect a romantic attachment; and, in fact, this can have been the only reason for clinging, year after year, to a pair of gloves that had become so very odorous, moth-eaten and generally nasty. Altogether, during the winter months, the cloak, the gloves, and a biretta worn at a rakish angle, combined to give the vicar of St Patrick's a somewhat bizarre, but dashing appearance.

He had gone through to see Miss Clare, who was now back with us, to tell her how sorry he was to accept her notice of resignation at the end of the term.

'I shall put the advertisement in *The Teachers' World* and possibly *The Times Educational Supplement* this week,' he said on his way back. 'I doubt if we shall get anyone to start in January, but Mrs Finch-Edwards may be willing to come until we get suited.' He paused and stroked the gloves nervously. Loose fur, I noted with distaste, began to settle heavily on *The Wind in the Willows* lying ready for the English Literature lesson on my desk. 'How do you get on with her?'

'Very well,' I said firmly, and he departed, looking relieved. I blew my desk clean and called peremptorily for a little less noise from my class.

During these last few weeks of term preparations for the concert kept us in a bustle. Mrs Finch-Edwards called in one afternoon a week to coach the infants in the plays and the action songs she had chosen for them. She and Mrs Moffat were spending almost every afternoon snipping and sewing the costumes, shouting cheerfully above the hum of their machines and becoming fast friends in the process.

'What I should like better than anything,' confessed Mrs Moffat one day to this new friend, who had banished the bogey of loneliness, 'would be to have a dress shop!'

'Me too!' rejoined Mrs Finch-Edwards, and they looked at each other with a wild surmise. There was a vibrating moment as their thoughts hovered over this mutual ambition.

'If it weren't for the family, and the house, and that,' finished Mrs Moffat, her eyes returning rather sadly to her seam.

'If it weren't for hubby,' echoed Mrs Finch-Edwards, gazing glumly at a gusset. They sewed in silence.

John Burton, Sylvia Long and Cathy Waites, who were all ten, sat for the first part of the examination which would determine their future schooling, one bitterly cold morning. The rest of the class were in Miss Clare's room, and the solemnity of the occasion and the need for complete quietness so that the three entrants would do their best, had been impressed upon the whole school.

It was very peaceful as the three children tackled the problems. It was an intelligence test, intended to sort out the children capable of attempting the papers to be set next February, from those who were not capable of attempting any further effort at all.

A wicked draught blew under the door, stirring the nature chart on the wall. The clock ticked ponderously, cinders clinked into the ash pan, and a rustling in the raffia cupboard sounded suspiciously like a mouse.

Cathy, frowning hard, went steadily through the paper; but John and Sylvia sighed, chewed their pens and occasionally gave a groan. At half-past eleven they finished, handed in their papers and smiled with relief at each other and vanished into the playground. John's paper, as I suspected, was sadly unfinished; Sylvia's was no better, but Cathy's looked much more hopeful.

The only dark child among the Waites' family had certainly more intelligence than her flaxen-haired brothers and sisters.

The day of the concert dawned and the afternoon was spent in getting the school ready for the hundred or so parents and friends we expected to be in the audience at seven o'clock.

The partition was pushed back, groaning and creaking, and Mr Willet, John Pringle, Mrs Pringle, Miss Clare and I erected the stage at the end of the infants' room and piled desks outside in the playground, praying that the weather would stay fine until the next morning.

The children had been sent home early, theoretically to rest, but a knot of them clustered open-mouthed in the playground to watch the preparations, despite increasingly sharp requests to go home and stay there.

Mrs Pringle, with a nice regard for social strata, had arranged the first row of chairs for the school managers and their friends. Armchairs from my house and her own, some tall, some squat, stood cheek by jowl with a settee that Mr Roberts had lent from the farm opposite. All this cushioned comfort would be shared by the vicar, who was chairman of the managers, his wife, Mr and Mrs Roberts, Colonel Wesley – very shaky and deaf but one of the more zealous managers – and wealthy Miss Parr, the only female manager.

'You'd better put two or three more comfortable chairs in case Mrs Moffat and Mrs Finch-Edwards get time to come in,' I told Mrs Pringle.

'This row's for the gentry,' pointed out Mrs Pringle. 'There's plenty of ordinary chairs for the rest.'

At the back of the hall, which was the side of my classroom, were rows of plain benches on which I knew the boys would stand and gape at the distant stage. We had never yet got through a concert without several deafening crashes, but so far we had had no injuries. I hoped our luck would hold.

The children were dressing in the lobby superintended by Mrs Moffat and Mrs Finch-Edwards, their mouths puckered up with holding pins. The air quivered with excitement.

Miss Clare, resolutely refusing to sit in the gentry's row, had her own chair set by the side of the stage and instituted herself as prompter and relief pianist.

Mr Annett had come over to help and I could hear him at the further lobby door collecting the shillings which were going to swell the school funds. The rows gradually filled and the air became thick with shag tobacco smoke.

A twittering row of fairies creaked excitedly up on to the platform behind the drawn curtain and I spoke to the vicar through the crack. He struggled up from the depths of Mr Roberts' settee, still clutching his leopard-skin gloves, and gave everyone present a warm welcome.

The fairies took a deep breath and up went the curtain in spasmodic jerks. The concert had begun.

It was a most successful evening. No one was hurt when three benches overturned, though a very loud word which was uttered at the time caused Joseph Coggs to look at me with eyes like saucers.

'You hear that man?' he whispered. 'He swored!'

Mr Annett told me that he had collected nearly five pounds at the door and that everyone had been most complimentary about the costumes. Mrs Moffat and Mrs Finch-Edwards bridled with pleasure when they heard this in the lobby where they were packing clothes wearily into baskets and boxes. The vicar took Miss Clare home and I reminded him of the Christmas party on the last day of term during the next week.

The night sky was thick with stars as the people dwindled away into the darkness.

'What about them desks, miss?' said Mr Willet at my elbow. 'They might get wet.'

'Forget them!' I said, turning the key in the school door. It had been a very long day.

On the last Saturday of term I caught the bus to Caxley to buy presents for the children with some of the concert money. I struggled round Woolworth's buying little dolls, balls, coloured pencils, clockwork mice and decorations for the Christmas tree, and spent the next hour searching the rest of the town for more elusive toys. In the market-place I came across Mr Annett.

'Do you want a lift?' he asked. 'I'm just off.'

I consulted my shopping list. There seemed nothing more of extreme urgency and I gratefully climbed into the car.

'I sometimes wonder about Christmas,' said Mr Annett meditatively, looking at my feet which I was resting, in an unlovely way, on their outer edges. We edged gingerly down the crowded High Street, demented shoppers darting before us, screaming at their children to 'Stay there – Lor' the traffic – Stay there!'

'The thing to do,' I said as we gained the lane that leads to Beech Green and Fairacre, 'is to get absolutely everything in the summer and lock it in a cupboard. Then order every scrap of food from a shop the week before Christmas and sit back and enjoy watching everyone else go mad. I've been meaning to do it for years.'

'Come and have tea with me,' said Mr Annett, swerving into the school playground before I had a chance to answer. His school-house was bigger than mine and also had a bathroom, but poor Mr Annett's towels were grey, I noticed, and the floor needed cleaning. The dust of several days lingered on the banisters, and it was quite obvious that his housekeeper did not overwork herself.

His sitting-room, however, though dusty, was light and sunny, with an enormous radiogram in one corner and two long shelves above it stacked with gramophone records. In the other corner was his 'cello, and I remembered that Mr Annett was a keen member of the Caxley orchestra.

Mrs Nairn, a wispy little Scotswoman, brought in the tea, and smiled upon me graciously.

'Your brother rang up while you was out,' she said to Mr Annett, 'and said to tell you he'll be down next Friday tea-time, and he's bringing two bottles of whisky and a bird ready cooked.'

This news delighted Mr Annett. 'Good, good!' he said, dropping four lumps of sugar carefully into my cup. 'That's wonderful! He's here with me for a week or more over Christmas. He's just had a book published in America, you know, and he's expecting big sales.'

As I knew that his brother was a professor of mathematics at one of the northern universities and occasionally brought out books with such titles as *The Quadrilateral Theory and its Relation to the Quantitative Binomial Cosine*, I felt unequal to any cosy chit-chat about the new publication, and contented myself with polite noises at this good news.

I did not get back until seven and spent the rest of the evening packing presents in blue tissue paper for boys and pink for girls and thanking my stars that there were only forty children in Fairacre School.

It was the last afternoon and the Christmas party was in full swing. Lemonade glasses were empty, paper hats askew, and the children's faces flushed with excitement. They sat at their disordered tables, which were their workaday desks pushed up together in fours and camouflaged with Christmas tablecloths. Their eyes were fixed on the Christmas tree in the centre of the room, glittering and sparkling with frosted baubles and tinsel.

Miss Clare had insisted on dressing it on her own, and had spent all the previous evening in the shadowy schoolroom alone with the tree and her thoughts. The pink and blue parcels dangled temptingly and a cheer went up as the vicar advanced with the school cutting-out scissors.

Round the room were parents and friends, who had come to share the fun of the party and to see the presentation of a clock and a cheque to Miss Clare on this her last school day.

The children had all brought a penny or two for a magnificent bouquet which was now hidden under the sink in the lobby, out of harm's way. The youngest little girl, John Burton's sister, was already in a fine state of nerves at the thought of presenting it at the end of the proceedings.

The floor was a welter of paper, bent straws and crumbs, and I saw Mrs Pringle's mouth drooping down, tortoise-fashion, as she surveyed the wreckage. Luckily the vicar clapped his hands for silence before she had a chance for any damping remark.

The room was very quiet as he spoke, simply and movingly, of all that Miss Clare had meant in the lives of those of us there that afternoon. It was impossible to repay years of selfless devotion, but we would like her to have a token of our affection. Here, he looked helplessly round for the parcel and envelope, which Mrs Pringle found for him and thrust hastily into his hand as though they were hot potatoes.

Miss Clare undid them with shaking fingers, while a little whisper of excitement ran round the room. There was the sudden clang of the paint bucket from the lobby, and little Eileen Burton emerged triumphantly with the bouquet and presented it with a commendable curtsey, amid a storm of clapping.

Miss Clare replied with composure, and I never admired her more than on this occasion. A reserved woman herself, I think that this was the first time that she realized how warmly we all felt towards her. She thanked us simply and quietly, and only the brightness of her eyes as she looked at the happy children told of the tears that could so easily have come to a less courageous woman.

PART TWO

Spring Term

* * * *

10. WINTER FEVERS

The Christmas holidays had slid away all too quickly. On the morning after we had broken up, I was busy writing Christmas cards, when a hammering had come at the front door.

On the step stood Linda and Anne. Linda carried a small parcel with much care, and when I invited them in she put it on the table among the half-finished cards.

'It's from both of us,' she announced proudly.

It turned out to be a bottle of scent called 'Dusky Allure.' A female of mature charms pranced on the label, inadequately clad in what looked like a yard of cheese-muslin. A palm tree and a few stars added point to the title. The children beamed at me as I unscrewed the top.

'It's simply wonderful!' I told them, when I had got over the coughing attack. 'And very, very kind of you.'

I pressed biscuits and lemonade upon them, and they sat on the edges of their chairs, demure and gratified, while I finished off the cards. In the quiet room one's lemonade went down with a gurgle, and they exchanged mirthful looks and turned pink.

We parted with various good wishes for Christmas and they skipped away taking with them my cards to post.

On Christmas Eve I had had more visitors. The carol-singers arrived on a clear, frosty night, bearing three hurricane lamps on long poles, and pushing a little harmonium which Mrs Pratt played. Mr Annett conducted them with vigour, and in the light of one of the lamps I saw that brother Ted had been prevailed upon to bring his flute. The fresh country voices were at their best in the cold night air, and even Mr Annett seemed pleased with his choir's efforts.

'Splendid!' he said vigorously, as 'Hark, the herald angels sing' dwindled to a close, and he beamed upon them all with such goodwill that I wondered if brother Ted's two bottles had been broached before they had set off, or whether it was indeed the spirit of Christmas that had softened him to include even Mrs Pringle in his expansive smile.

The new term found a depleted school, for measles had broken out in the village. In the infants' room Mrs Finch-Edwards had only twelve children to teach, out of eighteen, and I had only twenty out of twenty-two.

The weather was bitterly cold, with an east wind that flattened the grass and shrivelled the wallflower plants against the school wall. The skylight had undergone its usual repairs during the holiday, and though we had had no rain yet to test its endurance to the weather, it certainly let in a more fiendish draught than usual, which gave me a stiff neck.

The children did not want to go out into the playground, and with the weather as it was I doubted whether they would gain much from the airing; but being school-bound made them quarrelsome and cantankerous. Tempers were short and Mrs Pringle more annoying than ever with her fancied grievances and nagging at the children.

We all longed for the spring, for sunshine and flowers, and the thought that we were only in January made that prospect all the more hopeless.

It was during arithmetic one morning, when I had been teaching the middle group to multiply with two figures, that John Burton came out with the astonishing remark: 'I'm done! Can't do no more!'

He threw his pen down on to the desk, leant back and closed his eyes. He, as a top group member, had been working quietly at some problems from the blackboard, and this outburst made us all stop and stare.

'If you can't do any more of those, John,' I said, 'try some from Exercise Six.'

'I've said, ain't I, that I can't do no more?' shouted John, glaring at me. This was quite unlike his usual docile manner and I felt annoyed.

'What nonsense—' I began, when, to my amazement, he burst into tears, resting his head on his arms on the desk.

The children were much shocked that John, the head boy, the school bellringer, the biggest boy there, should indulge in such childish weakness! Their eyes and mouths were like so many O's.

I went over to him and raised his head. It was difficult to tell from the tears and congestion if he were feverish or not, but his forehead was burning.

'Have you had measles?'

'No, miss.'

'Is your mother at home?'

'No, miss. She's got a job at Caxley this week.'

'Anyone at home?'

'Not till four o'clock.'

I went to see Mrs Finch-Edwards.

'I'll leave the door open while I take him over to the house, if you'll keep an eye on them. What about Eileen?'

His little sister looked perfectly normal. She had not had measles, but technically she was now in quarantine if, as was fairly obvious, her brother had got it. We decided to compromise by putting her desk in front, away from the others, for the rest of the day.

John looked very sorry for himself as he lay on the sofa under a rug, with the thermometer protruding from his mouth.

'Did you say your mother was serving at Sutton's the fish-shop?'

John nodded, as he was effectively gagged with the thermo-meter. I looked up the telephone number as we waited, thinking, not for the first time, how sad it is when mothers with young children have to take full-time jobs, and how impossible it is to try and be a substitute.

The thermometer stood at 102 degrees when I took it from his mouth. I tucked him up more securely in his rug, poked up the fire and went out into the hall to telephone to his mother.

'Speak to Mrs Burton?' said a voice, which I supposed to be the fishmonger's. 'She's serving at the moment.'

'Then I'll hang on,' I said, 'but this is urgent. Her little boy is ill and she will have to come immediately.'

'It's most inconvenient,' said the fishmonger severely, 'but I'll tell her.'

Mrs Burton was sensible and practical. She would be on the next bus, and intimated that if Mr S. didn't like it he could lump it. I went back to tell John the good news, but he had fallen asleep, breathing heavily, his forehead damp with sweat, so I crept out and across to the school.

It is this sort of occasion that makes one realize how absolutely necessary it is for every school, however small, to have two people who can take charge. Without Mrs Finch-Edwards there to superintend the children, any sort of accident might have happened; and I thought of several schoolmistresses that I knew, in the charge of perhaps twenty or more children, with no adult help within call, who might be coping at this very moment with such an emergency and with all the added mental distress of their lonely circumstances. It is a position in which no teacher should have to find herself, and yet it is, alas, a common one in our country areas.

It was during this bleak and plague-ridden period that Mr Willet appeared one morning with his hand heavily swaddled in strips of shirt-tail.

'We 'ad a very rough night, miss, very rough! Very rough indeed!' he said in reply to my inquiries. 'That Arthur Coggs, miss, is nothing more than a crying disgrace to Fairacre.'

It had all begun, evidently, at Caxley during the dinner hour. It was market day, and a member of one of the more rabid and obscure evangelical sects had set up his rostrum between a fishmonger with lungs of brass, and a purple-faced gentleman who threatened to smash up teapots and repair them again, with the aid of the miraculous paste which he held in his hand.

When twelve o'clock struck, Mr Willet told me, 'This 'ere 'eathen-jelly was as hoarse as a crow and took his tracts and that round to the building site where Arthur Coggs and his mates had just knocked off. They was sitting about on wheelbarrows and such, having their grub.'

So blood-curdling, evidently, were the "eathen-jelly's descriptions of the after-life that they could confidently look forward to, that Arthur was seriously perturbed. Early memories of his stern old father, who had held much the same beliefs as the earnest soul before him, came flooding back, and he resolved in a flash to give up drinking, swearing, wife-and-child beating, and to become an example of right-living to all Fairacre.

During the afternoon, as he stacked bricks in a leisurely way, he decided that his new life might profitably begin on the morrow. This evening he would have a farewell round of drinks with his cronies at 'The Beetle and Wedge,' and tell them of his changed ways. Who knows, he might even persuade some of those lost, black sheep to return to the fold with him?

He was, of course, chipped unmercifully by the hardened sinners in the pub that night. Spirits were high, language ripe and fruity, and beer flowed more generously than usual, as 'This was poor old Arthur's last drink!' By closing-time Arthur was decidedly drunk, and inflamed with his mission for reclaiming lost souls.

'You better save old Willet,' suggested one boisterous reveller, as they approached the Willets' prim cottage.

Mr and Mrs Willet had been in what Mr Willet called 'a lovely sleep,' when the rumpus began. Afire with good works, Arthur belaboured the paint-encrusted knocker, with all the might of the righteous. His companions were divided between mirth and shame. Some egged him on, while the more sober did their best to get him away from the door.

'What the Hanover!' said Mr Willet, creaking out of bed. He leant out of the window. 'Get off home! Waking up sleeping folks! Get off with you!'

'You come on down!' rejoined Arthur, 'I got something to ask you urgent!'

Mr Willet pulled on his socks, using language that Mrs Willet had never heard him use before in all their twenty-eight years of married life and regular church-going. She followed him timidly down to the last few steps of the box staircase, holding the door at the bottom open a chink to see that no harm came to her husband.

'Well, what is it?' asked Mr Willet testily, as he unbolted the front door. The cat, so recently put out, now streaked in, with a cry of alarm, followed by Arthur Coggs.

His companions melted rapidly away into the darkness. It appeared to them that Mr Willet, standing there in his billowing flannel shirt that served him by night and day for six days of the week, and with his sturdy legs bristling like gooseberries in the night air, could well cope alone with his visitor.

Arthur came very close to Mr Willet and scrutinized his unwelcoming visage.

'Mr Willet,' he said with something between a sob and a hiccup, 'I got something to ask you.'

'Well, git on with it,' said Mr Willet sharply. The draught from the door was cruel.

Arthur Coggs looked behind him furtively, then advanced another step. 'Willet, are you saved?' he pleaded earnestly.

Mr Willet's patience snapped at this insult to as steady-going a churchman as the village boasted.

'Saved?' he echoed. 'I'm a durn sight more saved than you are, you gobbering great fool!' And he attempted to push Arthur through the door. But, with the strength of one who burns with nine pints of beer and religious convictions, Arthur thrust him aside, closed the door with a backward kick, and came further into the room. He leant heavily on the table and looked across at the incensed Mr Willet.

'But 'ave you seen the light?' he persisted. 'Do your limbs tremble when you think of what's to come?'

Mr Willet's limbs were trembling enough, as it was, with cold and fury. He opened his mouth to speak, but was shouted down.

'Gird on your armour, Willet!' bellowed Arthur, his breath coming in beery waves across the table. He brandished his arms wildly, knocking down a very old fly-paper, that fell glutinously across the red serge tablecloth.

'Gird on your sword! Gird on your 'elmet, Willet!' His eye lit upon two stuffed owls that dominated the dresser by the fireplace. Carefully he lifted the heavy glass cover from them, and, with a glad cry, dropped it over his own head. The stuffed owls swayed on their dead branch, and Mrs Willet gave a little wail, and came down the last three stairs.

Like some enormous goldfish Arthur rounded on her, eyes gleaming through the cover.

'You saved?' he bellowed suspiciously to the newcomer, steaming up the glass as he spoke.

'Yes, thank you,' murmured Mrs Willet faintly, shrinking behind her husband.

'Then put on your 'elmet,' advised Arthur, tapping the glass by his right ear. 'Gird your loins—!'

''Ere, that's enough of that!' shouted Mr Willet, enraged. He caught hold of the dome above Arthur's shoulders and attempted to force it off; but so heavy was it, and so much taller was his visitor, that he found it impossible to accomplish.

'Sit you down, will 'ee?' screamed Mr Willet, giving the glass a vicious slap and Mr Coggs a most unorthodox blow in the stomach. Arthur folded up neatly and sat, winded, on the horsehair sofa.

Speechless with fury Mr Willet pulled the cover off and handed it to his wife, who tiptoed across the room and replaced it lovingly over the owls.

'If I wasn't in me night-shirt,' said Mr Willet wrathfully, 'I'd 'old your fat 'ead under the pump! You git off home to your poor wife!'

Arthur's militant spirit had evaporated suddenly, and at the mention of his wife a maudlin smile curved his moist mouth.

'Me poor wife!' he repeated, and sat considering this for a full minute. 'Me *only* wife,' he said, looking up in some surprise. He lurched to his feet and caught Mr Willet by the neck of his shirt.

'And do you know what?' he boomed, his face thrust close to his host's, 'she ain't saved, poor weasel! Me *only* wife, and she ain't saved!'

Mr Willet broke away and flung open the door.

'Then you can dam' well clear off 'ome and save her! Coming in 'ere kicking up like this! Be off with you, Arthur Coggs!'

With inexpressible dignity Arthur drew himself up and crossed the threshold.

'I 'opes,' he said coldly, swaying on the doorstep, 'that I knows when I'm not welcome. Arthur Coggs ain't the sort that pushes in where 'e's not wanted!'

And with a shattering hiccup, he passed out into the night.

This dreadful scene had direct repercussions on our school life, for Joseph Coggs was absent the next morning, spoiling the week's record of attendance for the infants' room. 'Me dad overdone it,' he explained in the afternoon, 'and we was all late up.'

Worse still, Mr Willet had been 'so shook up by the rough night' that he cut his thumb badly as he was opening a tin of baked beans for breakfast and, as I have told, had to attend to his school duties with a heavily-bandaged hand for the rest of the week.

So discouraged was Arthur Coggs by the unpopularity of his mission work, that he lapsed into his normal regrettable ways, much to the relief of the whole village.

11. THE NEW TEACHER

There were only three applicants for the post advertised at Fairacre School, although the advertisement had appeared in both *The Teachers' World* and *The Times Educational Supplement* for several weeks.

The vicar had called a managers' meeting to interview the three applicants on a Thursday afternoon, late in January. It was to be held at two-thirty in the vicar's dining-room, and I was invited to be present. I appreciated this courtesy, which is not always extended to the headmaster or headmistress when new staff is being appointed, and arranged with Mrs Finch-Edwards a combined crayoning class of the whole school. As an added incentive to good behaviour I produced a box of small silver stars to be gummed on the best work, and from the children's rapt expressions when I told them of these joys I fully expected that Mrs Finch-Edwards would have a peaceful afternoon while I was at the vicarage.

I walked across the churchyard to the meeting. Mr Partridge's vicarage stands in an enormous garden which abuts on to the graveyard. Mr Willet, who is St Patrick's sexton as well as our caretaker, was tidying up the graves, straightening a loose kerb-stone, breaking off a dead rose or setting an overturned flower vase upright again.

'Snow on the way, miss,' he greeted me. 'Look at them clouds!' He pointed to the gilded weathercock that gleamed like gold against a pile of heavy, ominous clouds behind St Patrick's. 'Wind's dropped too.'

He fell into step beside me and we walked across to the wicket-gate that opened into a shrubbery in the vicar's garden.

'The graves look very nice and tidy,' I said, making conversation.

Mr Willet looked gratified. He stopped by a particularly ugly memorial cross made from pinkish polished granite. It reminded me of brawn. 'My uncle Alf,' he said, patting it lovingly. 'Stands the weather well.'

The vicarage is a large Georgian house of warm red brick, standing among sloping lawns and looking out upon two fine cedar trees. It has a square, pillared porch and a beautiful fanlight over the door. I was glad to see that the iron bell-pull which I had rung on my first visit there, and which had disconcerted me by coming away in my hand, had been replaced by a bell-push on the jamb of the door.

The dining-table was set out with the applicants' papers at the head of it, and chairs set primly round. The vicar, as chairman, welcomed us and resumed his place at the head of the table. Miss Parr was already there, an old lady of nearly eighty, who lives at the other end of Fairacre in a house built in the reign of Queen Anne. The villagers maintain that she is fabulously wealthy. Certainly she is generous, and none going to her for financial help is disappointed. She says that she is fond of children, 'even these modern ones that do nothing but eat gum,' but so far as I know, she has never set foot in the school of which she has been a manager for nearly thirty years, during a school session.

Colonel Wesley, also nearing his eightieth birthday, sat beside her. He calls in to see the children on occasions, and is, of course, invited to all school functions, as are all the managers.

Both Miss Parr and the Colonel, despite their age and frequent indispositions, attend managers' meetings regularly. It will be difficult when these two leave the board of managers to find two people in the village who will come forward to take their place. Neither Miss Parr's nieces and nephews, nor Colonel Wesley's three sons and numerous grandchildren have ever used the state schools for any part of their education. Few people nowadays, even if they have close ties with their local school, have either the time or the desire to take on these voluntary duties which an earlier generation shouldered with the feeling of *noblesse oblige*.

Mr Roberts the youngest school manager had attended an elementary school in Caxley as a small boy, and gone on from there to the local grammar school. He has a first-hand knowledge of elementary education and he, with the vicar, has a close understanding of the practical needs of the school in their care.

Behind the vicar's chair, on the wall, hangs a portrait of one of his ancestors. He has a peevish expression and is holding out a piece of paper as though he were saying petulantly, 'Now, could you read this writing? Isn't it appalling?'

The vicar is inordinately proud of this picture and the letter, he claims, was written by Charles II to his ancestor to thank him for services rendered during his exile. Be that as it may, the old gentleman would not appear to be overjoyed at its perusal.

I was studying it again when the vicar said, 'I think we should begin. The applicants are Mrs Davis, who has come from Kent . . .' He paused, and looked at us over his glasses. 'Er . . . this lady has not had experience with infants, but would like to try. She has two children of her own, I believe.' From his tone it was clear that her application had not impressed him very favourably.

'The second applicant,' he went on, 'is a little older and has had experience in infant and junior schools in several towns in the Midlands. She is, at the moment, teaching in Wolverhampton. She could begin in March.'

'What's the last like?' asked Mr Roberts, stretching his long legs out under the table suddenly.

'A Miss Gray, very much younger, still in her twenties. She left the teaching profession last summer—'

'No disgrace, I hope?' said Miss Parr.

'Oh, no, indeed, no, no, no! Nothing of that sort,' the vicar assured her hastily. 'I understand she nursed her mother for some months, but is now free to take a post.'

'Does she come from a distance?' asked the Colonel. 'Any chance of her living at home, I mean; or will she have to have digs in the village?'

'I expect it will have to be Mrs Pratt's,' answered the vicar. 'I have approached her and she has a very nice bedroom—'

'Well, let's see these gals,' said Miss Parr, putting her gloves down on the table with an impatient slap. I suspected that she had given up an afternoon nap for this meeting, for she seemed restless and had stifled yawns.

'Well, there we are,' said the vicar, gazing round at us all. 'I rather feel that Miss Gray will be our best choice, judging from her application; but we will ask them in and see for ourselves. Shall we have the lady from Kent in first?'

There were grunts of approval and the vicar went across the hall to ask Mrs Davis in.

They returned together. The vicar took his place at the end of the table again and Mrs Davis sat nervously at the other. We all wished her 'Good afternoon,' and smiled at her encouragingly.

She was a large woman with a shiny face. Her neck was flushed red with embarrassment and she answered the vicar's questions breathlessly.

'May I ask something?' she said. 'Where is the nearest station?'

'Why, Caxley!' said Mr Roberts in surprise.

'And what sort of bus service?' she asked. The Colonel told her and her mouth dropped open.

'I'm afraid that quite settles it,' she said with decision. 'I thought, coming along, how far away from everything it was; but if that's the situation – well, I'm sorry, but I would rather withdraw my application. I've got my two girls to think of, you know. We can't be buried miles from anywhere!'

The vicar looked regretful.

'Well, Mrs Davis,' he began, 'I know Fairacre is a little remote but—'

'I'm sorry, I'm sure, for all the trouble I've given; but my mind's made up. I had a look round the village this morning and it's not a bit like Kent, you know.' Her tone was reproachful.

The vicar said he was sorry, but if Mrs Davis was quite decided . . . He paused, his voice a query.

Mrs Davis rose from the dining-room chair and said, 'I'm afraid I must say "No," but I'm grateful to you for calling me up for interview.'

She smiled round at us; we made sounds of regret, and the vicar escorted her into the hall inviting her to stop for tea before she faced her long journey, but, like a freed bird, Mrs Davis was anxious to fly back to her nest in Kent and we heard her steps on the gravel path as she hurried to catch the three o'clock bus.

'Well, well,' said the vicar, with a note of relief in his voice as he sorted out the next application form, 'a pity about Mrs Davis, but of course she must consider her family.'

'Would never have done, anyway,' said Miss Parr flatly, voicing the secret thoughts of us all.

The vicar cleared his throat noisily. 'I'll fetch Miss Winter now. The lady from Wolverhampton,' he reminded us, as he set off across the hall again.

Miss Winter was as pale as Mrs Davis had been rosy. Grey wisps of hair escaped from a grey hat, her gloved hands fluttered and her pale lips twitched with nervousness. She did not heed our greetings nor our smiles, as she was quite incapable of meeting our eyes.

It transpired that she was run-down. She had had very large classes for many years and found them too much for her. It was quite apparent that they would be. Her discipline, I suspected, was non-existent, and even our local children, docile and amenable as they are by most standards, would soon take advantage of this poor, fluttering soul.

'I think I could manage young children,' she said, in answer to the vicar. 'Oh, yes, a small class of *good* young children . . . I should enjoy that! And I'm sure my health would improve in the country! The doctor himself suggested that I needed a much less trying post. Town children can be very unruly, you know!'

The managers asked a few more questions. The Colonel asked his stock one: 'A communicant, of course?'; and Miss Parr her stock one: 'I do so hope you are interested in needlework? Good, *plain* needlework – the number of girls these days with no idea of simple stitchery—'

Miss Winter was asked to wait again in the drawing-room while we interviewed the last applicant.

Miss Isobel Gray was twenty-nine, tall and dark. She was not good-looking, but had a pleasant pale face and a fine pair of grey eyes. We all felt more hopeful as she answered the vicar's questions calmly and concisely.

'I see that you gave up teaching to nurse your mother. I gather that she is well enough for you to feel that you can apply for a permanent post?'

'My mother, I'm afraid, died in the autumn. I did not feel like going back to teaching immediately, but I should like to now.'

We all made noises of sympathy and the vicar made a kind little speech.

Yes, she was a communicant, she replied to the Colonel, and yes, she was most interested in plain needlework and made many of her own garments, she told Miss Parr. There were a few more practical questions before the vicar escorted her back to the drawing-room.

'Well?' he asked, when he returned.

'Best of the bunch,' said Mr Roberts, stretching his legs again.

'A very nice, ladylike gal,' said Miss Parr approvingly.

'I liked her,' said the Colonel.

The Vicar turned to me. 'Miss Read, you have to work with our choice – what do you feel about it?'

'I like her too,' I said; and the vicar, nodding happily, made his final trip across the hall to acquaint Miss Gray with her good fortune and offer Miss Winter solace in a cup of tea.

Soon after five o'clock that day the vicar called at my house, bringing Miss Gray with him.

'Could you show Miss Gray over the school?' he asked, 'and I wondered if you would be able to go down to Mrs Pratt's with her to arrange about board and lodging. I wish there were more choice,' he added, turning to the new teacher, 'but accommodation in a village is always difficult – very difficult!' He stroked his leopard-skin gloves sadly, and some stray fur fluttered down with his sigh. 'But I'm sure you will be very happy here with us,' he went on, bracing up, 'Fairacre is an example of cheerful living to our neighbouring villages. Don't you agree, Miss Read?'

I assured him truthfully that I had been happy in Fairacre, but I wondered if Mrs Pringle and a few other such gloomy sprites could fairly be called examples of cheerful living.

The vicar said good-bye and went off down the path with a swirl of his cloak. A few snowflakes fluttered in the light from the porch.

'You haven't got to make the journey home tonight, I hope?' I asked Miss Gray.

'No, I'm staying with friends in Caxley. If I catch the 6.15 bus that will suit them very well.'

I put on my coat and we went across to the dark school.

'I wish you could have seen it in sunshine,' I said, 'it looks much better.'

'But I have,' she said, to my surprise. 'When I thought of applying I came over from Caxley and looked at the school and the village. I liked it all so much that that made up my mind for me. I know the neighbourhood fairly well through staying with friends. They have a good deal to do with the orchestra in Caxley.'

'Do you play at all?'

'Yes, the violin and the piano. I should like to join the orchestra if it is easy to get in and out of Caxley.'

The school was very still and unreal. The tidy rows of desks, the children's drawings, the pot of Roman hyacinths in flower on my desk all looked like stage properties awaiting the actor's presence to lend them validity. The artificial light heightened this effect.

Our shoes echoed noisily on the boards as we went through to the infants' room that would be Miss Gray's own.

'I wonder *why* they built the windows so horribly high!' exclaimed Miss Gray, looking at the narrow arches set up in the wall. 'Well, I know they didn't want the children to look out, but really – such a peculiar mentality!'

She walked round her new domain, examining pictures and

looking at books in the cupboards. Her pale face had grown quite pink with excitement and she looked almost pretty. It seemed a pity to take her away from it all, but if she had to catch the Caxley bus and we had to face Mrs Pratt first, there was no time to spare.

'You are coming to us on the first of February, I believe?' I asked.

'Yes, it seems best. I've no notice to give in, but it means that I shall have just over a week to settle in the village, and it gives your supply teacher a little notice.'

So we arranged that she would come over one day before the beginning of February to see about syllabuses, schemes of work, children's records, reading methods and all the other interesting school matters, but that now, with time pressing, we must hurry down the road to Mrs Pratt's house, before that lady began putting her two little children to bed.

Jasmine Villa had been built some eighty years ago by a prosperous retired tradesman from Caxley. His grandson still ran the business there, but let this property to Mr and Mrs Pratt for a rental so small that it was next to impossible for him to keep the house in adequate repair.

It was square and grey with a slated roof. A verandah ran across its width, and over this in the summer-time grew masses of the shrub which gave the house its name. So dilapidated was this iron verandah that its curling trellis-work and the jasmine appeared to give each other much-needed mutual support. A neat black and white tiled path, edged with undulating grey stone coping, like so many penny buns in rows, led from the iron gate to the front door. It was an incongruous house to find in this village. It might have been lifted bodily from Finsbury Park or Shepherd's Bush and dropped down between the thatched row of cottages belonging to Mr Roberts' farm on the one side, and the warm red bulk of 'The Beetle and Wedge' on the other.

Mrs Pratt, a plain cheerful woman in her thirties, opened the door to us. Her face always gleams like a polished apple, so tight and shiny is her well-scrubbed skin.

'Come into the front room,' she invited us, 'I'm afraid the fire's not in – we live at the back mostly, and my husband's just having his tea out there.' An appetizing smell of grilled herring wreathed around us as she spoke.

I explained why I had come and introduced the two to each other. Mrs Pratt began to rattle away about cooked breakfasts, bathing arrangements, washing and ironing, retention fees, door keys and all the other technical details that landladies need to discuss with prospective tenants, while Miss Gray listened and nodded and occasionally asked a question.

The room was lit by a central hanging bulb. It was very cold and I was glad that Mrs Pratt's business methods were so brisk that I might reasonably get back to my fire within half an hour.

Against one wall stood an upright piano on which Mrs Pratt practised her church music. A copy of 'The Crucifixion' was open on the stand. Mr Annett evidently started practising his Good Friday oratorio in good time. Two large photographs dominated the top. One showed a wasp-waisted young woman, with a bustle, leaning against a pedestal, in a sideways-bend position which must have given her ribs agony as her corsets could not have failed to dig in cruelly at the top. The same young woman appeared in the second photograph. She was in a wedding dress, and stood behind an ornately carved chair, in which sat a bewildered little man with a captured expression. One large capable hand rested on his shoulder, the other grasped the chair-back, and on her face was a look of triumph. Between the two photographs was a long green dish of thick china, shaped like a monstrous lettuce leaf, with three china tomatoes clustering at one end.

I turned my fascinated gaze to the sideboard as Mrs Pratt's voice rose and fell. Here there was more distorted pottery to the square foot of sideboard top than I have ever encountered. Toby jugs jostled with teapots shaped like houses, jam pots shaped like beehives, apples and oranges, jugs like rabbits and other animals, and one particularly horrid one taking the form of a bird – the milk coming from the beak as one grasped the tail for a handle. A shiny black cat, with a very long neck, supported a candle on its head and leered across at a speckled china hedgehog whose back bristled with coloured spills. A bloated white fish with its mouth wide open had 'ASHES' printed down its back and faced a frog who was yawning, I imagine, for the same purpose. At any minute one imagined that Disneyish music would start to play and these fantastic characters would begin a grotesque life of their own, hobbling, squeaking, lumbering, hinnying – poor deformed players in a nightmare.

'I do like pretty things,' said Mrs Pratt complacently, following my gaze. 'Shall we go up and see the bedroom?'

It was surprisingly attractive, with white walls and velvet curtains – 'bought at a sale,' explained Mrs Pratt – which had faded to a gentle blue. The room, like the one below it which we had just left, was big and lofty, but much less cluttered with furniture. Miss Gray seemed pleased with it. There were only three drawbacks, and they were all easily removed; a plaster statuette of a little girl with a pronounced spinal curvature and a protruding stomach, who held out her skirts winsomely as she gazed out of the window; and two pictures, equally distressing.

One showed a generously-proportioned young woman with eyes piously upraised. She was lashed securely to a stake set in the midst of a raging river, for what reason was not apparent. There were some verses, however, beneath this picture and I determined to read them when visiting Miss Gray in the future. The other picture was even more upsetting, showing a dog lying in a welter of blood, the whites of its eyes showing frantically. Its young master, in a velvet suit, was caressing it in farewell. I knew I should never hope for a wink of sleep in the presence of such scenes and only prayed that Miss Gray might not be so easily affected.

We followed Mrs Pratt down the stairs to the front door. Snow-flakes whirled in as she opened it.

'I will let you know definitely by Monday,' said Miss Gray. 'Will that do?'

'Perfectly, perfectly!' answered Mrs Pratt happily, 'and we can always alter anything you know – I mean, if you want to bring your own books or pictures we could come to some arrangement—'

We nodded and waved our way through the snowflakes down

to the gate and into the lane. The snow was beginning to settle and muffled the sounds of our footsteps.

'I suppose,' Miss Gray began diffidently, 'that there is nowhere else to go?'

'I don't know of any other place,' I replied, and went on to explain how difficult it is to get suitable lodgings for a single girl in a village. The cottages are too small and are usually overcrowded as it is, and the people who have large houses would never dream of letting a room to a school-teacher. It is a very serious problem for rural schools to face. It is not easy for a girl to find suitable companionship in a small village, and if it is any considerable distance from a town there may be very little to keep her occupied and happy in such a restricted community. It is not surprising that young single women, far from their own homes, do not stay for any length of time in country schools.

'Those pictures must go!' said Miss Gray decidedly, as we stood sheltering against Mr Roberts's wall waiting for the bus.

'They must,' I agreed, with feeling.

'She's asking two pounds ten a week,' pursued Miss Gray, 'which seems fair enough I think.' I thought so too, and we were busy telling each other how much better it would all look with a fire going and perhaps some of the china tactfully removed 'for safety's sake,' and one's own books and possessions about, when the bus slithered to a stop in the snow. Miss Gray boarded it, promising to telephone to me, and was borne away round the bend of the lane.

12. SNOW AND SKATES

It snowed steadily throughout the night and I woke next morning to see a cold pallid light reflected on the ceiling from the white world outside. It was deathly quiet everywhere. Nothing moved and no birds sang. The school garden, the playground, the neighbouring fields and the distant majesty of the downs were clothed in deep snow; and although no flakes were falling in the early morning light, the sullen grey sky gave promise of more to come.

Mrs Pringle was spreading sacks on the floor of the lobby when I went over to the school.

'Might save a bit,' she remarked morosely, 'though with the way children throws their boots about these days, never thinking of those that has to clear up after them, I expect it's all love's labour lost.' She followed me, limping heavily, into the school-room. I prepared for the worst.

'This cold weather catches my bad leg cruel. I said to Pringle this morning, "For two pins I'd lay up today, but I don't like to let Miss Read down." He said I was too good-hearted, always putting other people first – but I'm like that. Have been ever since a girl; and a good thing I did come!' She paused for dramatic effect. I knew my cue.

'Why? What's gone wrong?'

'The stove in the infants' room.' Her smile was triumphant. 'Something stuck up the flue, shouldn't wonder. That Mrs Finch-Edwards does nothing but burn paper, paper, paper on it! Never see such ash! And as for pencil sharpenings! Thick all round the fireguard, they are! Miss Clare, now, always sharpened on to a newspaper, and put it all, neat as neat, in the basket, but I wouldn't like to tell you some of the stuff I've riddled out of that stove at nights since madam's been in there!'

She buttoned up her mouth primly and gave me such a dark look that one might have thought she'd been fishing charred children's bones out of the thing.

I assumed my brisk tone. 'It won't light at all?'

'Tried three times!' attested Mrs Pringle, with maddening complacency. 'Fair belches smoke, pardon the language! Best get Mr Rogers to it. Mr Willet's got no idea with machinery. Remember how he done in the vicar's lawn-mower?'

I did, and said we must certainly get Mr Rogers to come and look at the stove. Mrs Pringle noticed the use of the first person plural and hastened to extricate herself.

'If my leg wasn't giving me such a tousling I'd offer to go straight away, miss, as you well know. For as Pringle says, never was there such a one for doing a good turn to others, but it's as much as I can do to drag myself round now. As you can see!' she added, moving crabwise to straighten the fire-irons, and flinching as she went.

'The children will all have to be in here together this morning, so I shall go down myself,' I said. 'With this weather, and the epidemic still flourishing, I doubt if we shall get many at school in any case.'

'If only he was on the 'phone,' said Mrs Pringle, 'it would save you a walk. But there, when you're young and spry a walk in the snow's a real pleasure!'

She trotted briskly back to the lobby, the limp having miraculously vanished, as she heard children's voices in the distance.

'And don't bring none of that dirty old snow in my clean school,' I heard her scolding them. 'Look where you're treading now – scuffling about all over! Anyone'd think I was made of sacks.'

There were only eighteen children in school that day. Little wet gloves, soaked through snowballing, and a row of wet socks and steaming shoes lined the fire-guard round the stove in my room.

I left Mrs Finch-Edwards to cope with a test on the multiplication tables and set out to see Mr Rogers who is the local blacksmith and odd-job man.

His forge is near Tyler's Row and I walked down the deserted village street thinking how dirty the white paint, normally immaculate, of Mr Roberts' palings looked against the dazzle of the snow. I passed Mrs Pratt's house and 'The Beetle and Wedge,' where I caught a glimpse of Mrs Coggs on her knees, with a stout sack for an apron and a massive scrubbing-brush in her hand.

'Sut!' said Mr Rogers, when I told him. 'Corroded sut!' He was hammering a red-hot bar, as he spoke, and his words jerked from him to an accompanying shower of sparks. 'That's it, you'll see! Corroded sut in the flue-pipe!' He suddenly flung the bar into a heap of twisted iron in a dark recess, and drawing a very dirty red handkerchief from his pocket, he blew his nose violently. I waited while he finished this operation, which involved a great deal of polishing, mopping and finally flicking of the end of his flexible nose, from side to side.

At last he was done, and he stuffed his handkerchief away, with some post-operative sniffs, saying: 'Be up there during your dinner hour, miss; clobber and all! Nothing but sut, I'll lay!'

The schoolroom was cheerful and warm to return to. There was a real family feeling in the air this morning, engendered by the small number of children and the wider range of age, from the five-year-olds like Joseph and Jimmy to the ten-year-old Cathy and John Burton.

They were sitting close to the stove, on which the milk saucepan steamed, with their mugs in their hands. After the bleak landscape outside this domestic interior made a comforting picture. They chattered busily to each other, recounting their adventures on the perilous journey to school, and tales grew taller and taller.

'Why, up Dunnett's there's a tractor buried, and you can't see nothing of it, it's that deep!'

'You ought to see them ricks up our way! Snow's right up the top, one side!'

'Us fell in a drift outside the church where that ol' drain is! Poor ol' Joe here he was pretty near up to his armpits, wasn't you? Didn't half make me laugh!'

'They won't run no more Caxley buses today, my dad said. It's higher'n a house atween here and Beech Green!'

Their eyes were round and shining with excitement as they sought to impress each other. Sipping and munching their elevenses, they gossiped away, heroes all, travellers in a strange world today, whose perils they had overcome by sheer intrepidity.

Playtime over, I brought out the massive globe from the cupboard and set it on the table. I told them about hot countries and cold, about tropical trees and steaming jungles, and about vast tracts of ice and snow, colder and more terrifying than any sights they had seen that morning. Together we ranged the world, while I tried to describe the diverse glories of tropic seas and majestic mountain ranges, the milling vivid crowds of the Indian cities and the lonely solitude of the trapper's shack; all the variety of beauty to be found in our world, here represented by this fascinating brass-bound ball in a country classroom.

'And all the time,' I told them, 'the world is going round and round, like this!' I twirled the globe vigorously, with one finger on the Russian Steppes. 'Which accounts for the night and the day,' I added. I regretted this remark as soon as I saw the bewildered faces before me, for this meant a further lesson, and one, as I knew from bitter experience, that was always difficult.

'How d'you mean – night and day?' came the inevitable query.

I looked at the clock. Ten minutes before the dinner van was due to arrive – I launched into the deep.

'Come and stand over here, John, and be the sun. Don't move at all. Now watch!' I twirled the globe again. 'Here's England, facing John – the sun, that is. It's bright and warm here, shining on England, but as I turn the globe what happens?'

There was a stupefied silence. The older children were thinking hard, but the babies, very sensibly, had ceased to listen to such dull stuff and were sucking thumbs happily, their eyes roving round the unaccustomed pictures of their older brothers' and sisters' room.

'England moves away?' hazarded one groping soul.

'Yes, it moves further and further round, until it is in darkness. It's night-time now for us.'

'Well, who's got the sun now?' asked someone who was really getting the hang of this mystery.

'Australia, New Zealand, all the countries on this side of the globe. Then, as the world turns, they gradually revolve back into darkness and we come round again. And so on!' I twisted the globe merrily, and they watched it spin with silent satisfaction.

'You know,' said John at last, summing up the wonder succinctly, 'someone thought that out pretty good!'

The dinner van was twenty minutes late and I began to feel worried. Throughout the geography lesson the clang and scrape of Mr Willet's spade had been heard as he cleared a path through the playground. I went out now to see if he had any news.

He stumped off to the road for me and I heard voices in the distance. His face was alight with the importance of bad news when he returned.

'They've just rung Mr Roberts, miss. He's taking his tractor out to Bember's Corner to try and right the van. It come off the road into the ditch, they says!' He puffed his moustache in and out in pleasurable excitement.

'Is Mrs Crossley all right?'

'Couldn't say, I'm sure; but not likely, is it? I mean, bound to be shook up, if there ain't nothing broken, which is only to be expected.' He fairly glowed with the countryman's morbid delight in someone elses's misfortune. I thought of my hungry family.

'Mr Willet,' I begged, 'do please go to the shop and get some bread for the children and tins of stew.' I made rapid mental calculations. About six would be able to go home and find their mothers there, but I should have at least twelve to provide for.

'Yes,' I continued, 'two loaves, six tins of stewed steak and two pounds of apples. And half a pound of toffees, please.' It seemed a good mixed diet and I doubted whether the vitamin content would be as well balanced as it should be; but it would be nourishing and quickly prepared. I provided him with money and a basket and returned to send home the children that I could and to break the news to the others.

Dinner was a huge success. Mrs Finch-Edwards and the children had heaved one of the long tables from the infants' room and set it by the stove, while I opened tins of steak and mixed up Oxo cubes and cut bread, over in my kitchen, with Cathy Waites and little Jimmy as awed assistants. Jimmy wandered round the kitchen inspecting the equipment.

'And what's this, miss?'

'That's for mashing potatoes.'

'My mum uses a fork. What's this?'

'A tea-strainer. Pass the salt, Cathy.'

'What for?'

'To catch the tea-leaves. And the pepper, dear.'

'What do you want to catch tea-leaves for?'

'Because I don't like them in my teacup. I think we'll start the other loaf now.'

'What do you do with them when you've caught them?'

'Throw them away.'

'Well, why catch them if you throws them out after?'

'Cathy,' I said firmly, 'take the tea-strainer to the sink and show him with water and bits of bread crumb, while I finish this off!'

The demonstration was successful, and when I presented Jimmy with an old strainer, to keep the tea-leaves out of his own cup at home, he was enraptured.

Dinner was eaten amid great good-humour and to the accompaniment of metallic hammerings from next door, where Mr Rogers, complete with 'clobber' was attacking the flue-pipe. It was, as he had foretold, simply corroded soot which had flaked away and fallen across a turn in the pipe, preventing a draught, and he departed in a comfortable glow of self-esteem.

The snow had begun to fall again, and Mrs Pringle, when she arrived to wash-up, was plastered with snow where she had faced the wind. Her expression was martyred and her limp much accentuated.

'If it's no better by half-past two,' I said to Mrs Finch-Edwards, as we watched the snow whirling in eddies across Mr Willet's newly-made path, 'we'll close school and get them home early.'

'I shall have to wheel my bicycle most of the way to Spring-bourne,' said Mrs Finch-Edwards. 'My hubby was awfully wor-ried about me coming on it this morning. Like a hen with one chick, he is!' She dusted her massive torso down with a gratified smirk. 'I sometimes wonder how he ever got along before he met me – with nothing to worry over, the silly boy!'

I was about to say that, surely, she had told me herself that he used to keep pigs, but thinking that this might be misconstrued, I held my tongue.

At half-past two the weather was even worse, and we buttoned children into coats, turned up collars, crossed woolly scarves over bulging fronts and tied them into fringed bustles behind, sorted out gloves and wellingtons and with final exhortations to keep together, to go *straight* home and (forlorn hope!) to desist from snowballing each other on the way, we sent the little band out into the wind and storm.

For three days and three nights the countryside was swept by snowstorms. Only three children arrived one morning and I rang the local education office for permission to close school. The snow-ploughs came out from Caxley to clear the main roads and a breakdown lorry was able to get to the abandoned dinner van and tow it back to the garage. Mrs Crossley, despite blood-curdling rumours, was luckily unhurt.

At last the snow stopped, and on the fourth day the sun shone from a sky as limpid as a June morning's. The snow glittered like sugar icing, but the temperature remained so low that there was no hope of a thaw. Mr Roberts had his duck-pond swept clear of snow and invited the village to skate. As the pond is a large one, and nowhere deeper than two feet, mothers were only too delighted to send the children who had been milling about their feet for the past few days, and once school was over – for we opened again when the snowstorms stopped – the children raced joyfully across the road to a superb slide at one edge of the pond.

The older generation dug out skates, and so keen were they that Mr Roberts switched on the headlights of his lorry and evening parties swirled and skimmed like rare winter swallows while the ice held.

Dr Martin and his wife brought Miss Clare, and the vicar, in a dashing red and white ski-ing jacket over his clerical greys and the inevitable leopard-skin gloves encasing his hands, brought his wife. Miss Parr came, with a sister who must have been eighty, and all these elderly people came into their own. They waltzed, they glided, they swerved magnificently in figures-of-eight, while we younger ones tottered tensely round on borrowed skates, or, more ignobly still, pushed old kitchen chairs before us and marvelled at the grace and beauty of those who were our seniors by thirty years or more.

Mrs Roberts, with true farmhouse hospitality, threw open her great kitchen, and sizzling sausages and hard-boiled eggs and hot dripping toast were offered to the hungry skaters, with beer or cocoa to wash down the welcome food. For a week the fun continued; then the church weathercock slewed round, a warm west wind rushed to us across the downs, the roofs began to drip and little rivers trickled and gurgled along the lanes of Fairacre.

The thaw had come; we packed away our skates, and Mr Roberts' ducks went back to their pond again.

13. SAD AFFAIR OF THE EGGS

Joseph Coggs sidled round the half-shut door of his cottage. The baby's pram was just inside and wedged the door securely. After the February sunshine the little house was dark, and smelt of babies' washing and burnt potatoes.

Joseph put the cap that he was carrying very carefully on the table.

'Mum!' he shouted hopefully. There was no reply. He went through to the lean-to scullery and saw his mother through the open door feeling baby clothes against her cheek. Around her, on the ragged hedge and on the unkempt gooseberry bushes were innumerable tattered garments, drying as best they could.

'Got something for you!' said Joseph, in his hoarse cracked voice. His eyes gleamed with excitement.

'What? Some old trash from school again?' queried his mother crossly.

'Ah! I got a little house I done a's'afternoon – but I got something special for you!' He tugged at her arm, and, snatching a few garments from the bushes as she went, his mother submitted to being pulled back to the house.

Proudly Joseph displayed the contents of his cap – five brown eggs, with the bloom of that day's laying still upon them.

'Where d'you get'em?' inquired his mother suspiciously.

'Mrs Roberts give 'em to me,' said her son, but his fingers drummed uncomfortably on the table edge and his eyes remained downcast. His mother thought quickly. Five eggs would be a godsend with things as they were. Now that Arthur was back regular at 'The Beetle and Wedge,' there was mighty little handed over to her for food.

It was a pity they'd stopped teasing her husband about that night at Willet's, for while that had been going on Arthur had only dared to call in for a quick one and had escaped from their ribald tongues as hastily as he could. She'd noticed the difference in her housekeeping money. She looked again at the tempting eggs. Why, she could make something real nice for the kids with them, and Mrs Roberts wasn't likely to miss them anyway. She spoke kindly to her son.

'That was nice of her – a real lady, Mrs Roberts! I'll put 'em safe in the cupboard.' And she whisked them hastily away. She didn't want awkward questions from Arthur anyway, and somehow, well – out of sight was out of mind, wasn't it? And least said, soonest mended! Sensible sayings, both of 'em!

'And this is what I done today,' Joseph's voice broke in on her thoughts. 'Miss Gray done the door for me, but I cut up the lines myself.' He held up a small paper house, grubby and woefully askew. His face glowed with the pride of creation. 'Ain't it lovely?'

'Pity they don't learn you nothing better than that stuff,' said his mother shortly, still smarting from a guilty conscience. 'Them new teachers don't half fill you up with rubbish. Time you was learnt something useful.' But she suffered him to prop it on the window-sill and there he leant, gazing through the tiny open door, at the window beyond. Tomorrow he'd cut out little men and women from the paper, he told himself happily, and they could all live together in his house, his very own house. He sighed blissfully at the thought of all the joy ahead.

Next door Jimmy and Cathy Waites were at tea. This was what Mrs Waites called 'A scratch meal,' as they would be having high tea soon after six when the rest of the family returned from Caxley.

As the children chattered together and munched bread and shop honey, she studied an advertisement in her favourite women's weekly magazine.

'I've half a mind to,' she murmured to herself, 'only one and three! It's a saving really; that last lot of nail-varnish was never rightly my colour.' She inspected her hands minutely. Despite housework and vegetable peeling they were still pretty.

'Don't want to let myself go,' she told herself peering down at her reflection in the glass-bottomed tray. 'Be as slummocky as the creature next door!' And with one of her sharp nails she began to claw out 'This Week's Amazing Offer To Our Readers.'

Jimmy was intent on the label on the honey jar. He now knew his sounds and was beginning to find that, by piecing them together, real words sometimes evolved. He was agog to read, to be able to sit, as Cathy did, with her head in a book, sometimes looking sad, sometimes laughing, flicking over the magic pages that unrolled a story for her.

'MAD FROM—' he began painfully.

'It's got an E on it,' said Cathy exasperatedly. 'You know what Miss Gray said! It says its *name* not its sound! Not "MAD," silly, "MADE!"'

'MADE FROM' repeated Jimmy meekly, and began maddeningly on 'PURE' with all its phonetic pitfalls.

Cathy fidgeted restlessly, as he struggled. A thought struck her. 'Mum, I never told you yesterday! I've got to do the next bit of that exam, next week, Miss Read says. If I gets through I can go to Caxley.'

Mrs Waites looked up from the scraps of paper, round-eyed.

'Well, aren't you a one! My, I'm glad, Cath! You do your best, love, and if you gets it we'll let you go somehow.'

Visions of uniforms, hockey sticks, satchels and other paraphernalia flickered before her. It would cost a mint of money. But
there, others managed, didn't they? And if the kid was clever
enough to get to Caxley High School, or whatever its new-
fangled name was, she'd see she was turned out nice. She looked
again at her daughter's dark head, close to Jimmy's flaxen one, as
she explained the intricacies of 'SUGAR' to him; and let herself
dwell, for an indulgent minute, on the memory of the dark good
looks of Cathy's father.

'He was a card, and no mistake,' she thought, blushing slightly.
She pulled herself together and rose to clear the table. No good
thinking on things past. Some people would say she'd been bad,
but she didn't believe anything that could make you so happy
could be *all* bad. She stood still, butter-dish in hand, puzzling
over the niceties of moral conduct.

'Ah, well!' she said, at length, giving up the struggle to
straighten the tangled skein, 'I've got a real good husband to
think about now!' And shutting the memory away in the secret
drawer that all pretty women have, she went to put on the
potatoes for his supper.

Mrs Finch-Edwards was sitting on Mrs Moffat's couch, admiring
the new rug which lay before the tiled hearth, and listening to
Mrs Moffat's account of Linda's progress under Miss Read.

'She can read anything, you know. Never had any difficulty
with that; but surely she ought to know all her tables by eight
years old! Didn't you teach them that in your room?'

'Only a few,' said Mrs Finch-Edwards. 'These days they don't
expect children to start all that stuff as young as we did.'

'Then it's time things were altered,' said Mrs Moffat decidedly.
'How's Linda going to tackle the arithmetic paper in the exam, if
she's still feeling her way round stuff she should have learnt in the
infants' room? What we'll do if she doesn't get through to Caxley
High School, I don't know. You know my husband's not one to
worry, but I know money's short. This house took more than we
thought, and the shop's not doing too well.'

Mrs Finch-Edwards studied her friend's worried countenance
and offered what comfort she could.

'You don't have to worry about Linda. She's got a couple of

years yet, and she's bright enough. As for money, well, we all worry about that, don't we?'

'Yes, but this is worse than usual! I've promised Linda she shall have dancing lessons next term at Caxley and now – well, I really don't know how we can do it! And she's that set on it!'

And so are you, thought Mrs Finch-Edwards, torn between pity and exasperation at this exhibition of maternal ambition.

'Can't you take in a bit of dressmaking?' she asked dubiously.

Mrs Moffat looked slightly offended.

'It's not quite the thing, is it? A little shop, now – the sort of idea we've talked about – that's different! But there again, you need capital. I don't like to say too much to Len, he always takes me up so short, saying other people can do on what we get. I tell him maybe they've no desire to better themselves.'

There were footsteps outside and Linda burst in.

'Hello, auntie, hello, mum!' She stood there, panting and sniffing.

'Wipe your nose!' said her mother, rather put out at her daughter's tousled appearance before a visitor. Linda rubbed her nose along her knuckles in a perfunctory way.

Mrs Moffat's voice rose to a horrified scream. 'For pity's sake, Linda! Where do you pick up such ways? That common school—!' She turned a scandalized glance at Mrs Finch-Edwards. 'Where's your hanky?'

'Lost it!' returned her daughter.

'Then go and get one!' said her mother, 'and wash yourself and do your hair!' she called after the retreating child. 'You see what I mean?' she appealed to her friend. 'She's getting as bad as the rest of them, and what can I do about it? If only I could get her to those dancing classes – she might meet some better-class children there.'

She rose to get the tea ready. At the door she turned with a refined shudder. 'I never thought to see a daughter of mine – COMMON!' she said.

It was arithmetic lesson and the classroom was quiet. Both blackboards were covered with sums, and the three groups groaned over such diverse problems as '½ lb. butter at 4s. lb.' in the lowest group, to '6d. as a decimal of £' in the highest one.

Beside me sat Cathy who was being shown once again the mysteries of long multiplication. She had some difficulty with this type of sum, though normally intelligent enough, and with the examination so near I felt we really must master this particular problem.

We were interrupted by the clang of the paint-bucket and heavy footsteps in the lobby, Mr Roberts' large head came round the door.

'Sorry to interrupt,' he said, in what he fondly imagined was a whisper. The children looked up, delighted at this welcome interruption. Who knows, Mr Roberts might have the old black-board down again, their eyes sparkled to each other! And what could be more delightful than that, in the middle of an arithmetic test?

'Can I have a word with you alone?' he asked.

I sent Cathy back to her desk, with a long multiplication sum to attempt, and followed him into the lobby.

His big face was distressed. 'Look here!' he began, 'I don't like suspecting people, as you know.' He stopped and studied his boot so long that I felt he needed some assistance.

'Well, come on! Out with it!' I said peremptorily, 'they'll be copying wholesale in there if I don't get back quickly.'

Mr Roberts shifted uncomfortably, took a deep breath and rattled it all out. It appeared that he had been missing eggs from the hen-house and had marked some very early that morning and put them back in the nest. He went to collect them at half-past nine and they had vanished. Would I mind . . . (here he peered earnestly at me and turned a deep red) if he looked through the children's pockets?

I said I thought we should ask the children first if they knew anything about the missing eggs; then they would have the chance to own up.

An unhappy silence greeted my inquiries. No, no one knew anything about the eggs. Blue eyes, brown eyes, hazel eyes, met mine in turn as I looked at their upturned faces. I nodded to Mr Roberts who returned miserably to the lobby. This was obviously hurting him as much as it hurt us, I thought with some amusement.

'Get on with your work again,' I said, and pens were resumed abstractedly, tongues twirled from the corners of mouths, and superficially, at least, all seemed normal; but there was a tension in the air. The door opened again and Mr Roberts beckoned me out with an enormous forefinger.

'Oh, miss!' came a choked cry as I went towards the door. It was Eric who had called out – his normally pale face suffused with a pink flush. Tears stood in his eyes.

'What is it, Eric?'

'Nothing, miss, nothing!' he said with a sob. And putting his head down in his arms his shoulders began to shake. His neighbours looked at him in astonishment and pity.

Out in the lobby Mr Roberts held open the pocket of Eric's raincoat. There, carefully wrapped in dock-leaves were three eggs. Each had a tiny cross on its side from Mr Roberts' pencil.

'Will you deal directly with this,' I asked, 'or shall I make it a caning job?'

Mr Roberts' unhappy face became aghast. 'Oh, by no means! Not caning! Such little children—' he began incoherently.

'They're quite big enough to know the difference between right and wrong,' I said firmly, 'but if you feel that way about it I shall hand him over to you and content myself with a short lecture about this.'

Mr Roberts twisted his great hands together and I felt a twinge of compunction for his soft heart as I opened the classroom door.

'Eric,' I called, 'come here a moment!'

With a dreadful shuddering sigh Eric lifted his mottled face. Slowly he came towards the lobby where Mr Roberts awaited him with quite as much agitation of spirit. I looked at them both as the distance between them dwindled, and then returned to the classroom, leaving the coats and hats to witness the meeting between accuser and accused.

'And I give a few to little Joe Coggs,' Eric had sniffed to me later, '''cos he saw me taking 'em and I never wanted him to say nothing.'

History lesson, about a little Roman boy, to whom the children were becoming much attached, was sacrificed to a lecture on respect for other people's property, common honesty, the power of example and the evil of leading others into bad ways. It was a much-chastened class that settled down to its nature lesson about the common newt, several of which disported themselves in a glass tank at the side of the room. I left them drawing sharply-spiked backs and starfish feet, and went into the next room to bring home to Joseph Coggs the wickedness of his crime.

'And another two?' Miss Gray was asking, stacking milk bottles in pairs into the crate.

'Four!' chorused the group clustered round her.

'And another two?'

'Six!'

'And two more?' The milk bottles clinked again.

'Eight!' This rather more doubtfully. Miss Gray left them to count again, and straightened her back to greet me. I told her the story and asked if I might take Joseph out into her lobby.

'I wanted to see you about my digs,' said Miss Gray, who had been with us now for about a fortnight.

'Us makes it seven!' shouted one of the mathematicians by the milk crate.

'Count again,' advised Miss Gray. 'We're getting ready for the two times table tomorrow, but heavens, what murder it is!'

'What is the matter at Mrs Pratt's?' I asked.

'Well, you know how it is—' she began uncomfortably.

'Tell me later,' I said taking Joseph's sticky hand and leading him from the class to the quiet order of the lobby.

Mrs Pringle's copper was humming merrily as I drew from Joseph the sorry tale of his part in the egg crime. Fat tears coursed down his face and splashed on to his dirty jersey.

'And my mum put 'em in the cupboard and we had one each for breakfast when our dad 'ad gone to work.' His tears flowed afresh as he burst out, 'Nothing ain't nice today! My little house, what I took home . . . my dad used it to light his pipe this morning . . . he never cared, he never cared!'

Truly Joseph Coggs suffered much. When the storm had spent itself I gave what tardy consolation I could by telling him that it was treacle tart for dinner and he might make another little house. The tears dried miraculously.

'But mind,' I added, in a firm school-marm voice, 'there's to be no more stealing. You understand?'

'Yes, miss,' answered Joseph with a repentant sniff; but I noticed that his eyes were on the school oven.

14. THE JUMBLE SALE

For the past week, posters announcing the jumble sale to be held in the schoolroom in aid of the Church Roof Fund had fluttered from the wall by the bus stop, the grocer's window, and from a hook in the butcher's shop.

At the end of afternoon school, Miss Gray and I pushed back the creaking partition between our rooms, and trundled the heavy desks into a long L-shaped counter, in readiness for the people who were coming to price the jumble before the public were admitted at seven o'clock.

'I wish I could help you with the pricing,' Miss Gray said, puffing slightly with her exertions, 'but I do so want to go to the orchestra practice and it begins at 6.30.'

'How are you getting into Caxley?'

'Mr Annett said he would fetch me and bring me back. I knew him a little through the people I used to stay with in Caxley. They play in the orchestra too.'

We sat down on the desks to get our breath and surveyed our filthy hands.

'Miss Clare's coming to tea,' I said, 'she's helping with the jumble sale. Can you stop for tea with us?'

'I'd rather not, many thanks. I must collect my violin and music; and I shall need to change. Which reminds me . . . It looks as though I shall have to leave Mrs Pratt's, I'm afraid.'

'Isn't it working out well? I know it's not ideal, but digs are hopeless in a village.'

'It's partly that; although I hadn't thought of complaining.' She gave me a sidelong smile, 'I hang a towel over the nymph in the river each night, and my petticoat over the dying dog – I really haven't the heart to say anything to Mrs Pratt about removing them.'

'Is it the food?'

'Lord, no! I get more than I want. No . . . Mrs Pratt's mother has just died over at Springbourne and they'll want my room for her father. He's evidently going to make his home with them. In a way, it solves my problem – but what on earth shall I do about other digs? I feel I can't live too far away. I can't afford a car and the buses from Caxley just don't fit in with school hours.'

'You can have my spare bedroom until you find somewhere that you really like. I'll make more inquiries, but don't worry unduly. If Mrs Pratt wants you out quickly, come to me for a time.'

Her thanks were cut short by the arrival of Miss Clare who was propping up her venerable bicycle in its old accustomed spot by the stone sink in the lobby. She looked well and rested and greeted us in her gentle voice.

'We don't begin pricing until five o'clock,' I told her, 'so we've plenty of time to go and build our strength up with tea!'

Miss Gray made her farewells and hastened off to Mrs Pratt's to get ready for Mr Annett, and Miss Clare and I dawdled, arm in arm, in the playground to watch the rooks as they wheeled about the elms, sticks in beaks, busily furbishing up their nests for the arrival of the new young occupants.

Mrs Pringle and the vicar's wife, Mrs Partridge, were already shaking out vests and sorting out shoes when Miss Clare and I went over to the school. We each carried a blue marking-pencil, shamelessly purloined from the school stock cupboard, paper, scissors and pins.

'Good evening, good evening!' Mrs Partridge greeted us, bustling along the line of desks with a pair of antique dancing shoes in her hand. They were pale grey in colour, with a strap and two buttons. The toes were sharply pointed with heels of the Louis type, and they looked about size two. It would be interesting to see who bought them.

'Such lovely things,' continued Mrs Partridge, with professional enthusiasm, 'so very good of people to give so generously.' Mrs Partridge, from years of experience, knew the necessity of praising everything sent to a jumble sale, for, to be sure, any adverse comment is bound to be overheard, if not by the donor, then by some dear friend who feels impelled to impart the tidings. Life in a village demands a guard on the tongue, and none knows this better than the vicar's wife.

'Now shall we put the things out first? Men's clothing here, women's there, and children's at the end? We thought shoes on this form near the door, and hats – such an attractive collection, don't you think? – in the far corner.'

'What about admission money?' asked Mrs Pringle. 'Who's taking that?'

Mrs Partridge looked a little flummoxed. 'The posters haven't said anything about admission. I think we must let the people in free.'

'A great mistake, in my opinion,' rejoined Mrs Pringle heavily. Her mouth began to turn down ominously. 'At Caxley last week the Baptists charged threepence; and no ill-feeling. But there, if you don't want the money—' Mrs Pringle shrugged her massive shoulders, as one who washes her hands of the whole affair, and began worrying at the tape that bound several pairs of men's corduroy trousers together.

'Well, well, well, well!' clucked Mrs Partridge in a conciliatory way, 'and this shall be the junk stall – china, you know, and jewellery and any odds and ends. Mr Willet has very kindly offered to sell raffle tickets for this basket of eggs. Mr Roberts sent them over – so kind, so kind!'

We all trotted to and fro, carrying everything, from derelict footstools to babies' binders, to their appointed places. A particularly hideous table, with three and a half legs and a top so mutilated with Indian carving as to render it quite useless, impeded us seriously in our movements.

'Who on earth,' said Mrs Partridge, shaken from her normal caution, 'sent that dreadful thing?'

Mrs Pringle's breathing became more stertorous than usual and her eyes glittered dangerously. Trembling, our fingers fluttering with the price tickets and our heads down bent, Miss Clare and I awaited the breaking of the storm.

'That table,' began Mrs Pringle, with awful deliberation, 'that *beautiful* table, was a wedding present to Pringle's mother, from her mistress that she worked for from the age of twelve. And as loyal a girl her mistress could never have wished for!'

Mrs Partridge was beginning her apologies, but they were brushed aside.

'*And furthermore,*' went on Mrs Pringle, very loudly indeed, and with one hand upraised as though taking the oath, 'the dear old lady had it stood by her bedside till her dying day. She had her Bible on it, close to her hand, and all her other needs.'

She paused for breath, and Mrs Partridge hastened in with: 'I'm sure, Mrs Pringle, I meant nothing derogatory—'

'*Such as,*' continued Mrs Pringle in a fearsome boom, 'her indigestion tablets, her teeth, her glasses and a very fine clock given her by Pringle and myself on the occasion of her eightieth birthday, and much admired by all her visitors. As well it might be, considering the shocking price that shark in Caxley asked for it!'

'Well, I'm sorry that you should be upset,' persisted Mrs Partridge, 'and I hope you will accept my apology.'

Mrs Pringle bared her teeth for a moment and inclined her head graciously.

'It has *associations,* that table, and I don't like to hear ill spoke of it. A friend of the family, you might say.'

'Quite, quite!' said the vicar's wife in a final kind of way, and she and Mrs Pringle continued in silence to pin tickets along the men's stall, while Miss Clare and I, who had retired in a cowardly way with our blue pencils to the hat department, tried to appear unconcerned and efficient, and failed, I fear, to look either.

*

At seven o'clock the door was opened and a gratifyingly large crowd swarmed in. Capacious shopping bags of every shape and colour dangled from the women's arms. The first rush, as always, was for the children's clothes.

'Do nice for my sister's youngest.'

'Ah, that's just right for our Edna for next summer! Always liked a bit of frilling on knickers for little girls, myself!'

'Hold up, Annie, and let's try this for size! Pull your stummick back, child! How's a body to tell, else?'

The clothes were churned over by busy hands, snatched from one to the other, admired, deprecated and subjected to close and searching scrutiny. Pennies, sixpences, shillings and half-crowns changed hands, and the pudding basins provided by the vicar's wife on each stall were soon filling with contributions to Fairacre Church Roof Fund.

Prominent in the mob of women jostling for position was Mrs Bryant, a tall, imposing gipsy, wearing a man's trilby hat squarely upon her coiled greasy plaits. Heavy gold earrings gleamed against her dusky cheeks and she carried a formidable ebony stick. Behind hovered the lesser fry of her family, daughters, young wives and a bevy of dark-eyed children who watched everything in solemn silence. Mrs Bryant was known to strike a hard bargain and when she approached the men's stall, where Miss Clare and I were struggling to find change for a pound note and sell waistcoats and socks at the same time, we girded ourselves for the fray.

With the end of her ebony stick Mrs Bryant lifted a pair of grey flannel trousers. She gazed at the dangling objects with contempt, and then said: 'Give you sixpence for these.'

'The price is marked on them, Mrs Bryant,' replied Miss Clare, without looking up from her counting.

'They's only rubbish! Not fit for nothing but dusters!' persisted Mrs Bryant.

'In that case I advise you not to buy them,' answered Miss Clare politely, handing change to a customer and not bothering to glance in the gipsy's direction.

'Shillun!' snapped Mrs Bryant. Several of the women had paused in their buying to watch with amusement and also with some admiration for Miss Clare's handling of the situation.

'What price are they?' asked one, looking aloft at the suspended garments. In one swift movement Miss Clare twitched them free, surveyed the ticket, and handed them over to the questioner, saying, 'Half a crown.' There were sly smiles all round at this neat manoeuvre. Mrs Bryant said, 'Some folks buys any old rags, I sees!' and strode off with a face like thunder.

Mr Roberts towered above the throng and his mighty laugh could be heard above all the hubbub. He was present in his triple role of school manager, churchwarden and donor of the raffle prize.

'How are you doing, Mr Willet?' I heard him shout cheerfully.

Mr Willet was laboriously writing out the counterfoil of a raffle ticket, licking his pencil frequently, and, as it was an indelible one, gradually dyeing the edge of his ragged moustache a sinister purple. His tongue, by now an awe-inspiring sight, would have done credit to a prize chow.

'Made ten shillings already,' answered Mr Willet, with some pride.

'Fine, fine! You'll be able to buy one of my tickets for the Grand National draw. Come on now, Mr Willet,' said Mr Roberts tugging a book from his pocket, 'All in a good cause – Caxley Old Folks' Outing.'

'Mr Roberts,' he answered with dignity, 'you should know I'm not a betting man! It's the devil's work! I promised my poor old mother, years ago – and I hope she can hear me now wherever she may be – that I would never have no hand in betting and lottery!'

'Then what the blazes are you doing with the raffle tickets?' demanded Mr Roberts, trying to control his mirth.

Mr Willet's purple mouth opened and shut once or twice.

'As a sidesman, Mr Roberts, I hope I know my duty to the church,' he answered with fine illogicality, 'I'm putting my personal feelings on one side. The church must come first!'

'Well said!' replied Mr Roberts, 'and I'll have two tickets for my own eggs.' Mr Willet's pencil returned to his mouth as he settled the book of tickets more conveniently on the basket-handle.

'In that case, sir, I'm sure my poor old mother would wish me to contribute to the Caxley Old Folks,' said Mr Willet as he tore out the tickets. And fishing in their pockets the two men found each a shilling and exchanged them with due civility.

One blue and white spring morning, soon after the jumble sale, the sunlight streamed so temptingly through our high Gothic windows and the rooks cawed so encouragingly from the elm trees, that I decided that it was cruelty to children – and teachers – to coop ourselves up any longer.

'Put your books away,' I told the delighted class, 'and we'll go out for a nature walk and see how many exciting things we can find.'

They bustled into the lobby, chattering busily, while they put on their coats. I went through to Miss Gray's room.

'This is too good to miss,' I said, indicating the window. 'Would you like to bring them out for half an hour?'

We buttoned coats and tied shoelaces amidst cheerful confusion; then two by two, with John Burton and Cathy Waites as leaders, we took our excited family out into the spring sunshine.

Mr Roberts was laying a hedge with expert strokes of a chopping knife. He straightened up and smiled at the procession as it dawdled by him. There was a chorus of greeting.

'Morning, sir. Hello, sir. We's out for a walk! Too good to stop in, Miss Read says!'

'Never heard of such a thing!' said Mr Roberts, trying to appear deeply shocked at this news. 'No slipping out of school when I was a boy! Where are you going?'

'I thought I'd take them down to the wood to see if there are any early primroses and violets. We should get some catkins; but I don't want to be too long in case the managers find out!'

Mr Roberts' mighty laugh at this mild sally made little Eileen Barton run to the side of her big brother in alarm, and we left him, still smiling, to continue his work.

Our progress down the village street was greeted by cries and friendly shouts from windows and gardens. Mothers, making beds and dusting window-sills, called to us, the toddlers, fingers in mouths, watched us round-eyed. Mr Willet, who was inspecting a row of young broad beans, waved to us from his garden, and we all bounded along quite heady with this unwonted freedom, feeling devil-may-care at having escaped from school and revelling in the surprise we were occasioning by our incursion into the morning life of Fairacre.

We turned left at 'The Beetle and Wedge' along a narrow lane that led to a small copse at the foot of the downs. Beyond the copse the lane rose, becoming narrower and grassier, until it petered out into an indistinct footpath on the bare heights. A fresh wind tossed the children's hair and the catkins that streamed, like banners, from the hazels in the hedge.

In the dry fine grass of the banks, the violets' heart-shaped leaves were showing, and the little girls searched industriously for the blue and white blossoms, holding their thread-like stems tightly in their small cold fingers, and sniffing at their bunches hungrily. Starved of flowers through the long winter months, now the full joy of this sensuous feast broke upon them.

High above us, in a fold of the windy downs, we could see the shepherd's hut and the lambing pens made from square bales of straw set together to make a shelter from the weather. Now and again we could hear the distant tinkle of a sheep-bell, and the children would stop short, heads cocked sideways to listen.

'It's my grandpa, up there with the sheep,' John Burton told me. 'I takes his tea up sometimes after school. He give me this yesterday.' Fishing in his pocket he drew out a little boat fashioned from half a cork. By its odour, the cork had once served to seal a bottle of sheep disinfectant. Three masts adorned it and sets of paper sails, and rigging contrived, I guessed, from unravelled binder twine, completed the ship.

'He give Eileen the other one,' went on John, 'but she floated hers out in the road last night and it went down the drain.' His voice was full of scorn.

By now we had reached the copse, and some of the children sat in the shelter of the trees to rest, while others picked early primroses and anemones, or found other treasures . . . birds' feathers, oak-apples, coloured stones, or the large, pale-grey shells of the Roman snails that frequent the downlands.

I leant against a post and watched a tractor, looking like a toy in the distance, creeping slowly across a field. Half the field was already ploughed, and behind the tractor wheeled and fluttered a flock of hungry rooks, scrutinizing the fresh-turned ribs of earth for food. They were too far away to hear, but their black shapes rose and scattered like flakes of burnt paper from a bonfire.

Reluctantly, we returned bearing our trophies with us, with flushed faces and tangled hair. As we turned the bend of the lane I saw the school nurse's car outside our gate.

Nurse Barham, a plump motherly woman, with a Yorkshire brogue, calls periodically to inspect heads and keep an eye open for any other infection.

I watched her as she parted locks and ruffled the boys' hair, keeping up a comforting monologue the whole time.

'Beautiful hair, dear, keep it brushed well. Now your hands. Spread out your fingers. Nice nails, not bitten, I see. Don't forget to wash them before dinner.'

The children do not seem to mind being subjected to this examination. Only the nail-biters look rather fearfully at Nurse's face as they proffer their stubby fingers for inspection. Nurse's main concern, when she looks at hands, is for scabies, but she is also a foe to nail-biters.

'You don't know of anyone who could put our new young teacher up, I suppose?' I asked her, as she worked. Nurse Barham knows the neighbourhood well and realizes the difficulty of getting digs. 'Miss Clare suggested Mrs Moffat – a newcomer here. I don't know whether she will be able to, I'm sure.'

'I can't think of anyone suitable,' said Nurse thoughtfully, 'but I'll remember to let you know if I come across anyone. I've met Miss Gray at music practices. She seems very nice indeed. Mr Annett seems to think so, anyway,' she added mischievously and whisked off to her duties in the infants' room.

I felt vaguely annoyed by this last remark. Really, village gossip is downright irritating, I thought. The poor girl has only to be given a lift home by a neighbour and the village has them wedded, bedded and all the children named for them. It was too bad, and I was a little cool with Nurse when she bustled back.

'Only the new little boy, Joseph Coggs,' she informed me, 'I'll go and call on his mother now if she'll be in.'

I glanced at the clock. Mrs Coggs would be back from her floor-scrubbing at 'The Beetle and Wedge,' I told Nurse.

'What sort of home?' she asked. I told her what I knew of the Coggs family and she departed to Tyler's Row to see what advice and help she could give, and to leave a large bottle of noxious-smelling liquid for the anointing of Joseph's head.

Miss Gray had liked the idea of going to Mrs Moffat's bungalow if it could be arranged. Miss Clare, with true village caution, had advised us against going to Mrs Moffat too precipitately.

'Let me mention it to Mrs Finch-Edwards,' she had said, 'and let her sound Mrs Moffat. Then we can follow her lead.'

I was glad about this arrangement, for although I was willing to have Miss Gray at my house, I realized that it was not an ideal plan. We had to work together during school hours and I felt it would be better for both of us to have our leisure times apart. Our relationship at school could not be happier, and I did not want to subject it to too rigorous a trial.

Mrs Finch-Edwards had approached the subject of Miss Gray's future occupation of the spare bedroom with some wariness, but Mrs Moffat welcomed the idea.

'It would be a help with the housekeeping,' she said gratefully, 'and I only use that room for my needlework and the machine. All those things could easily go in the dining-room cupboard.' She pondered for a while. 'And she's a real lady-like girl,' she added, 'set a good example to Linda, and that sort of thing. I'll talk it over with Len tonight and let you know tomorrow.'

And so it had been settled. Miss Gray had called at the bungalow and inspected the bedroom, happily picture-free, and admired the bathroom – a refinement which Mrs Pratt's house lacked, and which had meant two trips a week to the friends in Caxley – they had discussed terms, to their mutual satisfaction, and Miss Gray was to move into her new home in a fortnight's time, with a very much lighter heart.

15. THE BELL TOLLS

Three energetic little girls were skipping in the playground. Two took it in turns to twist the rope, arms flailing round, while the third bobbed merrily up and down, hair and skirts dancing, in the twirling rope.

'Salt, mustard, vinegar, pepper!
One, two, three, four, five . . .'

they chanted breathlessly, until the skipping child caught a foot or stopped from sheer exhaustion.

The rest of the children played more quietly, for the spell of fine weather continued and the spring sunshine beating back from the school walls sent most of them to the shade of the elm trees. Here they crouched, some playing with marbles, beautiful, whorled, glass treasures kept carefully in little bags of strong calico or striped ticking; some tossing five-stones, red, blue, green, orange and white, up into the air and catching them expertly on the back of their hands before going on to further complicated man-oeuvres. These movements had old quaint names like 'Nelson, Crabses and Lobsters,' and involved much dexterity, patience and quickness of eye.

Among the roots, the little ones played the timeless make-believe games: mothers-and-fathers, hospitals, schools and keeping house. Above them the tight, rosy buds of the elms were beginning to break out into tiny green fans, and in the school garden the polyanthus, which the children here call 'spring flowers,' and early daffodils and grape hyacinths all nodded gently in the warm sunshine.

Against the north wall, in the cool shade, Cathy played two-ball intently by herself. Her cotton skirt was stuffed inelegantly into her knickers, for some of the seven movements of this game involved bouncing the balls and catching them between one's legs, and a skirt was a severe obstruction. She counted aloud, her dark eyes fixed on the two flying balls, and as she twirled and threw, and bounced and caught, she thought about the exam-ination papers that she had attempted that morning . . . papers that would decide her future.

She had sat at her usual desk, with only Miss Read for silent company, while the rest of the class had taken their work into Miss Gray's room next door. She had felt lonely, but important, left behind, with only the clock's heavy ticking and the rustle of her papers to break the silence; but once begun she had forgotten everything in her steady work. If this was the way to get to Caxley High School with its untold joys and games, gymnastics, acting and never-ending supply of library books, why, then she'd work hard and get there! That determination, which set her apart from the other members of her family, whose sweet placidity she lacked, carried her triumphantly through that morning's labours; and when, at last, she put down her pen and stretched her cramped fingers, she was conscious of work well done.

In all the schools around Caxley preparations were going forward for the annual Caxley Musical Festival, which is held in the Corn Exchange each May.

Miss Gray and I had spent a long singing lesson picking our choir. This was not an easy task, as all the children were bursting to take part, but Miss Gray, with considerable tact, managed to weed out the real growlers, with no tears shed.

'A little louder,' she said to Eric, 'now once again,' And Eric would honk again, in his tuneless, timeless way, while Miss Gray listened solemnly and with the utmost attention. Then, 'Yes,' she said, in a considering way, 'it's certainly a *strong* voice, Eric dear, and you do *try*: but I'm afraid we must leave you out this time. We must have voices that blend well together.'

'He really is the Tuneless Wonder!' she said to me later, with awe in her voice. 'I've never known any child quite so tone-deaf.'

I told her that Eric was also quite incapable of keeping in step to music; the two things often going together. Miss Gray had not come across this before and was suitably impressed.

'When you think how hard it is NOT to prance along the pavement in time with a barrel-organ,' she remarked, 'it seems almost clever!'

I handed over the choir to her care as she was a much more competent musician than I was, and for weeks the papers on the walls rustled to the vibrations of 'Over the Sea to Skye' and 'I'll Go No More A-Roving,' and the horrid intricacies of the round 'Come, Follow, Follow, Follow, Follow, Follow, Follow Me.' This last was usually punctuated with dreadful crashings of Miss Gray's ruler and despairing cries from the children who had failed to come in at the right bar, battled against overwhelming odds, faltered to a faint piping, and finally finished with a wail of lamentation. The thought that this sort of thing was going on in dozens of neighbouring schools was enough to daunt the stoutest heart; but Miss Gray, with youth and ardour to sustain her, struggled bravely on.

One afternoon, while the choir was carolling away with Miss Gray at the piano, and I was watching the infants and 'growlers' drawing pictures of any scene they liked from 'Cinderella' in the next room, the bells gave out a muffled peal from St Patrick's spire close by. The peal was followed by solemn tolling. Next door the music continued cheerfully enough, but in my room the children looked up with startled faces, pencils held poised in their hands.

On and on tolled the great bell, beating out its slow measure over the listening village. Out across the sunny fields floated the sound and men looked up from their hedging and harrowing to count the strokes. In the cottages housewives paused in their ironing or cooking, and stood, tools in hand, as the tolling went on. Sixty . . . seventy . . . still the bell tolled . . . and little children squatting by backdoor steps suddenly became conscious of the tension in the air and ran in, fearfully, to seek the comfort of familiar things.

'Come follow, follow, follow . . .' the children's voices stumbled next door; and Mrs Pringle's face appeared at the window opposite. I heard her in the lobby and went out to see her.

'Forgot my apron,' she volunteered. 'They say poor Miss Parr's passed on.' She stuffed her checked apron into a black shiny bag and I noticed that her hands, wrinkled and puffy with her recent washing-up, were trembling slightly. 'I was in service with her, as a girl . . . just for a bit, you know . . . she was good to me, very good.'

I said I was sure she had been, and it was sad to hear the bell tolling. Mrs Pringle appeared not to hear these lame remarks. She was gazing, with unseeing eyes, at the pile of coke in the playground.

'Always paid well too, and was generous with her clothes, and that. I've still got a scarf she give me . . . mauve, it is. Yes, never grudged nothing to me, I must say—' Her voice faltered, and she turned hastily away to pick up the black bag from the draining board. When she faced me again it was with her usual dour expression.

'Ah, well! No good grieving over times past, I suppose. And after all, if she couldn't afford to be generous with the lot she'd got, who could?'

This uncharitable comment seemed to give Mrs Pringle some comfort; but I could see that this seeming indifference, this harshly-expressed philosophy, was Mrs Pringle's challenge to something which had shaken her more than she cared to show. Her parting comment was a truer indication of her feelings.

'I suppose we've all got to go, but somehow . . . that old bell! I mean, it brings it home to you, don't it? It brings it home!' As she stumped off, the black bag swaying on her arm, I felt for Mrs Pringle, my old sparring partner, a rare pang of pity.

Miss Parr's funeral was held on an afternoon as glorious as that on which she had died.

The children had brought bunches of cottage flowers, daffodils, polyanthus, wallflowers, and little posies from the woods and banks, primroses, blue and white violets and early cowslips. We put them all in my gardening trug, which was lined with moss, and Cathy wrote on a card, 'With love from the children at Fairacre School,' in her most painstaking hand, and we laid it among the blooms. Mr Willet was entrusted with it, and he set off to deliver it at the house.

As the playground is in full view of the churchyard, I decided to let the children have an early playtime, and then be comfortably indoors while the service was going on.

We had begun *The Wind in the Willows*, and I thought, as I waited for the children to settle down after playtime, what a perfect afternoon it was to hear about the adventures of Water Rat and Mole. An exhilarating wind was blowing the rooks about the blue and white sky. Somewhere, in the vicarage garden, a blackbird whistled, and an early bee, bumbling lazily up and down the window-pane, gave a foretaste of summer joys.

Together, the children and I set out into that enchanted world where the river laps eternally and the green banks form the changeless setting for Mole's adventures. The sun dappled the children's heads as it shone through the tossing boughs into the schoolroom. Around them lay the sunshine, and within them too, as they contemplated, with their mind's eye, the sunlit landscape conjured up by magic words.

I was conscious, as I read steadily on, of ominous sounds from the churchyard, slow footsteps on the scrunching gravel, a snatch or two of solemn phrase in Mr Partridge's gentle voice, blown this way by the exuberant breeze, and the muffled thumpings of heavy wood lowered into the earth. Very near at hand a lark soared madly upwards, singing in a frenzy of joy, with the sun warm on its little back. It seemed hard, I thought, to have to be buried on such an uprushing afternoon.

Out there, in the churchyard, the black silent figures would be standing immobile around the dark hole. Above them, no less black, the rooks would be wheeling and crying, unheeded by the mourners. They would stand there, heads downbent, with who knows what emotions stirring them . . . pity, regret, the realization of the swiftness of life's passage, the inevitability of death. While here, in the classroom, sitting in a golden trance, our thoughts were of a sun-dappled stream, of willows and whiskers, of water-bubbles and boats . . . and, I venture to think, that of all those impressions which were being made on that spring afternoon, ours, for all their being transmitted, as it were, second-hand, would be more lasting in their fresh glory.

Thoughts by a graveside are too dark and deep to be sustained for any length of time. Sooner or later the hurt mind turns to the sun for healing, and this is as it should be, for otherwise, what future could any of us hope for, but madness?

16. APRIL BIRTHDAY PARTY

April had come; one of the most beautiful within living memory. The long spell of sunshine and the unusually warm nights had brought early rows of carrots and peas and sturdy broad beans into all the cottage gardens.

'Unseasonable!' announced Mr Willet. 'We'll pay for it later, mark me, now! Just get the fruit blossom out and there'll be a mort of frosts. Seen it happen time without number!' He seemed to gain some morbid satisfaction from this augury.

The children were glorying in it and were already tanned and freckled. They came in from the playground and spreading their hot arms along the cool wood of the desks, they sniffed luxuriously at the warm, biscuity smell that the sun had drawn from their scorched skins.

In a week's time the Easter holidays would begin, and I hoped that the fine weather would hold, for my garden was weedy and the hedges, usually clipped at the beginning of May, were already needing attention.

On this particular afternoon the girls were busy with their sewing and the boys were making raffia mats or cane baskets or bowls according to their ability. The last few stitches were being put, by Linda Moffat, into a kettle-holder of especial importance; and as the other children worked they watched Linda with excitement.

The kettle-holder was their own present to Miss Clare who celebrated her birthday that day. All the children in the school had put several stitches in it – some, I fear, which Miss Clare would privately think of as 'cat's teeth' – and I had promised to take it to her when I went to her tea-party that afternoon.

Linda cut the cotton with a satisfying snip of the scissors and came out to the front of the class, bearing it as if it were the Holy Grail itself. It certainly was a magnificent object, made of a piece of vivid material, in deep reds and blues of a paisley pattern. It was edged with scarlet binding and had a rather bumpy loop to hang it by.

Linda held it up for the children to admire and they looked at it with reverence.

'Us've done it real nice!'

'Don't it look good!'

'Miss Clare'll like that all right!'

'Ah! Even if she's got a little old kettle-holder, she can always do with another one!'

They nodded wisely to each other, exchanging sagacious remarks like old women at a market stall.

John Burton, who was the neatest-fingered child, had the enviable task of wrapping it in tissue paper and tying it with a piece of red raffia. The children, handwork neglected, clustered round his desk to watch the delicate operation and to give advice.

'You pulls it too tight, mate!'

'He's right, you know . . . you'll have it all twizzled up inside!'

'If you leaves it to me,' said John soberly and without any rancour, 'I'll do it all right. It ain't no good getting excited-like when you doos parcels.' He tied a neat bow with unhurrying fingers, and I put it in a prominent position on top of the piano, so that they could gloat over it until it was time to go home.

There were four of us sitting at Miss Clare's round table that afternoon.

A cloth of incredible whiteness, bordered with a deep edging of Miss Clare's mother's crocheting, covered the table, and in the middle stood a bowl of primroses. The best tea-service, patterned with pansies, was in use, and cut-glass dishes held damson cheese and lemon curd of Miss Clare's own making. The bread and butter was cut so thin as to be almost transparent.

'I've a special old carving-knife,' explained Miss Clare earnestly, 'and I always sharpen it on the bottom step up to the lawn. It's really quite simple.'

The kettle-holder had been much admired and hung on a hook by the fire-place. Miss Clare glanced at it fondly from time to time.

'I shan't dirty it, you know. I've an old one I shall use . . . no, I really don't feel I could soil that one!'

Miss Gray and Mrs Finch-Edwards were with us and the conversation turned to Miss Gray's new home.

'No complaints anywhere!' announced Miss Gray. 'Except perhaps over-feeding. She's a wonderful cook.'

'And dressmaker,' added Miss Clare, peering into the depths of the teapot.

'She's making me some silk frocks,' began Mrs Finch-Edwards, then stopped suddenly. Her face became a warm red and she crumbled her cake.

'For any special occasion?' asked Miss Gray, who seemed unaware of her neighbour's sudden shyness.

Mrs Finch-Edwards looked up from her crumbling. 'I want them in September. I . . . that is, my hubby and I . . . are looking forward to a baby then.'

We were all delighted and a hubbub of questioning broke out

about knitting needs, the desirability of real wool for first-size vests, no matter what time of the year the baby was born . . . the advantages of high prams over low prams, and draped cots over plain ones . . . until it dawned on us three spinsters how fervent we were being with our advice to the only member of the party, who, presumably, knew more about the business than the rest of us put together.

The tea-party gained immensely in hilarity and animation after this disclosure, Miss Clare even going so far as to scold her guest for cycling over 'in her present state . . . very naughty indeed!' And she was inclined to get her brother to take her back in his car!

While we were thus cosily gossiping Mr Annett came up the path with a basket of eggs.

Mrs Partridge helped at the Women's Institute stall for two hours each market day, and I used to see the vicar's ancient car nosing its way round the bend by the school just before ten each Thursday morning. In the back would be piled Fairacre Women's Institute's contributions. During the holidays, Miss Clare had always enjoyed helping the vicar's wife, and now, having retired, she helped regularly at the stall.

On their way they would stop at Beech Green School. Mr Annett's older boys produced a weekly supply of eggs, vegetables, herbs and flowers which were sold on a stall in the market, belonging to a local market gardener. With the proceeds they bought seeds, plants, netting, tools and so on to carry on this good work. By the time the boys had loaded up their products Miss Clare and Mrs Partridge would be seated in a bower of greenery, peering above bunches of scrubbed carrots and turnips, and feeling for the gears among the cabbages.

At this time of year the school garden was not producing enough to be sent in, so that Mr Annett brought the eggs to Miss Clare to pack with hers overnight to save the car stopping again.

He sat himself down by Miss Gray and ate birthday cake. He looked very much more relaxed and happy, and could be called almost good-looking, I decided, when he smiled at his neighbour. If only he were fed properly and did not drive himself so hard at everything . . . if only he could find a thoroughly nice wife . . . I found myself looking at Miss Gray speculatively and pulled myself up sharply. Really, I was quite as bad as Nurse!

But for all that I was glad to see how very much at ease they were in each other's company, and although I didn't go so far as to name their children for them, I must admit that I was favouring a draped creamy wedding-dress for Miss Gray, rather than a white, when Miss Clare brought me back to earth by inquiring kindly if I had found the cake perhaps a trifle too rich.

The children were busy copying a notice from the blackboard. It said:

> 'Spring term ends on April 9th.
> School will reopen on Tuesday, April 28th.'

Pens were being wielded with especial care for their parents would receive these joyous communications and the children were aware that criticism, kindly or adverse, would greet their handwriting.

My class had to do two copies apiece; the best writers might even have the honour of writing a third, for Miss Gray's children could not yet be relied upon for a fair copy and the older children would supply theirs.

As they rattled their nibs in the inkwells and thumped their blotting paper with fat fists, I marked the compositions which had been written that morning. The subject was 'A Hot Day.' John Burton who has a maddening habit of transposing letters had written:

A Hot Day

I feels tried when it is hot. I likes it best to be just rihgt not to hot not to clod. I wears my thin clothes when it is hot and my shaddy linen hat we bouhgt at a jumble sale it is a treat.

I called him to my desk and corrected this piece of work while he watched.

'You must make an effort with these "ght" words,' I told him, writing 'bought' and 'right' for him to copy three times. I explained, yet again, the intricacies of 'to, too and two' and wrote 'too hot and too cold' to be copied thrice.

There has been much discussion recently on the methods of marking compositions. Some hold that the child should be allowed to pour out its thoughts without bothering overmuch about spelling and punctuation. Others are as vehement in their assurances that each word misspelt and incorrectly used should be put right immediately. I think a middle course is best. On most occasions I correct and mark the work with the child by me, explaining things as I did to John, but sometimes I tell the children before they begin that I want to see how much they can write, and although I should appreciate correct spelling, I would rather they got on with the narrative and spelled phonetically than hold up their good work by inquiring how to spell a particular word. In this way I can assess any literary ability more easily and encourage that fluency, both written and spoken, which is so sorely lacking in this country school.

As a rule, the girls find it easier to express themselves than the boys. Their pens cover the page more quickly, they use a wider choice of adjective, and make use too of imagery, which the boys seldom do. The boys' essays are usually short, painstakingly dull and state facts. John Burton's account of a hot day is a fair example of the boys' attempts.

Cathy's contribution on the same subject made much more interesting reading:

A HOT DAY

There are no clouds today and we shall have P.T. in the playground which I like. I like to run and jump and feel the wind through my hair. But I hope Miss Read does not make us sit with our legs crossed up for our exsersises because my knees get all sticky at the back on a hot day.

On the way home we all walk in the shade by the hedge. The cows stand under the trees and swish their tails to keep the flies off.

My mother likes hot days because her washing bleeches

white as snow, much whiter than the flowers on the elder bush
where she always spreads out our hankys.

Everyone is happy when the sun shines on a hot day.

The glorious weather continued unbroken and here in the schoolroom were all the tokens of an early spring. The nature table
against the wall bore primroses, cowslips and bluebells. The
tadpoles were growing their legs with alarming rapidity and
were due to depart, any day now, for the pond.

The weather chart pinned on the wall above the table showed a
succession of yellow suns, bright as daisies, and out in the lobby a
few cotton hats and light cardigans were an indication of the
heat. To Mrs Pringle's well-disguised gratification the stoves had
been unlit for two or three weeks and the most that she could find
to grumble at was the wallflower petals that fluttered from the jug
on the window-sill to the floor.

After the hard winter it seemed an enchanted time, and the
reading of *The Wind in the Willows* on those blissful afternoons
matched both the freshness and youth of the listeners and the
spring world outside.

Through the partition I could hear the hum of Miss Gray's class
at work. She seemed happy and in better health than when she
arrived. Mrs Moffat had turned out to be the perfect landlady,
and was herself much happier now that she had an appreciative
lodger to admire her cooking, needlework and the other domestic
virtues which her husband was apt to take for granted.

I hoped very much that Miss Gray would stay with me at
Fairacre School. The children adored her and responded well to
her quiet but cheerful manner. I could see that she was providing
for them, as Miss Clare had done, an atmosphere of security and
peaceful happiness in which even the most nervous child could
put forth its best. With her top group's reading, particularly, she
had worked well, and I was looking forward to having them in
September in my class, confident that they would be able to hold
their own with the older children. It was a fortunate day indeed, I
told myself, when Miss Gray was appointed to Fairacre School
and I hoped that she would stay with us for many years. A small
doubt arose in my mind – wordless, but shaped like a question
mark.

'Well, naturally . . . if that happened—' I answered aloud, and had to change the mutter to a cough, as the children's eyes met mine in some bewilderment.

April 9th came at last, and the excitement of the last day of term kept the children chattering like starlings.

As I was giving out the hymn books for morning prayers, Eric appeared at the door, with his father behind him. Mr Turner was carrying in his arms a small girl, who could not have been more than three years old. He looked dishevelled and agitated, and motioning Eric to his desk, I went into the lobby with his father.

'I've come to ask a favour, miss,' he began anxiously, dumping the child by his knees. She put one arm round his legs and looked up at me wonderingly.

'If you want me to have your daughter for the day,' I answered – this sort of emergency crops up occasionally and I always enjoy these diversions – 'I shall be very pleased indeed.'

Mr Turner looked relieved and grinned down at the upturned face.

'Hear that, duck? You can stop at school along of Eric, like a big girl, and I'll fetch you as soon as I gets back from Caxley.'

'What's happened?' I asked.

'It's my wife. I had to get Mrs Roberts to ring up Doctor at five this morning, and she's been took to hospital. Appendix, they thinks it is, and I'm to go in early this afternoon. Mrs Roberts would have had the little 'un but for it being market day. Ah! She's a good sort – been real kind, give us breakfast in her kitchen and all. And you too, miss,' he added hastily, fearful lest I should take umbrage at his praise of Mrs Roberts and his neglect of me, 'I'm truly thankful, miss . . . you knows that!' He fumbled in his pocket and brought out some coppers. 'For Lucy's dinner, if that's all right.' He counted out the money carefully, promised to fetch his daughter before the end of afternoon school, if he could get away from the hospital in time, and, with a final knuckle-grinding shake of my hand, made his farewell.

All through the morning Lucy sat perched up on the seat by her brother. Eric had been sent through to Miss Gray's room for a box of bricks, a doll and a picture book and these she played with very happily, keeping up a soft running commentary on her activities.

The children were enchanted to have a baby in the classroom and made a great fuss of her, offering her their sweets at playtime and picking up the stray bricks that crashed to the floor.

They reflected the attitude of the grown-up village people in their relationship to young children. I am always amazed at the servitude of the parents in these parts to their children, particularly the little rascals between two and five years old. These engaging young scoundrels can twist their doting parents round their fingers by coaxing, whining or throwing a first-class tantrum. The parents thoroughly spoil them, and the older children are also encouraged to pander to their lightest whim. Sweets, ice-cream, apples, bananas, cakes and anything else edible that attracts the child's fancy flow in an uninterrupted stream down the child's throat, as well as normal meals and the quota of orange juice and cod liver oil which is collected from the monthly clinic at the village hall, and, I must say in all honesty, that a more healthy set of children it would be hard to find. They seem to stay up until the parents themselves go to bed, and I see them playing in their gardens, or more frequently in the lane outside their cottages, until dusk falls. Then, sometimes as late as ten o'clock on a summer's evening, they finally obey the calls to 'Come on in!' which have been issuing from the cottage unheeded for an hour or more, and dragging reluctant feet they resign themselves, still protesting, to bed.

And yet, as I have said, under these methods which are a direct violation of the rules of a well-regulated nursery, these children thrive. Furthermore, when they enter school at the age of five, one might reasonably expect some trouble in maintaining discipline; but this is not so.

They prove to be docile and charming, obedient and happy in their more restricted mode of life. The truth of the matter is, I think, that they feel the need for direction and authority, and if this is offered them with interest and kindness they are more than ready to co-operate.

They love to have an outlet for their creative ability. To be shown how to make a paper windmill, or a top that really works, to learn to sing a song with actions, to make a bead necklace for

themselves, or a rattle for a baby at home, or best of all, something for their mothers – a paper mat with their own bright
patterns adorning it – all these things give them infinite pleasure
because they have had an aim and they can see something for
their labours. Their pre-school play has on the whole been
aimless. Their parents buy for them expensive toys, dolls' prams,
tricycles, model cars and the like which have restricted scope in a
child's hands. Sand, water, clay and other creative media are not
encouraged. 'Too messy . . . don't you go mucking up that clean
frock now with that old mud,' you hear the parents call. 'Leave
them old stones be and come and nurse your dolly! What's the
good of me giving a pound for it if you never plays with it, eh?'
What indeed?

In the infants' room Miss Gray was unpinning the Easter frieze of
yellow chicks which had been the apple of the children's eyes for
the past fortnight. Her cupboards were packed full of the objects
which normally were stored in individual boxes under each
child's desk. Counters, plasticine, chalk, felt dusters, first readers,
boxes of letters and all the paraphernalia of infants' work had
been sorted, checked and repacked.

The dregs of powder paint had been poured away and gleaming jam jars awaited next term's mixture-as-before. Vases were
stacked on one shelf, and below them the great black clay tin,
weighing half a hundredweight, had been packed with moist
flannel to keep the balls in good condition for three weeks.

The babies were busy polishing their desks, on top and underneath, with pieces of rag brought from home and a dab from Miss
Gray's furniture polish tin.

'Waste of time and good polish!' was Mrs Pringle's sour
comment as she carried in the clean crockery to put away in the
tall cupboard. On top of this stood a mysterious cardboard box,
out of reach of prying hands. The label said 'Milk Chocolate
Easter Eggs' and was carefully turned to face away from the class.
Each one had a small label tied on, either blue or pink, and each
child had to find the one with his own name on it. Miss Gray was
going to hide them about the classroom while the children were
out at afternoon play.

'Which reminds me,' she said to me, grovelling painfully under a low desk for a stray drawing-pin, 'I must see that they bring the eggs to me to check up on the names. It will never do to eat the wrong egg!'

In my room there was an equally interesting container, but mine was a round moss-lined basket, like an enormous nest, filled with eggs wrapped in bright tinfoil. The arrival of Lucy in our midst would mean a trip across to the schoolhouse to fetch one more for the basket.

We too were in a fine bustle of clearing-up when the vicar came in at the door. His cloak and leopard-skin gloves had been put away with his other winter garments, and he presented a summery appearance in his pale grey flannel suit and panama hat.

'I wanted to remind you all of one or two things,' began the vicar, when the children had settled back into their desks and he went on to explain to them the significance of the next Sunday, Palm Sunday, and invited offerings of pussy-willow and spring flowers for the church.

He followed this by a brief homily on Easter, the significance of the eggs which they would receive, and the hope that they would be at church with their parents on both these days.

He then spent a few minutes looking at the Easter cards which the children had crayoned ready to take home to their parents, and deciding that this was as good a time as any to present the eggs, I fetched two extra from the house and then passed the basket round.

The children's faces were alight with joy as they chose their eggs, little Lucy having to be restrained from scooping all that were left into her pinafore.

When it was found that there was one left and I asked them if they could think who might like it, the children rose to their cue, and, as one man, chorused: 'The vicar, miss! The vicar!'

And so, with great cheerfulness we broke up, and the children of Fairacre School, clutching their treasures to them, clattered out into the spring sunshine – free for three weeks!

PART THREE
Summer Term

* * * *

17. Ancient History, Doctor and the Films

In the bottom drawer of my desk are three massive books, with leather covers and mottled edges. Embossed on their fronts are the words 'Log Book' and they cover, between them, the history of this school.

The third one, which is nearly filled, has been in use for the past twenty years. If anything of note happens, such as a visit from an inspector, the outbreak of an epidemic, or the early closing of school through bad weather, illness or any other reason, then I make a note to that effect in the book, following in the tradition of the former heads of Fairacre School.

The log books thus form a most interesting account of a school's adventures; the early ones are particularly fascinating and should, I sometimes feel, be handed over to the local archivist who would find them a valuable contribution to the affairs of the district.

Our first entry at Fairacre School is at the latter end of 1880 when the first headmistress set down the details of her appointment and that of her sister as 'An assistant in the Babies' Class.' It has thus been a two-teacher school since its inception.

These two ladies would appear to have been kindly, conscientious and religious. Their discipline seems to have been maintained with some difficulty, and the rule, laid down by the local authority and still in force, that canings must be entered in the log book, leads to several poignant entries. The ink has faded to fawn in this first battered book, but there, in rather agitated handwriting, we can read:

'February 2nd, 1881. Had occasion to cane John Pratt (3) for Disobedience.'

And a little later on:

'April 4th, 1881. After repeated warnings, which have in nowise been heeded, had occasion to punish Tom East (2), William Carter (2) and John Pratt (3) the Ringleader, for Insolence and Damage to School Property.'

The figures in brackets refer to the number of strokes of the cane, usually (2) or (3) seemed to be the rule, but gentle Miss Richards was evidently driven to distraction by John Pratt, for before long we read, in a badly-shaking hand:

'July, 1882. Found John Pratt standing on a Stool, putting on the Hands of the Clock with the greatest Audacity, he imagining himself unobserved. For this Impudence received six (6).'

During the following two years there are several entries about the sisters' ill-health and in 1885 a widow and daughter took over the school. Their first entry reads:

'April, 1885. Found conditions here in sore confusion. Children very backward and lacking, in some cases, the first Rudiments of Knowledge. Behaviour, too, much to be deplored.'

This is interesting because it is echoed, at every change of head, throughout the seventy-odd years of Fairacre School's history. The new head confesses himself appalled and shocked at his predecessor's slackness, sets down his intention of improving standards of work and conduct, runs his allotted time and goes, only to be replaced by just such another head, and just such another entry in the log book.

After a number of changes the headmistresses were replaced by a series of headmasters. One, Mr Hope, had his wife as assistant and their only child, Harriet, figures in the log book as the star pupil for several years.

'16th June, 1911. The Vicar presented the Bishop's prize to the best pupil, Harriet Hope. The Bishop was pleased to say that this child's ability and endeavour were outstanding.'

I like to think of Harriet accepting her prize Bible in this old schoolroom, her hair smoothed down and her pinafore dazzling white over a clean zephyr frock, while her classmates, resplendent in Norfolk or sailor suits for the occasion, clapped heartily.

But in 1913 come two tragic entries.

'January 20th, 1913. Have to record sad death of pupil (and only daughter) Harriet Hope,' and
'January 25th, 1913. School closed today on the occasion of the funeral of late pupil, Harriet Hope, aged twelve years and four months.'

Mr Hope's entries go on until 1919. He records his wife's long illness, his work throughout the Great War in the village, the school's War Savings accounts, the return of old pupils in uniform, the deaths of some in battle, and finally:

'May 18th, 1919. Have now to enter this last. My resignation having been accepted I leave Fairacre School for an appointment in Leicestershire.'

Mrs Willet filled in some of the gaps for me when I went down there to buy some rhubarb for bottling.

'I remember him well, of course, though I was only a child at the time; Harriet was a year or two older than I was. He went all to pieces after the child died. They both took it very hard. Mrs Hope was never well after it, and the headmaster – well, he just took to the bottle. I can remember him now bending down to mark something on my desk, his hand shaking like a leaf and his breath heavy with liquor. As soon as the school clock said ten, he'd put up another few sums on the blackboard, dare us to make a racket and then saunter down to 'The Beetle' for a drink. Us kids used to stand up on the desk seats and watch him go. The boys used to pretend to be upending the bottle and hiccup and that – all very naughty, I suppose, but you couldn't hardly blame them with that example set them, could you, miss?'

She wrapped the rhubarb securely in two of its own great leaves and tied the bundle with bass. From the dresser the owls gazed unblinkingly from under their glass case and I remembered the affair of Arthur Coggs.

As if she knew what was in my mind, Mrs Willet spoke: 'And I believe that's partly why my husband's so set against the drink. He saw what it done to poor Mr Hope – he was asked to leave the school you know, becoming too much of a byword – and took up some job up north as an ordinary teacher. They say he was never a headmaster again; which was a pity really, he being so clever. He wrote some lovely poetry and used to read it to us. Of course some of the boys laughed about it, but us girls liked it.'

'Was Mr Willet at school when you were?'

'Oh, yes, miss. He was always sweet on me. Pushed a little stone heart through the partition to me when I was still in the babies' room. There's a biggish gap in one part, you know.'

I did know. The children still poke odd things through to the adjoining room. The last object confiscated had been a stinging-nettle leaf cunningly gummed on to a long strip of cardboard.

Mrs Willet crossed to the dresser and brought back an oval china box. The lid bore a picture of Sandown and inside it was lined with red plush. She turned out the contents on to the serge tablecloth – jet brooches, military buttons, clasps, a gold locket and chain, and, among these trinkets, a small pebble, shaped like a heart, which had been picked up in the playground by the ardent young Willet so many years ago.

After admiring the treasures I made my farewells and set off up the lane with the heavy cold bundle on my bare arm.

'I suppose you're thinking of a full store-cupboard,' shouted Mr Roberts across the hedge. But my thoughts were of the man who had lived once in my house, whose daughter had died, whose wife had ailed, whose poems had been laughed at by the only people he had found to listen to them. The log books, with their sparse entries, tell truly of 'old, unhappy, far-off things, and battles long ago.'

Dr Ruth Curtis, who is our school doctor, employed by the County Council, is a man-hater. Or perhaps it would be better to say that she is a man-despiser, for she would scorn to whip up so much emotion against the lowly creatures as hatred. The men maintain, with their habitual modesty, that this is because she has not been lucky enough to secure one of them for a husband.

'Stands to reason,' they assert, soberly, 'that she feels frustrated! "Unfulfilled" is the word, isn't it?' And I try and look as solemn as they do, as I listen to them.

We women hold different views, but we don't air them quite so readily in front of the men. After all, as we say to each other, we all have to live together, don't we? No good making bad blood.

Dr Curtis arrived early in the summer term to examine the new children, Joseph, Jimmy and Linda, and the children who would be leaving at the end of the term, Cathy, Sylvia and John Burton.

The parents of these children had been notified of the time of the appointment and had been invited to be present. Chairs had been set in the lobby and Doctor had my room for the examination. The chart for sight testing was pinned up on to the partition, the scales were in evidence, and the wooden measure was fixed to the back of the door to record the heights of the six children.

Doctor was busy sorting out the cards which record each child's medical history throughout its school life. Cathy's, John's and Sylvia's would be forwarded to their new schools at the end of this term.

'Sorry I'm late,' growled Dr Curtis. 'My brother's staying with me and wanted me to change an adhesive dressing on his leg before I came away. Really, the fuss! I'd just started to pull it when he made enough noise for six stuck pigs! "Here!" I said, "take the scissors and hot water and get it off yourself!" So I've left him soaking the stuff, trying not to hurt himself. I told him one good sharp tear would soon get it off, but what can you do with men?'

I assumed that this question was rhetorical and asked her if she would like to see Mrs Coggs first with Joseph, as I knew she would want to get down to 'The Beetle and Wedge' for her scrubbing.

Joseph's eyes were wide with alarm throughout his examination. His apprehension, as he stood with his back to the door and felt the wooden marker descending on to his head, was pitiful to see. But no tears fell, even when Doctor stood him on a desk to see if his feet were flat.

'A very nice arch,' she said, squinting at Joseph's grubby foot. 'Very nice!' she added, and I caught the note of disappointment in her voice. Obviously flat feet were going to be 'the thing' this year, and I imagined half the children in the county walking about on the sides of their feet, as they did remedial exercises for the next few months.

Last year, hollow backs had been our doctor's obsession, and the year before, I remember, we were all exhorted to swim whenever possible to improve our physique. I could imagine the conversation when a few headmasters and mistresses met together later on in the term:

'And how many flat feet in your school?'

'Ten out of twenty.'

'Oh, we did better than that! We scored five out of six!'

Sure enough, the true fanatic gleam came into the doctor's eye only when she approached the feet this time. She left these to the last, in each case, working conscientiously on sight, hearing, hearts, posture, throats, height and weight, rather as a child works steadily through its pudding keeping the chocolate sauce intact to eat at the end.

John Burton was the only child who obliged Doctor on this day, but his feet were so triumphantly flat as to make up for the disappointingly springy feet of the other five. Mrs Burton was asked to take him to the clinic at Caxley where she would be shown the exercises he would need to do; and so Doctor's visit came to a successful close.

The lobby was empty, the chairs returned to the schoolroom

and the smell of disinfectant from the tumbler on Doctor's desk, which had held the spatula that she used when inspecting throats, gradually faded away.

'A really bad case, that last one,' said Doctor with much gratification, snapping her case closed. 'I'll keep an eye on that boy. I really don't think I've ever seen anything flatter!'

Quite exhilarated, she waved good-bye from her little car, and I returned to the schoolroom reflecting that we do indeed take our pleasures variously.

Mrs Pringle's bad leg always took a turn for the worse on the first Wednesday of each month.

On this afternoon the mobile film van called at Fairacre School to the joy of all but Mrs Pringle.

I could never quite understand the grounds for Mrs Pringle's dislike of these educational films. She had hinted darkly once of a terror-laden afternoon when her sister had heard the shout of 'Fire!' go up at the Caxley cinema and had had a corn trodden on painfully in the general stampede to the exit. But this second-hand adventure could not have accounted entirely for the regular monthly 'flare-up' of her own afflicted member. I think the general disorganization upset her, for we had to trundle back the partition and arrange the chairs in rows at the infants' end, leaving my part free for the screen to stand. The black-out curtains were drawn and, except for the unbiddable skylight which defied all attempts to shroud it, very little light penetrated. The children loved this mysterious twilight, and excitement always ran high, until the purring of the projector quietened them.

'Waste of the ratepayers' money,' snorted Mrs Pringle as, limping heavily, she clattered plates into the crockery cupboard. 'Do the children more good, I'd say, to be learnt something useful. Spelling, for instance. We always had spelling lists every Wednesday afternoon in Mr Hope's time. And he knew how to spell them himself without having to look 'em up!'

Mrs Pringle had been scandalized to see me looking up a word in the dictionary the week before. I think she had seriously considered reporting me to the omnipotent 'office' for inefficiency.

'Never see Mr Hope with a rubbishy thing like a dictionary,' continued Mrs Pringle, shooting forks with quick-fire precision into their box, and shouting above the racket.

'Perhaps he kept it at home,' I replied amiably.

'And another thing,' boomed Mrs Pringle, 'some of these films are downright improper. I saw one once at Caxley, with two people kissing each other, and though I daresay they were well on the road to a straightforward wedding, I didn't care for it myself and come out at once. Very unpleasant remarks I had to put up with too, I may say, from other people in the row who should have known better by the flashy way they were dressed up.'

I wondered whether it was worth while shouting myself hoarse against the clatter by explaining that the afternoon's programme consisted of a film about the building of a Norman castle, which would link up with the history lessons of this term, a second film about the herring industry, which might widen the outlook of some of these children who had only just seen the sea, although it lay less than eighty miles away; and a short film about the animals at the London Zoo. I decided to save my breath, and, leaving Mrs Pringle to her dark mutterings, I went to welcome Mr Pugh who was staggering in carrying heavy equipment. Behind him followed a train of admiring children who had had strict orders to stay in the playground until called, but were drawn to Mr Pugh's imposing collection of tin cases, cables, stands, the rolled-up screen and so on, like needles to a magnet.

Mr Pugh is a small, volatile Welshman who takes his work very seriously. His job is really to bring the films and to show them, but he takes such a passionate interest in every one of them that any sort of adverse criticism throws him into Celtic protestations. One would imagine that he had produced, directed and acted in all the films that flicker in our murky classroom, so quick is he in their defence. Luckily, he is soothed by cups of tea, and I make sure that the tray is set and the kettle filled in readiness, on the first Wednesday afternoon of each month.

At last the room was ready, the children were called in and exhorted by me in the playground to step carefully over the cable, and by Miss Gray inside to sit down and sit still. Mr Pugh flicked a switch, the projector purred, the pictures wavered before us and the old magic had begun again. After each film the children clapped energetically. The most popular, of course, was the animal film. Some of the children had already been to the Zoo and I knew that others might go in the near future with the Mothers' Union outing.

A satisfied sigh went up from the school as the last film ended. Miss Gray and I drew back the curtains and surveyed our family, sitting in rows and blinking like little owls in the unaccustomed light.

While Mr Pugh dismantled his paraphernalia, Miss Gray went to switch on the kettle and I led the children out to play, their heads buzzing with castles, herrings and hippopotami. Tomorrow I should have to sort out these troubled images for them, as best I could, and I made a mental note that another trip across to the church to see the Norman window there, would be a good thing to do in the morning.

These visits from the film unit are of inestimable value to the country school. The choice of films is wide and gives an added fillip to the classroom lessons which follow them.

Perhaps the welcome that the children give to Mr Pugh and his fellows is the surest indication of their success.

18. THE MUSICAL FESTIVAL

There was a bus drawn up in the lane outside Fairacre School. It quivered and vibrated in the May sunlight; and beside it, in their best clothes, the children clustered hopping with excitement. It was the great day of the Caxley Musical Festival and Miss Gray, who was to conduct the choir, was doing her best to fight down her own stage-fright and calm her charges.

She wore a pale-green linen frock which had been much admired by the children.

'Real smashing!' said John Burton.

'It suits her lovely!' said the girls, head on one side; and Linda Moffat said, with much pride: 'My mum helped her with it. You never saw so many darts in the bodice! That's what makes it fit so good.'

'Now you understand,' I addressed the children when they were finally seated, 'you are to be on your best behaviour. All the other schools will be there at the Corn Exchange. Let them see how polite and helpful you are!'

Whether these admonitions were heeded I doubt, for the excitement of the occasion was almost unendurable, but the driver climbed in, was greeted cheerfully by the children, for he was a local boy, and the bus began to grind along the flower-starred lanes to Caxley.

'Miss,' said Eric, 'what happens when we want a drink?'

'Or we feels sick?' added Ernest.

'Or wants to be excused?' asked Linda in a prim, but anxious whisper.

We assured them that Caxley Corn Exchange offered facilities which could cope with all these contingencies, and we begged them to cease to worry, to relax, to rest their throats or otherwise they would forget their songs or sing horribly sharp with anxiety.

At last we chugged into the market-place. There, outside the Corn Exchange which dominates one side of the square, were queues of excited children slowly edging through the wide doorway.

Shepherding their flocks were determinedly patient teachers, the women with their hair freshly set, wearing undramatic summer dresses and their best sandals, and the men almost unrecognizable in formal suits . . . their beloved shapeless grey flannels and jejune hacking jackets mercifully left behind on the backs of their bedroom chairs.

We collected our twittering children and joined the mob.

Caxley Corn Exchange is described as 'an imposing pile' by the local guide-book and perhaps it is as well to leave it at that. Certainly one's feelings on first catching sight of it are incredulity and then pity for so much misapplied labour.

Inside, the walls are of bare brick. The windows are glazed with a greenish glass and these admit a curious underwater light which adds to the general feeling of submersion. On each side of the windows are brick curlicues, like gigantic barley-sugar sticks, and at the end of the hall looms a massive statue of one of the benefactors of the town. This forbidding person, who is twelve feet high, gazes with bewhiskered severity at the crowd below him, and holds in his hand a watch, for all the world as if he is saying: 'Late again, eh? This must be reported!'

The hall was rapidly filling with schoolchildren from more than twenty schools. We found our places and gazed about us.

In the centre of the hall was a dais with a large table, a microphone, masses of papers and a handbell. Here the judges were to sit. Near the stage was the grand piano with banks of hydrangeas at its feet.

'Real beautiful, ain't it?' said Sylvia in an awed whisper – her eyes on the barley sugar sticks.

'Been here often!' announced John Burton casually, with a cosmopolitan air. 'Come with my dad for the chrysanthemum show last autumn. There's a bigger place than this up London.'

A respectful silence greeted this piece of news.

At last Eric spoke. 'Show off!' he said witheringly, and had the satisfaction of seeing John turn pink, but whether from rage or discomfiture no one knew.

The morning wore on. We sailed over the sea to Skye at various paces from staccato to near-static. We follow-follow-followed till we were dizzy and our heads throbbed. The air inside the Corn Exchange grew thicker despite the open windows, which had yielded grudgingly, with dreadful groanings, to much heavy battering.

But the Fairacre children looked bright-eyed as squirrels as they waited on the stage to begin their songs. Miss Gray's green linen back registered acute anxiety and her baton trembled when she raised it first, but once they were launched all went well and they beamed smugly at the applause which followed their efforts. Swaggering slightly, they simpered back to their places. Mr Annett, who had somehow managed to seat himself near our school, murmured congratulations into Miss Gray's ear as she returned, and hitched his chair a foot closer.

The chairman rose on the dais.

'We'll stop now for lunch. Everyone back here please at one-thirty sharp. Thank you all very much,' This welcome announcement brought the biggest clap of the morning.

After lunch Miss Gray and I took the children to a nearby park. They made a rush for the paddling pool, for in the downland village of Fairacre there is very little water to play in.

The sun was warm and a dragon-fly hovered, vibrating and iridescent over the water. I sat on the grass to watch our children as they gazed at the lucky owners of toy boats who were running importantly round the edge with long sticks.

At the other end of the park I could see the Beech Green children, with Miss Young and Mr Annett. He appeared to be scanning the horizon in a purposeful way, and at length he detached himself from his school and, leaving poor Miss Young to cope with the entire school, advanced rapidly upon Miss Gray who was sitting composedly upon a bench under a poplar tree.

'There's fish here!' screamed Joseph Coggs, across the pond, in great excitement. 'Little 'uns, miss. You come and see!'

'There's real fish what you can eat in that ditch behind you,' a tall boy told him, in a voice that trembled between soprano and baritone, indicating a little stream that slips along the side of the park to join the river that flows through Caxley. At this moment hubbub broke forth behind me and there, emerging dripping from the pool, with hair sleeked down like a seal and mouth agape for bawling, stood Jimmy Waites.

His beautiful white shirt and grey flannel shorts were soaking, and spattered with flotsam from the surface. In fact, the only dry things about him were his socks and sandals which Cathy had helped him to remove for a surreptitious paddle while my eye was averted. Crying herself, with vexation and shock, she knelt beside her little brother.

I hallooed to Miss Gray who was still sitting on the bench studying her shoes demurely while Mr Annett chattered away beside her. Really, I thought with some exasperation, it was too bad of them to be so blissfully removed from the vexations of this life. Somewhat peremptorily, I told Miss Gray that I was taking Jimmy to the lavatory to mop him up and would she keep an eye on the others. Mr Annett returned hastily to this world from the elysium where he had been floating, and had the good sense to offer to run the child home in his car when I had dried him.

'Lord!' said the attendant with relish, 'he hasn't half got his clothes mucked up! Won't your mother say something to you, my lad!' At which, the hideous bawling which I had calmed with much difficulty, broke forth anew.

Between us we rubbed the shivering child dry and Cathy was despatched to fetch Mr Annett's car rug to wrap him in.

We emerged from the shrubbery, which decently drapes our Caxley lavatories, with Jimmy looking like a little Red Indian, the fringe of the rug trailing behind him. We gathered the rest of the children together and with Mr Annett carrying Jimmy, and Miss Gray beside him, leading the way, we returned to the Corn Exchange.

As we crossed the market square I noticed John Burton walking closely behind Mr Annett. He was mimicking the schoolmaster's springy steps, and with eyes crossed and mouth idiotically open he was giving a striking and hideous representation of a love-sick swain, much to the admiration of his companions.

'John Burton!' I called sharply. He hastily returned to normal. 'What on earth,' I continued, using that tone of shocked bewilderment that comes so easily to any teacher, 'what on earth, boy, are you supposed to be doing?'

'Nothing, miss!' he answered meekly, and, lamb-like, walked with decorous steps back to his place in the Corn Exchange. We watched Mr Annett and his bundle drive away towards Fairacre and followed the children for the afternoon session.

'Well, we've had enough excitement to last us today,' I commented to Miss Gray, as we subsided into our seats. She smiled at me in reply, with such sweet and lunatic vagueness, that I realized that she was still many miles away, on the road to Fairacre, in fact. Love, I thought crossly, can be very tiresome; and, looking to the stage for some relief, found none; for, with awful purpose writ large upon their youthful faces, twenty children were there assembled, and each bore a violin.

It was not until after Mr Annett's return that the second shock of the day fell. He had assured me, in a tickling whisper, that Jimmy was safely with his mother and I had whispered back my gratitude and allowed my tense muscles to relax with some relief. At that moment I thought of Joseph Coggs, scanned the rows before and behind me and could see nothing of him. On the stage the excruciating sawing went on, and under the cover of its discord I sent agitated messages to Miss Gray. Had she seen him? Had he slipped out to the lavatory? Did he come back with us? Had she counted the children when she collected them in the park? How many were there then?

Miss Gray's gentle gaze rested upon me without a hint of perturbation. She wore the expression of one who, returning from an anaesthetic, leaves some bright world behind with infinite regret. Only the fact that she turned her eyes in my direction gave any hint that she had heard me.

No help there, I thought to myself, and added in a savage whisper: 'I'm going out to look for him.' Several shocked glances from my more musically-conscious colleagues were cast at me as I retreated from the hall, and a look, more in sorrow than in anger, from the only female judge.

'Are you all right? Can I fetch you some water?' inquired a kindly headmaster near the door. I felt inclined to tell him that I was on the verge of an apoplectic fit, brought on through exasperation, and that nothing less than half a tumbler of neat brandy could touch me – but, knowing how these things get misconstrued in a small community, I restrained myself, thanked him, and escaped into the market square.

The park was much less crowded now and presented a peaceful appearance. Mothers sat beside prams, knitting or gossiping, while their infants slept or hurled toys blissfully to the ground.

The paddling pool had only a few small female occupants, who were wading with their frocks tucked into bulging knickers. Joseph was not among them.

In the distance the park-keeper was spearing odd pieces of paper with a spiked stick. I hurried towards him.

'I've lost a child—' I began breathlessly.

'No need to take on so, ma!' replied the man. 'You ain't the first to mislay your kiddy, believe me. The mothers we get, coming up here to me, hollering same as you—'

'I am unmarried—' I said with what dignity I could muster.

'Well, well,' soothed the insufferable fellow comfortingly, 'we all makes mistakes sometimes.'

'I mean,' I said with emphasis, wondering how long my sanity could stand up to these repeated bludgeonings of an unkind fate, 'that I am a schoolteacher.'

'That accounts for it, miss,' the man assured me. 'School-teachers, unless they're caught very young, never hardly gets married. Funny when you come to think of it!'

His eyes became glazed as he dwelt upon this natural phenomenon, and I adopted a brisk tone to bring him round.

'One of my children . . . my class . . . a little boy, was left behind when we went back to the Corn Exchange this afternoon. A dark child – about five.'

'About five,' repeated the man slowly, stropping his chin with a dirty hand. He thought for a few minutes and then looked up brightly. 'He's probably lost!' he said.

Controlling myself with a superhuman effort, I told him to take the child if he found him to Miss Gray at the Corn Exchange, where he would be suitably rewarded. Turning my back on him, with some relief, I set out to the little stream where I guessed that those 'fish big enough to eat' had probably drawn the truant from Fairacre School.

The stream was bordered with dense reeds, lit here and there by yellow irises and kingcups. The early swallows and swifts flashed back and forth, squealing, the sun glinting on their dark-blue backs. On any other afternoon I should have thought this willow-lined retreat a paradise, but anxiety dulled its beauties, as I squelched by the water's edge to the detriment of my white shoes.

'Joseph! Joseph!' I called, but the only answering cry was from the birds around me. Somehow I felt sure that the child was near here . . . that the stream had attracted him.

Supposing, I thought suddenly, something dreadful had happened to him! Morbid pictures of a small body awash among the duckweed, or entangled among willow roots, or, worse still, gradually being sucked down into the treacherous mud at the stream's edge, all flitted through my mind.

'For pity's sake,' I begged myself crossly, 'don't add to it! You'll be choosing the hymns for the funeral next.'

The stream made a sharp right-angled bend by a fine black poplar tree whose white fluff blew about the grass beneath it. Huddled against its trunk, terrifyingly still, lay Joseph.

Unable to speak, and with mounting agitation, I approached him. To my infinite relief I could hear him snoring.

His cheeks were flushed with sleep, but there were shiny streaks, like snail tracks, where the salt tears had dried. His long black lashes were still wet and his pink mouth slightly open. Beside him, in a jam jar, swam two frenzied minnows in about half an inch of water.

I sat down on the grass beside the sleeping figure to regain my composure. Tears of relief blurred the shining landscape, my legs ached and I felt, suddenly, very old and shaky.

While I was recovering, Joseph stirred. He opened his eyes and stared straight above him at the rustling leaves. Then, without moving his body, he rolled his head over and looked long and solemnly at me. Slowly a very loving smile curved his lips, he put out a grubby hand and held fast to my clean dress.

'Oh, Joseph!' was all I could say, giving him a hug.

'I got lost,' growled Joseph, 'and a boy give me this jar to go fishing with. Ain't they lovely?' He held the jar up to the sunshine while the two unhappy occupants flapped more madly than before.

I rose to my feet, and we went to the water's edge to fill the jar. There was no doubt about it . . . the minnows were destined to spend the rest of their short lives in Joseph's doting care.

Together we wandered back along the stream, hand in hand, Joseph pausing from time to time to croon over the top of the jar. His sandals oozed black slime at every step, his eyes were still swollen with crying, but he was a very happy little boy, safe again, and with two new playmates.

The market square was dazzling in the sunlight and it was good to get back to the cool under-water gloom of the Corn Exchange. Thankfully, I realized that the violins had finished during my absence, but my relief was short-lived.

'And now,' announced the chairman, with misplaced enthusiasm, as we regained our seats, 'we begin the percussion classes!'

The children sang on the way home in the bus. They sang all the songs that they had learnt for the Festival, some they had heard on the wireless, and some regrettable numbers that someone's father had taught them in an expansive moment. Miss Gray and I sat silent, I with exhaustion and she, it seemed, with unmodified rapture. Occasionally a happy little sigh escaped her lips. Occasionally, when my feet obtruded their discomfort particularly, I sighed too.

At Mrs Moffat's bungalow we stopped and she spoke.

'Shall I come on to the school with you? Can I be of any help?'

'No,' I answered, 'I can manage. It's been a long day – you'll want your tea and a rest I expect.'

'It's been a heavenly day,' replied Miss Gray ardently, 'and I'm not a bit tired. In fact, I've arranged to go out for the evening with Mr Annett . . . we thought . . . well, yes! I'm going out with Mr Annett.'

I said that would be very nice indeed and that I would see her in the morning.

John Burton, who had overheard this conversation, and fondly imagined that he was unobserved, now saw fit to repeat his famous dying-duck-in-a-thunderstorm act and began to blow languid kisses about the bus to his delighted friends.

The door closed behind Linda and Miss Gray. I leant forward and, without any warning, gave John Burton a sharp box on the ear.

It was, I found, the best moment of the day.

19. THE FÊTE

In the infants' room a crayoning lesson was in progress. Joseph Coggs, now recovering from his adventure, was busily drawing little boys dancing. They all had three buttons down their egg-shaped bodies, large teeth and hands like rakes. From their trunks up they presented a wooden and fearsome appearance; but their legs were thrown about in attitudes of wild abandonment.

'Be very careful,' Miss Gray warned them, 'the best ones will be pinned up on the blackboard, and put in the tent for everyone to see, on the day of the Fête.'

'Will we get prizes?' asked Jimmy Waites.

'Very likely; and even if you don't, you want your parents to see how well you can draw. Keep them clean,' added Miss Gray, and went back to her cupboard-tidying, humming to herself.

Joseph liked to hear her humming. She hummed a lot these days, and seemed, he thought, to be kinder than ever. As he drew a large yellow circle for the sun, he thought of all the things she had taught him.

He could add up numbers up to ten and take them away too, though this was hard sometimes. He knew all the sounds the letters made and some words as well. He could copy his name from the card Miss Gray had made for him, and he knew lots of songs and poems that he sang and recited to his little sisters at home. And as for making paper houses, like the first one his father had used for a pipe lighter, why, he'd made dozens since then and each better than the last. Yes, he decided, he liked school and . . . blow it all, he'd bust his crayon!

'Lend us yer yaller,' he hissed to Eileen Burton beside him, but she was uppish this afternoon, and shook her head.

'I wants it,' she said firmly, putting down the green one she had been using for grass. The subject was 'A Summer's Day,' and all the green crayons were wearing down fast. She snatched up her yellow crayon close to her chest. 'I wants it,' she repeated, and then leaning over surveyed Joseph's picture closely. 'I wants it for the sun,' she announced triumphantly, and began to draw a yellow circle, exactly like Joseph's, on her paper.

This annoyed him, and, gripping Eileen's fragile wrist, he tried to prise the crayon from her fingers. Miss Gray, humming still, and sitting on her heels with her head in the cupboard, remained oblivious of the gathering storm.

'You ol' devil!' breathed Joseph, scarlet in the face. 'You copy-cat! You give it here!'

With a wrench, Eileen gained possession of the crayon again, and holding it above her head, she put out an impudent pink tongue at her pursuer. Maddened, Joseph lowered his dark head and butted her on the shoulder, and then, fastening his teeth in her arm he bit as hard as he could.

A terrible screaming broke out from Eileen and cries from the rest of the class. Miss Gray, rushed into action, slapped Joseph and released Eileen who inspected her wounds and howled afresh at the neat teeth marks on her tender flesh.

'He swored, Miss,' volunteered Jimmy Waites, 'he said "Devil," Miss, didn't he? Didn't he swear, then?'

Yes, he had, agreed everybody, rather smugly. Joseph Coggs had swored and tried to take Eileen's crayon and bit her when she wouldn't let him have it. Joseph Coggs was a naughty boy, wasn't he? Joseph Coggs wouldn't be allowed to go to the Fête, would he? Joseph Coggs, in the opinion of his self-righteous classmates, was not fit to mix with them.

Miss Gray silenced them peremptorily, sent Joseph to stand by her desk and Eileen to wash her arm in the lobby.

The artists continued in comparative silence, but there were many accusing nods towards the culprit, who was having his version of the incident drawn from him by Miss Gray.

'It doesn't excuse you, Joseph,' said Miss Gray finally, 'you must say you are sorry to her and never do such a dreadful thing again. I shall have to write a note to Eileen's mother to explain her hurt arm, and you must sit on your own until we can trust you again.'

So Joseph sat in splendid isolation to finish his picture, and a few sad tears mingled with the daisies that he drew in the grass.

But once the hated apology was over, the crayons collected, and Miss Gray's *Mother Goose Nursery Rhymes* appeared again on her desk, his spirits revived.

Who cared what ol' Eileen Burton's mother said? She couldn't hurt him, and anyway it served her right for copying his sun. And he didn't call 'Devil' swearing – why, it was in the Bible the vicar read to them! Swearing indeed! With a glow of pride Joseph thought of all the real swear words his father used. He bet he knew more than anybody in the class, if it came to that!

Much heartened, he turned an attentive face to Miss Gray, who thought what a dear little boy he was, despite everything. And there she was right.

The fête was held on the first Saturday in May, in the Vicarage garden; 'Proceeds' said the posters, that fluttered from vantage points in the village, 'in aid of the Church Roof Fund.'

'And how slowly it grows!' sighed the vicar. 'We need another three hundred pounds at least, and the roof is deteriorating every day.'

He was in his shirt-sleeves, his mild, old face screwed up against the sunshine. He bore a wooden mallet for driving in the stakes which were to hold the various notices. In the distance we could hear the clatter of the lawn mower which Mr Willet was pushing over the tennis court.

This, the only flat piece of the vicar's garden, which lay on the slope of the downs, was to be used for bowling for the pig. Golden bales of straw were stacked at the side, ready to make an enclosure for the great skittles, when Mr Willet had finished his ministrations.

A breeze fluttered the crêpe paper along the edge of the stalls. Miss Clare was busy setting out dozens of crêpe paper dorothy bags filled with home-made candy, and tempting bottles and boxes of toffee, humbugs and boiled sweets. Rows of lollipops lined the edge of the stall and it was obvious that Miss Clare's old pupils would soon be flocking round her again.

She was having lunch with me; cold meat, new potatoes and salad, with gooseberry fool for sweet – a meal which, I surmised, would be echoed in most Fairacre homes that day – a direct result of a bumper gooseberry crop coupled with hectic last-minute preparations for the fête.

In Linda Moffat's house, Mrs Moffat, her mouth full of pins, was putting the final touches to her daughter's flowered head-dress. Linda was going to the fête dressed as a shepherdess, complete with blue satin panniers, sprigged apron and a shepherd's crook, borrowed from old Mr Burton and decked for the occasion with bunches of blue ribbons. Miss Gray stood by admiring. 'Sweet!' she said.

'Hold ftill!' said Mrs Moffat, much impeded in her speech by pins 'Ftand ftraight for juft a fecond more!'

And Linda, sighing deeply, but submitting to the fuss, only hoped that her long suffering might result in a prize in the fancy-dress competition that afternoon.

In Tyler's Row, at the Waites' cottage, there was great excitement, for a letter had come, with the education committee's seal on its envelope, bringing the good news that Cathy had been deemed fit for a place next September at Caxley County Grammar School for Girls.

'But I wanted to go to the High School!' protested Cathy, when this was read out to her.

'Same thing!' her mother assured her. 'Cathy, my love, you've done real well.'

Her father beamed at her, and feeling in his pocket, presented her with half a crown.

'Here, duck, that's for the fête this afternoon. I reckon you deserves a bit of a spree!'

The letter was propped carefully behind the tea-tin on the mantelpiece, and Cathy, rushing into the little garden turned cartwheel after cartwheel, her red checked knickers bright in the sunshine, letting off some of the high spirits that fizzed and bubbled within her.

Joseph Coggs, squatting on the ash path next door, watched these antics through the hedge. Beside him sat his two little sisters, crop-headed since Nurse's visit, busily stirring stones and mud together for a delightful dolls' pudding.

'Going up the fête?' asked Cathy, standing upright at last and staggering slightly as the garden slowed down around her.

'Dunno,' answered Joseph gruffly. The two little girls ceased their stirring, and advanced towards the gap in the hedge, wiping their hands down their bedraggled skirts.

'What fête?'

'Up the vicar's. You know, what we been practising for at school.'

Joseph suddenly remembered all he had been told about races, fancy-dress competitions, sweet-stalls, prizes and his own beautiful picture which had been pinned on to the board for the judges to see. Without a word he pounded up to the house, the sisters scampering, squeaking, behind him.

In the stuffy kitchen his mother was shaking the baby's bottle and looking at it with some impatience. The baby cried fitfully.

'Can us go to the fête?'

'Do let's, Mum; let's go! Say us can go, Mum!' they clamoured above the baby's crying.

'Oh, we'll see,' said their mother testily. 'You get off in the garden while I feeds baby. This bottle don't draw right.'

She sucked at it lustily and then turned it upside down, watching it critically.

'Oh, Mum, you might! Just for a bit. Please, Mum!' they pleaded.

The bottle was thrust into the baby's mouth, and peace reigned.

'I'll see how I gets on,' said Mrs Coggs grudgingly. 'I don't know as I've got enough clean clothes for you all to go up to the vicar's, with all the rain this week. You get on outside and play quiet for a bit. Perhaps we can.'

She joggled the baby on her arm. The children still waited.

'Oh, buzz off!' shouted Mrs Coggs with exasperation. 'I've said us might go, haven't I?'

And with this unsatisfactory answer ringing in their ears, the Coggs children returned reluctantly to the garden.

The vicar had prevailed upon a well-known novelist, Basil Bradley, who lived locally, to open the fête, and this he had done in a speech of charm and brevity.

Beside him, accommodated in the vicar's best armchair, sat his mother, an old lady in her ninety-third year, so wayward and so eccentric in her behaviour as to cause her celebrated son many moments of anxiety.

She was the widow of a brewer and was said to be very wealthy indeed.

It was common knowledge that her son had none of this money. He lived, comfortably enough, however, upon his earnings, and was wont to smile patiently when his mother said, as she did frequently, 'Why the dickens should the boy have any of my money? He'll have it when I'm gone – do him good to wait for it!'

It was her habit, however, to give him expensive, and often useless, presents at odd times, which he did his best to receive gratefully, for he was devoted to this maddening despot. Only this morning he had accepted, with well-simulated gratification, a quite hideous paper-rack, made of black bog-wood, which his mother had purchased from an antique dealer who should have known better.

'Speak up, Basil,' she had commanded, in a shrill pipe, towards the end of his speech, 'Mumble-mumble-mumble! Use your teeth and your tongue, boy! Where are your consonants!'

She was now at Miss Clare's stall inquiring the price of sweets, and expressing her horror at such outrageous charges.

'As a gel,' she said to the imperturbable Miss Clare, 'I bought pure home-made fig toffee for a halfpenny a quarter. Good wholesome food, with a wonderful purging property. Not this sort of rubbish!' She waved an ebony stick disdainfully at Miss

Clare's stall and turned away in disgust. Her son, smiling apologetically, bought humbugs and lollipops in such enormous quantities that Miss Clare wondered where on earth he would get rid of them.

Dr Martin, holding a large golliwog which he had won at hoop-la, was admiring the rose which climbed over the vicarage porch.

'That's a nice rose,' said the old lady, coming up behind him. 'A good old-fashioned rose. A nice flat face on it, you can get your nose into!'

The vicar basked in this sudden approval. 'A great favourite of mine, isn't it, Doctor? I planted it the autumn that my son was born.'

'Can't beat a Gloire de Dijon,' agreed the doctor, 'splendid scent!' And he bent a spray for the old lady to sniff.

'Allow me to pick you some,' said the vicar, and vanished into the house for the scissors.

'Most sensible man I've seen for a long time,' commented Mrs Bradley. 'Knows a good rose and gives you some too. Don't often get a bunch of flowers these days. Old people get neglected,' she added, squeezing a tear of quite unnecessary self-pity into her eye. Doctor Martin and poor Basil Bradley exchanged understanding looks. Doctor Martin thought of the numerous well-kept hot-houses in the Bradley grounds and forbore to make any comment; but taking the old lady's hand in his he patted it comfortingly.

The vicar bustled back and snipped energetically, taking great pains to cut off any thorns. He was very proud of his rose and delighted to find an admirer in this crusty old lady.

'And now,' she said, when the bouquet was tied with bass, 'I must give you something for your funds before my son takes me home. Go away, Basil,' she ordered the poor man, who had stepped forward to take her arm. 'Go away, boy, while I go into the vicarage to write a cheque. And don't fuss round me as though I were incapable!'

Her son meekly sat on the edge of the stone urn while the vicar, expostulating politely, led his visitor to the drawing-room. There, in a spiky handwriting, reminiscent of the French governess of her childhood, Mrs Bradley wrote a cheque and gave it to the vicar.

'But, my dear Mrs Bradley, I simply can't accept—' began that startled man.

'Stuff!' snapped Mrs Bradley, 'I haven't been given a bunch of roses like that for years. Stop fussing, man, and let me get home for my rest.'

She stepped out into the sunshine again and set off for the car.

Mr Partridge, much bewildered, held out the cheque for Basil Bradley's inspection.

'Your mother, so kind, but I feel perhaps . . . her great age, you know,' babbled the vicar incoherently.

The son reassured him. 'I'm so glad that she has given generously to such a good cause. Believe me, you have made her very happy this afternoon.'

'Hurry up, boy,' came a shrill voice from the car, 'don't waste the vicar's time when he's busy!' And, waving a claw-like hand, she was driven off.

Over on the tennis court, bowling-for-the-pig was doing a roaring trade. Mr Willet was in charge, perched up on the top of the straw bales, and hopping down, every now and again, to roll the heavy balls back to John Burton's father, who was taking the sixpences and handing out the balls.

Away, in the corner of the walled kitchen garden, stood the pigsty, usually empty, but now housing a small black Berkshire pig, who was accepting such dainties as apple cores, and even an occasional toffee-paper, from the children who stood round admiring him.

Mrs Bryant, her trilby hat a landmark, sat on the grass at the side of the tennis court, with several of her sons and daughters around her. All her boys were noted marksmen, and very few pigs from the local fêtes found other homes than with the Bryant tribe.

Malachi, a swarthy six-footer, in a maroon turtle-neck sweater, had just knocked seven of the nine skittles down with his three balls, and Ezekiel was now about to try his luck.

All Mrs Bryant's boys had Biblical names and as she had mastered the reading of capital letters, but had never gained the ability to read small ones, their names had been garnered from the headings of the books of the Bible. Her fifth son she had decided to call 'Acts' but was gently dissuaded from this by the vicar who had suggested that 'Amos' might be a happy substitute, and in this the old lady had concurred.

The tale got round, however, and Amos was nicknamed 'Acts' or rather, 'Axe,' from an early age. Now a man in his thirties, Axe Bryant ran a thriving fish and chip shop in Caxley, and was too busy this afternoon preparing his potatoes for the Saturday night rush to join his brothers at Fairacre in bowling for the pig.

After Ezekiel had had his turn, John Pringle arrived on the scene. He was popular, and everyone hoped he would give the Bryants a run for their money. With great cunning he bowled his three balls, and the last one, by some distortion of the pitch, knocked down three out of the remaining four standing.

'Eight!' went up the triumphant cry, 'Good old John! Eight!' And delighted glances were exchanged and much back-slapping. Even Mrs Pringle managed a faint congratulatory smile at her son, basking in his reflected glory. But the Bryant tribe looked grim.

'Malachi!' ordered Mrs Bryant in a voice of thunder, with a jerk of the trilby hat towards the balls. With his black brows drawn together, Malachi advanced with another sixpence, and after spitting on his hands, he sent down his first ball in answer to the challenge.

Mrs Moffat was receiving congratulations from the vicar's wife on her daughter's dress. Linda had won first prize of five shillings which she was now ploughing back into the fête funds by treating several small friends to ice-cream.

Several of the mothers had spoken to her and had said how pretty Linda looked. Fairacre, Mrs Moffat suddenly thought, was a very pleasant place, and, with an uprush of spirits, she remembered how gloomy she had been a year ago as a newcomer to the village. No, she decided, things were not too bad. Money was easier with Miss Gray boarding with her, Linda was happy at school, the house and garden were settled and she had made a staunch friend in Mrs Finch-Edwards. She moved among the crowd on the lawn, now one of Fairacre's inhabitants, accepted and content.

The schoolchildren in my class performed their play. John Burton's opening line, 'I am the Spirit of Summer,' which I had practised with him until it rang in my head from dawn to dusk, was, as I had feared, delivered in the perfunctory, off-hand mutter, that I had sweated blood to change to an arresting declamation. Everyone applauded heartily, however, and the infants gambolled on to perform their singing games under Miss Gray's direction.

In the vicar's drawing-room, Miss Clare sat at the piano, which had been pulled close to the french windows, and there she played the old nursery tunes, 'Here we go round the Mulberry Bush' and 'Poor Jenny is a-weeping,' and 'There was a Jolly Miller,' as she had done so many times for their fathers and mothers.

The babies clapped and sang, very delighted with themselves, gazing cheerfully over their shoulders at their parents all the time. The circle occasionally set off in the wrong direction and had to be steered by Miss Gray now and again, but the whole show was an enormous success, and I felt that Fairacre School had covered itself with glory.

A cold little wind sprang up after tea, rustling the leaves of the rhododendrons and sending the people back to their cottages. The stall-holders began to sell their wares at half-price, and the people in charge of Aunt Sally, fishing with a magnet, and rolling pennies, began to collect their paraphernalia and the pudding basins, heavy with money.

'It seems incredible,' said the vicar later, as he sat with neat piles of coins before him, 'but we seem to have made a hundred and fifty pounds! Of course, I know that that includes Mrs Bradley's most generous contribution, but even so . . . it is quite wonderful!' His face was glowing with happiness. He adored his church and the parlous state of the roof had afforded him much sorrow for some time. Now, well before the winter gales began, a start could be made.

Through the french windows he could see the bigger children, under Mr Willet's supervision, clearing up the debris. Mrs Coggs, with her young family, had made her appearance very late, but was now busily stuffing lettuces, gooseberries and spring cabbage into a string bag.

'It will be a relief to get rid of it,' the vicar's wife was assuring her. 'We can't keep it here and it will come in useful for the children, I hope.' She caught sight of Joseph's monkey eyes fixed mournfully upon her. 'Here, my dear, run over to Miss Clare and see if she has anything left on the sweet stall.' And to Joseph's speechless amazement he found himself on his way to Miss Clare with a sixpence warm in his hand.

John Pringle was trundling a wheelbarrow covered with a net out of the vicarage gate. Loud squealing accompanied him as he wheeled his pig home, and on each side of the barrow trotted admiring children.

Outside 'The Beetle and Wedge' lounged the Bryant menfolk. Mrs Bryant had stalked home in disgust some half-hour earlier, and the men were loth to face her acid tongue when they returned.

They watched the pig and its escort go by them, with hostile glances, but in stony silence. As the cavalcade turned the bend, Ezekiel spoke.

'Come and 'ave one, mates,' he muttered, and the brothers turned silently in at the pub door to gain consolation for past tribulations and strength to face those to come.

20. Perplexed Thoughts on Rural Education

'Heard about Springbourne?' asked Mr Willet. He was sheltering in the school doorway from a sharp spattering of hail. Beside him was propped a besom with which he had been sweeping the coke back to the pile. An outbreak of Cowboys-and-Indians, involving ambushes behind the pile and wild sorties over it, had spread the crunching mess far and wide.

'What about it?' I said, peering out to see if I could make a dash for the kettle. The spasmodic spatterings suddenly turned to a heavy bombardment. Hailstones danced frenziedly on the asphalt, so thick and fast, that it seemed as though a mist were rising. I leant against the stone sink in the lobby, ready to gossip.

'They say the school's closing down,' said Mr Willet. 'You heard that?'

I said I had.

'Well, it ain't good enough by half. The people over Springbourne are proper wild about it. After all, it's been there pretty near as long as this one.'

'But it's so expensive to keep up. Only fifteen children, I believe and the building in need of repair.'

'What about it? Got to go to school somewhere, ain't they? Can't walk this far, some of 'em only babies; now, can they? Besides, every village wants its own school. Stands to reason you wants your own children to run round the corner to where you went yourself.'

He blew out his stained moustache with vexation.

'And another thing,' he said, nodding like a mandarin, 'the bus'll cost a pretty penny to cart 'em over here. And what about poor old Miss Davis? Been there donkey's years. She and Miss Clare was pupil teachers together as girls. Where's she to go? Pushed off to some ol' school in Caxley, I've heard tell, with great ol' classes that'll shout her down, I shouldn't wonder!' He paused for breath, glowering out across the veiled playground.

'Mark my words, Miss Read,' he continued, wagging a finger, 'this'll be the death of that poor soul. Give her life up, she has, to Springbourne – and the people there won't let her go without a tussle. Run the cubs, played the organ, done the savings – Oh! I reckons it's cruel!'

I agreed that it was.

'And where's the poor ol' gel to live? There's rumours going that she'll be turned out of the school-house, where she's lived all these years. Look at the garden she's made! A real picture – and took her all her life! And that's another thing!' Mr Willet moved closer to me to emphasize his point. The ragged moustache was thrust aggressively near.

'Suppose these school people up the office ever wants to open that school again? Who's coming there, if they've sold the house? Tell me that?' he demanded. 'You know, miss, we've seen it time and time again – no house, no schoolteacher! And in the end it's the kids and the village what suffers. No one living there to take an interest and know everybody. "Yank 'em off in a bus," says the high-ups!' Mr Willet's tone changed to one of mincing refinement. ' "Push 'em all into one big school – it's economy we've got to think of!" '

I laughed, and was immediately sorry, for Mr Willet was so burning with righteous indignation that I could not explain that I was laughing at his impersonations and not at his sentiments.

'Economy!' Mr Willet spat out, with disgust. 'I don't call that economy! Economy's taking care of what you've got and making good use of it. And if shutting up the village schools for the sake of a bit of hard cash is what the high-ups call economy, they just wants to sit down quiet for a minute and think what real value means – not ol' money – that's the least of it – and then to think again and ask themselves "What are we throwing away?"'

The hail stopped with dramatic suddenness, and with Mr Willet's wisdom ringing in my ears I sped across to the kettle.

While Mrs Pringle was still flicking her duster the next morning. Miss Gray beckoned me into her empty room to show me a very beautiful sapphire ring snug in its little satin-lined box.

'I can't tell you how pleased I am!' I said, kissing her heartily, 'you'll suit each other so well—' A thought struck me. 'It is Mr Annett, I suppose?'

Miss Gray laughed, although her eyes were wet and she was rather tremulous. 'Yes, indeed, who else would it be?'

'I'm so glad. He deserves to be happy at last.'

'Poor man!' agreed Miss Gray, with a sigh so fraught with sympathy and pity that I foresaw a very maudlin few minutes. 'He has suffered terribly,' she went on, looking at me with anguished grey eyes. I composed my features and prepared to listen to the harrowing account of Mr Annett's past love-life and the hopes, declared with becoming downcast modesty, for his future. But luck was with me. The door burst open, and a gaggle of small children entered.

'Miss,' said Jimmy Waites breathlessly, 'Eileen Burton's knicker elastic's busted, and she won't come out of the lavatory she says, until you brings a pin!'

Miss Gray put the ring in her bag and hastened away, while I returned to my room to choose the morning hymn, observing, as I went, how seldom one can indulge in the inflation of any sort of emotion without life's little pin-pricks bursting the balloon.

'And a very good thing too,' I was moralizing to myself,

'emotions cannot be enjoyed without them becoming dangerous to one's sense of proportion,' and I was about to develop this lofty theme, when I caught sight of Ernest, and was obliged to break off to direct him to wipe his nose.

On Tuesday the *Caxley Chronicle* carried the announcement of the engagement and all the village was agog.

'Not that it wasn't plain to see for weeks,' was the general verdict. 'Let's hope they'll be happy.'

Mrs Pringle was at the top of her form when she heard the news.

'That poor girl!' she said, dragging her leg slightly, 'he's got through one wife and now he's setting about another!'

'Oh, come!' I protested, 'you make him sound a Bluebeard! It wasn't Mr Annett's fault, merely his misfortune, that his first wife was killed in an air-raid!'

'That's his story,' replied Mrs Pringle, darkly, 'and anyway who's to say we shan't get more air-raids?'

This piece of reasoning was quite beyond me, but I determined to let some light into the gloom of Mrs Pringle's argument.

'You are saying, in effect, Mrs Pringle, that anyone marrying Mr Annett lays themselves open either to slow-death-by-matrimony or sudden-death-by-air-raid.'

'What a wicked lie!' boomed Mrs Pringle indignantly, bristling and breathless. 'I simply said Mr Annett had got a good wife in Miss Gray and I hope she's got some idea of the state of the house she's taking over before she goes to it as a bride.'

Before this *volte-face* I was silent.

'And if she wants to know of a real good scrubber, my husband's niece over at Springbourne would be the one for the job, but would need to be supplied with old-fashioned bar soap, these new sudses, she says, brings her up all of a nettle-rash!' She paused for breath and assumed the look of piety which the choir-boys mimic so well.

'May she be very happy,' she said lugubriously, 'and I only pray she doesn't have her confinements in that front bedroom of Mr Annett's! Mortal damp, it is, mortal damp!'

'Delightful news,' said the vicar, beaming, 'so very suitable – a most charming pair! But, my dear Miss Read, Annett's gain must, of course, be Fairacre's loss, I fear. Has she mentioned anything to you? Whether she is willing to continue here I mean? At any rate for a few months, shall we say? Just until – well, in any case – does she want to go on teaching?'

I said that I had no idea.

'I must set about drafting another advertisement if she decides to leave us, I suppose. Such a short time since our last interviews. I wonder now if Mrs Finch-Edwards would help us out again?'

I pointed out that Mrs Finch-Edwards would be busy looking after a young baby by that time.

'Of course, of course,' nodded the vicar. 'More good news! I never can quite decide which I find the pleasanter – news of a wedding or a birth. Well, who can we think of?'

'Let's find out if Miss Gray is planning to leave or stay first,' I suggested.

At the back of the class I could see a picture, drawn by Ernest, being displayed secretly to his neighbour, under the desk. From a distance it looked remarkably like a caricature of the vicar and I felt the matter should be investigated immediately. I did my best to catch the malefactor's eye, but he was much too engrossed with his handiwork to bother about me.

'I'll call again,' said the vicar, setting off for the door, so preoccupied that he forgot his farewells to the children. At the door, he paused: 'Perhaps Miss Clare?' he suggested. His face was illuminated. He looked like a child who has just remembered that it is Christmas morning. With a happy sigh, he vanished round the door.

The warm weather had returned. On the window-sills, pinks, so tightly packed that they looked like cauliflowers, sent down warm waves of perfume to mingle with the scent of roses on my desk.

The elm trees in the corner of the playground cast comforting cool shadows, and beyond them, in the lower field that stretched away to the foot of the downs, the hay was being cut.

Vetch, marguerite and sorrel had coloured the thick grass and now they were falling together before the cutting-machine. Behind Mr Roberts' house was a field of beans in flower and every now and again we would take in a heady draught from that direction.

The pace of school work inevitably slowed down. The children were languid, their thoughts outside in the sunshine. It was the right time for day-dreaming, and I took as many lessons as possible in the open air.

One afternoon of summer heat we were disposed at the edge of the half-cut field under the elm trees' shade. The air was murmurous with the noise of the distant cutter and with myriads of small insects. Far away the downs shimmered in the heat, and little blue chalk butterflies hovered about us. In a distant cottage garden I could see an old woman bending down to tie lace curtains over her currant bushes to protect the fruit from the birds.

The lesson on the time-table was 'Silent Reading' and in various attitudes, some graceful and some not, the children sat or lay in the grass with their books propped before them. Some read avidly, flicking over the pages, their eyes scampering along the lines. But others lay on their stomachs, legs undulating, with their eyes fixed dreamily on the view before them, a grass between their lips, and eternity before them.

With so little encouragement to read at home, in overcrowded cottages and with young brothers and sisters clamouring round them until bedtime and after, these schoolchildren at Fairacre desperately need peace and an opportunity to read. But on this particular afternoon I wondered how much reading was being done and how much day-dreaming. My marking pencil slowed to a standstill and the geography test papers lay neglected in my lap. What an afternoon, I mused! When these boys and girls are old and look back to their childhood, it is the brightest hours that they will remember. This is one of those golden days to lay up as treasure for the future, I told myself, excusing our general idleness.

There were footsteps on the high playground behind us and one of the infants came to the edge and looked down upon us. He spoke importantly: 'Miss Gray says to tell you a man's come.'

'Oh, then I'll come and see him,' I said, putting down my papers reluctantly. The children hardly noticed my going, but lay docile and languorous as though a spell were upon them.

The child and I crossed the baking playground. The sun

beat here unmercifully and I spread my hand over the child's head.

'Do you know the man?' I asked him.

'It's not exactly a man,' he answered thoughtfully, and paused. I began to wonder what sort of monster had called.

'It's just John Burton's dad,' he added.

Alan Burton had called to discuss his son's future schooling. He was very disappointed that John had not been accepted for the Grammar School at Caxley, and did not want the boy to go on to Beech Green next term.

'Not that I've anything against Mr Annett. He's all right – but there's not the stuff there for training a boy like John who wants to do something with his hands. There's no woodwork shop and no metalwork place, and as far as I can see the building's just the same as it was years ago. Where's this technical school we were promised when young John was a baby in arms?'

I agreed that there was no sign of it.

'A man like me can't afford to send a boy away to school even if he wanted to. I could have managed the Grammar School in the old days and John would have been a credit to the place. He's good at games and he can make anything. I want something better than Beech Green for him now. Mr Annett has to take all sorts, and there's some among them downright vicious. And some thick-headed ones that are bound to hold the others back.'

All this was sound good sense and I felt very sorry for Alan Burton. It certainly was a calamity that the Caxley area had no technical school for boys of John's calibre. I could only suggest that he let him go to Beech Green where he would get a certain amount of handicraft training and then apprentice him at fifteen to a trade that he would enjoy.

'I suppose that's what it'll be,' he sighed and picked up his hat, 'but I'd have liked him to go to the Grammar School. I didn't go, because I was the youngest and my father had just died, but all my brothers went there. I know John's not over-bright, but he's a good lad and as bright as his uncles were. He'd have done well there.'

I said John would do well at Beech Green and wherever he went afterwards, but he was not to be comforted.

'There's something wrong somewhere,' he said, preparing to go. 'The Grammar School suffers in the end, as I see it; for it isn't always the cleverest boys that have most to give, is it? And why are the families with a bit more money than I have scraping up all they can to send their boys away to school? In the old days, they'd have been proud to send them to Caxley Grammar School. Why's that? I don't know much about schooling these days, but what I do know I don't feel happy about.'

Sadly he departed through the school gate, and I returned to collect my somnolent children from the elm tree's shade.

21. TERM IN FULL SWING

The last day of the month has a beauty of its own, for it is pay-day. Jim Bryant, a remote cousin of the Biblical Bryants, brings the post while I am still at breakfast, and the cheques arrive together in one envelope. There are four of them; one for Mrs Pringle's cleaning and washing-up ministrations, a smaller one for Mr Willet's unenviable but necessary duties, one for Miss Gray and the last for me.

Mrs Pringle never fails to remind me, in the most roundabout and delicate manner, that it is pay-day. She usually makes a remark about the post being late, or early, or has some information to impart about Jim Bryant, thus bringing the cheque to mind for me. Sometimes I am wicked enough to postpone handing over the money for a few minutes, in order to see what form the reminder will take. This morning, Mrs Pringle was standing up on a desk zealously flapping a duster round the top of the electric light shade, as I entered. She intended to let me see that she earned her money. Dust flew in clouds, and I felt it was a pity that her zeal was not spread more evenly through the month.

'Friday again!' was her greeting. 'Don't the time fly?' I said it did, unlocking the desk drawer. Mrs Pringle eyed the letters in my hand and I waited for the next move, my eyes averted.

'Midsummer Day past already!' said Mrs Pringle. I took out the register.

'Don't seem hardly possible that July's nearly here, do it?'

'No,' I said, and straightened the massive inkstand.

'Why, bless me, it's tomorrow!' gasped Mrs Pringle, with well-feigned astonishment. 'Last day of June today – last day of the month!' she continued with much emphasis.

I walked across to the piano and opened it. Mrs Pringle clambered down from the desk, with groans. 'Sometimes I wonder if I can stick this job out much longer, with my leg. The money's not all that good, though I must say it's regular.'

'Yes,' I said absently, turning over the leaves of the hymn-book.

There was a pause. Mrs Pringle changed her line of approach. 'Postman been yet?'

I gave in.

'Yes, Mrs Pringle, and he's brought your cheque.' I handed it over to her.

'Well, now,' said Mrs Pringle, with an affected laugh, 'and I'd forgotten all about it being pay-day!'

Mr Willet shows just as much delicacy of feeling over receiving his wages. He knows that I hand it over to him as soon as I can in the morning, but if, on the odd occasion, I have been unable to find him, he appears, without fail, in the afternoon of pay-day.

He would not dream of asking me outright for his rightful dues, but he finds some noisy job in the playground, close to the door or window, which focuses my attention upon him. He usually elects to scrape the coke up with a shovel – a perennial job in any playground – and, after a while, I realize what is happening and translate what I have dimly thought of as a passing nuisance into the cry for help which it really is. On one occasion, when coke was short, Mr Willet beat upon the iron shoe-scraper outside the lobby door, with a metal bar, and the clangour quickly brought me to my senses.

I always hurry out, overflowing with apologies, and Mr Willet invariably replies: 'No need to worry, Miss Read. It'd quite slipped my mind it was the last day of the month, but I'll take it now it's here.'

The ritual over, we part with compliments on either side.

*

As this day was not only the last day of the month, but also a Friday, it would be a busy one, for besides the disposal of cheques, there were attendance records to send into the office at Caxley, the dinner money accounts to check and send in with the cash in hand, and forms to be filled in stating the number of hours worked by Mrs Pringle and Mr Willet.

I was also engrossed in a lengthy document and numerous catalogues as this was the time to apply for the stock needed throughout the coming year. So much money is allocated to books, stationery and cleaning materials for each child, and it takes a considerable amount of time and heart-searching deciding how best to allot the stock. This year I felt that the infants' room should have the lion's share, for Miss Clare had never demanded much in the way of educational-play apparatus. In fact, I had had to introduce much there that she disapproved of and failed to use. Now that Miss Gray was in charge she had many good ideas for apparatus which I was only too glad to order. I only hoped that her successor would be as enterprising and enthusiastic.

Today she handed in her resignation from Fairacre School. Notice has to be given for three months, so that we should have her with us next term, as Mrs Annett, until the end of September. The marriage was to be at the beginning of August.

'And we both hope you'll be able to come to the wedding,' said Miss Gray, as I handed back the letter of resignation which she was posting to the office. 'We shall send you a proper invitation, of course, but do please come!'

I said that I should like nothing more, and was she wearing white?

'Not a *dead* white,' explained Miss Gray earnestly, 'I don't think I could take white satin, for instance; but I've decided on a cream chiffon, with a faille underslip, and a softly-swathed bodice.'

I was on the point of crying out that that was exactly what I had hoped she'd choose for her wedding dress when we were at Miss Clare's birthday party, but luckily I held my tongue in time.

'It sounds quite perfect,' I said enthusiastically; and we became engrossed in head-dresses, veils, bouquets, bridesmaids' ensembles and all the enthralling details of a well-equipped wedding, much to the pleasure of our classes, who took the opportunity to gossip happily among themselves, and had to be spoken to quite sharply.

John Burton and Cathy Waites were standing in front of the class, surveying their fellow-pupils with a judicious eye. They were picking sides for cricket, and as there were only nineteen children present I foresaw that I should be called upon to make up the number.

It was sultry weather. A hot little wind blew the dry grass and dust round and round the playground. The children scuffled their sandals in the dusty road as we crossed to Mr Roberts' field opposite, where we have his permission to play.

The wicket is not all it should be, but it is reasonably flat, and it is possible to give the children some elementary notion of the game and its rules. At the further end, Mr Roberts' house cow, a demure Guernsey named somewhat incongruously 'Samson,' was grazing peacefully.

She looked up at our approach, and advanced with tittupping gait and nodding head.

'It do seem wrong somehow,' observed Eric, 'to have that ol' cow round us cricket times.'

I pointed out that Samson had rather more right to the field than we had, and though no doubt the M.C.C. might look askance at our conditions of play, we were lucky to have any sort of pitch at all.

Eric and I were the opening batsmen, so that I should be able to take over my rightful duties as umpire with the least delay.

Cathy, a deadly under-arm bowler with a quite unpredictable pace, now rushed up to the wicket and hurled the ball at me. It flashed by me and Ernest, the wicket-keeper, and travelled at remarkable speed to Sylvia at longstop. She had been foolish enough to think herself too far away to be noticed and had squatted down happily by a grasshopper. They were surveying each other with mutual interest when the ball cracked upon her tender knee with the most fearsome report. Hubbub broke out.

'Serve you right! You did ought to be attending! It's your own fault!' said the hard-hearted ones.

'Do it hurt bad? Poor ol' Sylvie! Spit on it, mate, as quick as you can! Now, rub it well in!' said the more compassionate.

More scared than hurt, Sylvia struggled to her feet and the game was resumed. Cathy's second ball bowled me and I handed the bat to John Burton, with considerable relief.

The game wore on. Samson chewed the cud and watched our antics with a mild eye. In the next field the haycocks stood in rows and Mr Roberts' blue and red wagon had already started to collect them. Above us, black clouds were piling up ominously and I was wondering whether we should get our game finished and whether Mr Roberts would get his hay in before the rain came, when I noticed a stranger leaning over the gate, watching us with interest.

On seeing that he was observed, he opened the gate and crossed the grass towards me.

It transpired that the stranger was one of Her Majesty's Inspectors of Schools, newly appointed to this area. He had served before, he told me as we walked back to the school, in one of the home counties, where new estates had gone up rapidly since the war, and the new schools, despite their classes of forty or more children, were efficient in design and very well-equipped.

'You've no playing-field then,' he asked, 'although there are fields all round you? Do you think it's worth while trying to teach these children cricket under such conditions? Actually, you've not really enough people for two teams, I gather.'

I told him that I thought the effort was justified. At least the children knew the rules of the game, enjoyed it, and could, in their next school, feel that they could take part in the game with some knowledge and pleasure. Thanks to Mr Roberts, the children were able to get out of the small and badly-surfaced playground to take much of their exercise.

His gaze swept the lofty pitch-pine ceiling, the ecclesiastical high windows, and at last came to rest on the skylight.

'Do you find it dark in here?' he asked.

I said that I realized it was dark compared with the steel and glass schools of the present day, but that I didn't think the children's sight was impaired at all.

'Despite its architectural drawbacks,' I told him, 'there is something in this atmosphere conducive to quiet and to work. I know it is only right that children should have big, low windows that they can see through, but they can be very distracting.'

The inspector sighed, and I could see that he thought me prejudiced and a diehard, as he ambled round the room studying the wall-pictures. The children watched him furtively, their library books open but unread.

Outside, the wind had started to roar, and the black clouds which had gathered during the afternoon made the room murky enough to horrify any inspector. There was a flash of lightning, a few muffled squeals from the children, and then a long menacing rumble of distant thunder.

The rain suddenly burst upon us in torrents, lashing the windows and streaming down the skylight. In a few minutes the usual steady drip began into the classroom below. Without waiting to be told, Cathy went into the lobby, returned with the bucket, and folding a dishcloth neatly, she tucked it methodically in the base of the bucket to stop the clanging of the drops. Mr Arnold, the inspector, watched these smooth proceedings amusedly.

'How long has this been going on?' he nodded at the skylight.

'Seventy years,' I answered, and his laugh was drowned in another clap of thunder.

'Can I go through to the infants' room, before they go home?' he asked, and I took him in to meet Miss Gray, who was already buttoning children into coats and peering hopefully across the playground to see if any mothers had braved the rain with their children's mackintoshes. I left them discussing reading methods and returned to get my own class ready to face the weather.

There was a flurry in the lobby and the vicar burst in, his cloak pouring with silver streams from his dash across the playground.

'What a storm! What a storm!' he gasped, shaking his hat energetically. The children in the front row flinched as the cold rain splashed them, but otherwise endured this treatment with stoicism.

'I had to bring the hymn list and I thought I might stow some of the children who had no coats into my car and run them home.'

The children brightened up, sitting very straight with shining eyes. Here was adventure indeed! The prudent few, with mackintoshes waiting on the lobby pegs, cursed their own forethought which had deprived them of this treat.

'Some of their mothers may be coming,' I said, 'but, let's see . . . ! Who knows that their mothers won't be able to come? And who has no coat?'

John Burton and his little sister were in this category, and five more children. As they all lived roughly in the same direction along the Beech Green Road, they were called together, and under the vicar's outspread cloak it was decided to make a dash for his waiting car, when I remembered the inspector.

'Just a moment, children,' said the vicar, 'while I greet our visitor, and then we'll set off.' Cloak swirling, he sailed into the infants' room, and found Mr Arnold engrossed in a word-making game which he had found in the cupboard.

'Fat, mat, sat, cat, rat, hat . . .' he was muttering absorbedly to himself, turning a neat little cardboard wheel to make each new word. It seemed a pity to break in on his enjoyment, but I introduced the two men and left them while I interviewed a little knot of wet mothers who had just arrived.

The lobby floor ran with little rivulets from their mackintoshes and umbrellas. Outside, the playground streamed with water, and in the dip of the stone doorstep, worn with generations of sturdy country boots, a dark pool gleamed. The children who had been claimed were bright-eyed and garrulous, faces upturned and cheerful, as they suffered their heads to be shrouded and their collars buttoned. Those who still awaited rescue were anxious and forlorn, and their eyes, turned towards the school gate, were dark and mournful.

Mr Roberts' sheepdog, its coat plastered against its ribs, edged into the gateway and was implored by its urgent friends to come into the lobby for shelter.

'Bess, come on in!'

'Bess, Bess!'

'Poor ol' Bess. Soaking, ain't she?'

Hearing sympathetic voices, Bess joined the crowd in the lobby, her tail flicking drops as it wagged furiously, and confusion reigned supreme. Gradually the numbers thinned and the vicar, having made his farewells to Mr Arnold and Miss Gray, collected his charges on the doorstep, and with the black cloak outspread above them, they all set off across the playground. From the rear, the vicar looked like some monstrous black hen sheltering her chicks, as underneath each side of the outspread cloak a forest of little legs twinkled through the puddles to the car. With a parting toot they were off, heads and hands sticking out of all the windows, despite the downpour.

Mr Arnold engaged Miss Gray in conversation again, and I saw off those children who were well-equipped for the weather. Only Cathy, Jimmy and Joseph Coggs remained and I retrieved the old golf umbrella which shares a home with maps, modulators and other awkward objects in one of the cupboards, and opened it against the lashing rain on the doorstep.

'There you are, Cathy,' I said, handing over the red and green giant, 'hold it as low as you can over the three of you, and get to Tyler's Row in record time!'

I watched the umbrella bob along the lane at a smart trot, and then hurried back to my empty classroom.

Mr Arnold came through from the infants' room to make his farewells.

'I'm afraid I picked an unfortunate day for my first visit,' he said, 'but I should like to come again, quite soon, to see you all in action.'

He waved, and sprinted across to his car through the puddles and drove away through the downpour.

Mr Annett, with a solicitude for his future wife that was quite pretty to see, had deserted his schoolchildren promptly at four and dashed over in his car to collect Miss Gray. I prevailed upon them to share my tea and together we sat gossiping and eating home-made gingerbread in the school-house.

'As long as schools are dependent on local rates,' said Mr Annett decidedly, dusting far too many crumbs, for my peace of mind, from his lap to the carpet, 'there are bound to be serious disparities in buildings and equipment. My three little nieces started their schooling in Middlesex. Their first school was a model one, individual towels, combs, beds, and so on. There was a paddling pool, two chutes, stacks of first-class toys, mounds of paper, chalks and everything else a teacher or child could wish for. Now they've moved into this area, and their local village school is not only as antiquated in design and as primitive in its sanitation and water supply as this one, but is also looked upon, as far as I can see, by the families with whom they play, as only "good enough for other people's children." '

'Don't I know!' I agreed feelingly.

'My sister is looked upon as an oddity because her daughters are going to the village school,' he continued, 'but, as she and her husband point out, they have faith in our state education and believe they are doing a wise thing. They live within a stone's throw of the school and the girls are taught in small classes by teachers who are all qualified and certificated, and any complaints made by their parents as ratepayers, about conditions, have every chance of being considered and put right.'

'It's very difficult to argue about,' I answered, 'for in the end it boils down to the liberty of the individual. If parents prefer to pay for schooling, well, why shouldn't they? I, too, deplore this "the-village-school-is-good-enough-for-them" attitude, but short of state education for all, with no choice at all, what can be done?'

'I don't quite know,' said Mr Annett thoughtfully, accepting his fourth cup of tea in a preoccupied way, 'but there are one or two things that will have to come before very long. The discrepancies between different areas will have to be overcome to begin with. Just as the teachers' salaries have been made equal in different areas, so should the school conditions be evened up. And if only more intelligent parents would make use of their local school and take an interest in it, instead of complaining about the rates they have to pay, plus school fees that they need not, it might be a step in the right direction.'

'Owners of private schools won't think so,' I pointed out, as he rose to help Miss Gray with her coat. We made our way to the car. The storm had spent itself and the sides of the lane were running with little rivers, bearing twigs, leaves and other flotsam on their swirling surfaces.

The air was soft and fresh and a blackbird was singing its heart out in the cherry tree.

'We're very lucky,' I observed, breathing in the damp earthy smell, but Mr Annett was gazing at Miss Gray. It was some time before he spoke.

'Very, very lucky,' he echoed soberly.

22. THE OUTING

The first Saturday in July is always kept free in Fairacre for the combined Sunday School and Choir Outing.

'At one time,' said the vicar, 'the schools here closed for a fortnight at the end of June for a fruit-picking holiday, and as they were paid at the end of that time the outing was held then. And now, somehow, we just stick to the first Saturday in July. It seems to suit us all.'

He beamed happily round the coach, which was filled with thirty-three of his parishioners, of all shapes and sizes, each one dressed in his best.

Behind us chugged another coach equally full, for mothers were encouraged to accompany their children on this expedition. 'For really,' as the vicar remarked, 'it would be far too great a responsibility for my wife and the two Sunday school teachers to undertake; and it does give some of these poor house-bound women a breath of fresh air.'

Mrs Pratt, as organist, was there with her two children and behind her sat Mr Annett, as choir-master, and Miss Gray. They were both making heroic efforts to be civil and attentive to their fellow-travellers, for they were at that stage of mutual infatuation when the mere presence of other people is a burden. I wondered how quickly they would abandon us when we reached the seashore. They would certainly need a breathing-space on their own for an hour or two, after behaving with such admirable self-control under the gaze of thirty-one pairs of eyes.

Miss Clare sat beside me. There had been a few seats to spare and she had agreed to come 'just to smell the sea and collect a fresh seaweed ribbon to hang in the back porch,' so that she could tell the weather.

'Years ago,' she said, 'we used to have our outing in a brake with four horses to pull it. Of course, we never went far, to the sea, or any great distance like that. But we had wonderful times. For several years we went to Sir Edmund Hurley's park, beyond Springbourne, and we all loved that journey, because we had to splash through the ford at the bottom of the steep hill there. It was before they altered the road and built the new bridge.'

'Was that Sir Edmund who gave Fairacre School its piano?' I asked, a vision of that fretwork-fronted jangler rushing at me from forty miles behind us.

'That's the one,' cried Miss Clare, delighted at my knowledge. 'He was a great friend of the vicar's at that time – the late vicar – Canon Emslie, such a dear, and so musical! He was shocked to find the school without an instrument and mentioned it to Sir Edmund one day when he was visiting at Hurley Hall. The upshot was that the present piano was sent over from the Hall. Most generous, but then all the Hurleys have been renowned for their generosity.'

'My grandfather,' boomed Mrs Pringle, swivelling round on the seat in front, 'the one as made the choir-stalls that come in for some uncalled-for criticism by them as is ignorant of such things – my grandfather did a tidy bit of carpentering for Sir Edmund.' She cast a triumphant look at Mr Annett from under the brim of her brown straw hat, as one who says, 'And if Sir Edmund was satisfied with my grandfather's handiwork, then who are you to point the finger of scorn at his choir-stalls?'

But Mr Annett was too busy adjusting the window so that no harmful gale should blow upon his life's love, and the shaft went by him and left him unscathed.

'And what's more,' continued Mrs Pringle's penetrating bellow, 'Sir Edmund asked his advice for some jobs actually in The House!' She nodded her head belligerently, the bunch of cherries on her hat-brim just a split second behind in time. This bunch of cherries is an old and valued friend, nodding from straw in summer and felt in winter, and now so far gone in years as to show, here and there, a little split, through which the white stuffing oozes gently, like some exotic mildew.

'In the house?' echoed Miss Clare. 'Where did your grandfather do the carpentering then?'

'Kitchen cupboards!' said Mrs Pringle shortly and bounced

round again to face the front, the cherries quivering, but whether with indignation or family pride no one could say.

Barrisford, as everyone knows, is a genteel watering-place with wonderful, firm, broad sands, which would cause a less refined borough to advertise itself as 'A Paradise for Kiddies.'

The children were ready to rush to the sea's edge the minute that the coaches shuddered to a standstill, but were restrained by the vicar, who, using his bell-like pulpit voice, made an announcement.

'We shall disperse, dear people, until four-thirty when we shall meet at our old friend Bunce's, on the Esplanade. I gather that an excellent tea is to be prepared for us there, with cold ham and other meats, salad, cakes, ices and so on. We shall leave here at half-past five sharp.' He looked severely at his flock, knowing that punctuality is not one of our Fairacre virtues.

'At five-thirty,' he repeated, 'and even so we shall not be home, I fear, until nearly nine, which is rather late for our very young members.'

'Never mind, vicar,' called a cheerful mother at the rear of the coach, 'it's only Sunday, tomorrow . . . nothing to get up for!'

This remark must have been instantly regretted, so scandalized was the vicar's expression on hearing it, for as well as its derogatory tone about the importance of the Sabbath, he would be celebrating Holy Communion at 8 a.m., Matins at 11 a.m., Children's Service at 3 p.m., and Evensong at 6.30 p.m.

'Four-thirty at Bunce's then,' he repeated, in a somewhat shaken voice, 'and five-thirty here.'

He stood aside, and with whoops of joy and rattlings of buckets, the youth of Fairacre swept on to the beach with a reckless disregard for kerb drill that made their teacher's blood, if not their parents', run cold.

Miss Clare had decided to take a turn about the shops before going down to the sea and asked me if I would like to accompany her.

'But not, of course, if you would prefer to be elsewhere. It's only that I am looking out for a blue cardigan, something between a royal and a navy, to wear with my grey worsted skirt in the winter.'

I said that there was nothing I should like better than a turn about the shops.

'It would be so useful too, for school,' went on Miss Clare happily, her eyes sparkling at this prospect, 'just in case, you know, I am needed, from the time Miss Gray leaves, until Christmas. The vicar has been so very kind about it all, and I feel so much better for my rest, that I hope I can come back, even if it is only for a few weeks.'

It was nice to see Miss Clare so forward-looking again, and I hoped, for her sake, that the vacancy at Fairacre School would not be filled before the end of next term.

We had a successful shopping expedition. '*Most* suitable, madam,' the girl had gushed, 'and if madam ever indulged in a *blue rinse*, the effect would be quite, quite electrifying.' Digesting this piece of intelligence we made our way to the beach, where, scattered among other families, the Fairacre children could be seen digging, splashing and eating with the greatest enjoyment.

The tide was crawling slowly in over the warm sand, and Ernest was busy digging a channel to meet it. His spade was of sharp metal and cleaved the firm sand with a satisfying crunch. I thought regretfully of my own childhood's spade, a solid wooden affair much despised by me, but nothing would persuade my parents that I would not chop off my own toes and be a cripple for life if I were given a metal one, and so I had to battle on with my inadequate tool, while more fortunate children sliced away beside me with half the effort, and, as far as my jaundiced eye could see, their full complement of toes.

Ernest paused for a minute in his work.

'Wish we could stay longer here,' he said, 'a day's not long, is it?'

We settled ourselves near him and agreed that it wasn't very long.

'You'd better make up your mind to be a sailor,' I said, nodding to a boat drawn up at the edge of the beach. People were climbing in ready for a trip round the harbour.

'Oh, I wouldn't like that,' responded Ernest emphatically, 'I don't reckon the sea's safe, for one thing. I mean, you might easy get drownded, mightn't you?'

'A lot of people don't,' I assured him, but his brow remained perplexed, working out the countryman's suspicions of a new environment.

'And there don't seem enough grass and trees, somehow. Nor animals. Why, I didn't see any cows or sheep the last bit of the journey. No, I'd sooner live at Fairacre, I reckons, but I'd like to have a good long holiday here.'

Having come to terms with himself he began digging again with renewed effort, and I looked about to see how the other children fared.

The sky was blue but with a fair amount of cloud, which kept the temperature down. Despite this, most of the children seemed content to be in bathing costumes, but it was interesting to see with what respect and awe they treated the sea. Not one of them, it appeared, could swim – not surprising perhaps, when one considered that Fairacre was a downland village and the nearest swimming water was at Caxley, six miles distant.

I wished, not for the first time, that I could see my way clear to taking my older children into the Caxley Swimming Baths once a week, but the poor bus service, combined with the difficulties of rearranging the time-table to fit in this activity, made it impossible at the moment. Paddlers there were, in plenty, but not one of the Fairacre children went more than a yard or two from the beach edge into the surf, and while they stood with the swirling water round their ankles, they kept a weather eye cocked on dry land, ready to make a dash for safety if this strange, unfamiliar element should play any tricks with them.

At digging they came into their own. Armchairs, sandworks, channels, bridges and castles of incredible magnitude were constructed with patience and industry. The Fairacre children could handle tools, and had the plodding unhurried methods of the countryman that produce amazing results. Here was the perfect medium for their inborn skill. The golden sand was turned, raked, piled, patted and ornamented with shells and seaweed, until I seriously thought of importing a few loads into the playground at home to see what wonders they could perform there.

One or two went with their parents for a trip in the boat, but they sat, I noticed, very close to the maternal skirts, and looked at the green water rushing past them with respectful eyes.

The day passed cheerfully and without incident. Tea at Bunce's was the usual happy family affair, held in an upstairs room, with magnificent views of the harbour.

'Our Mr Edward Bunce,' as the waiter told us, was in personal attendance on our needs, an elegant figure in chalk-striped flannel and bow tie. Soft of voice and smooth of manner, he swooped around us with the teapot, the living emblem of the personal service which has made Bunce's the great tea-shop that it is.

At five-thirty, we were back in our coaches, with seaweed, shells and two or three unhappy crabs awash in buckets in an inch or two of seawater. The vicar, quite pink with the sea-air, was holding his gold half-hunter and counting heads earnestly.

Mr Annett and Miss Gray mounted the steps in a dazed way and resumed their seat amidst sympathetic smiles, and only one seat then remained empty.

'Mrs Pratt, vicar,' called someone, 'Mrs Pratt and her two little 'uns!'

'I think I see one of them, coming across from the chemist's shop,' answered the vicar. A fat little girl in a pink frock stumped across to the coach, panted heavily up the steps and to her place, and sat, swinging her legs cheerfully. We continued to wait.

The driver flipped back his little glass window and said: 'That the lot?'

'No, no,' answered Mr Partridge, rather flustered, 'one more and a little boy to come. Peggy, my dear,' he said to the elder Pratt child, 'is your mummy still in the chemist's?'

'Yes,' said the child, smiling smugly. 'Robin's got something in his eye.' She sounded both proud and pleased.

The vicar looked perturbed, and sought his wife's support anxiously. She rose, bustling, from her seat, leaving her gloves and bag neatly behind her.

'I'll just run across to her,' said the good lady and trotted across to the open door of the chemist's shop.

Dimly, in the murk of the interior, we could see figures grouped around a chair, on which, presumably, sat the patient. There were head-shakings and gesticulations, and at length Mrs Partridge came hurrying back with the news.

'The chemist seems to think that the child should see a doctor. He suggests that we take him to the out-patients' department at the hospital. It's quite near here evidently.'

There was what reporters call 'a sensation' at this dramatic announcement. Some were all for getting out of the coach, rushing across to fetch Robin and Mrs Pratt away from all these foreigners, and taking them straight home to their dear familiar Doctor Martin; others suggested that the chemist was a scaremonger, and that 'the bit of ol' whatever-it-is will soon slip out. You knows what eyes is – hell one minute, and all Sir Garnet the next!' But all factions were united in the greatest sympathy for the unfortunate family.

'The child is in great pain,' went on Mrs Partridge, looking quite distracted. 'Cigarette ash evidently, and it seems to have burnt the eye. I really feel that he should go to the hospital.'

'In that case, my dear,' said the vicar, making himself heard with difficulty above the outburst of lamentation that greeted this further disclosure, 'you and I had better stay with Mrs Pratt and see this thing through, while the rest of the party go back to Fairacre.'

'But tomorrow is Sunday!' pointed out his wife.

'Upon my word,' said the vicar, turning quite pink with embarrassment, 'it had slipped my mind.'

'Shall I stop?' I volunteered.

At the same time, a voice said: 'What about little Peggy here? Had she better come with us or stay with her mum?'

Bedlam broke out again as everyone offered advice, condolence or reminiscences of past experiences of a similar nature. The driver, who had had his head stuck through his little window, and had been following affairs with grave attention, now said heavily, 'I 'ates to 'urry you, sir, but I'm due back at nine to collect a party of folks after a dance in Caxley; and we're running it a bit fine, if you'll pardon me mentioning it.'

The vicar said that, of course, of course, he quite understood, and then outlined his plan.

'If you will stop with Mrs Pratt and Robin,' he said to his wife, 'I'm sure our good friend Mr Bunce will be able to find you a night's lodging – I will hurry there myself, if the driver thinks we can spare ten minutes.' He looked inquiringly at the driver and received a reassuring nod. He produced his wallet, and there was a flutter of notes between him and Mrs Partridge, 'And then hire a taxi, my dear, to bring you all back tomorrow.' He looked suddenly stricken. 'I shall have to remember to set the alarm clock for early service, of course. I must tie a knot in my hand-kerchief to remind me.'

This masterly arrangement was applauded by all and we were sitting back congratulating ourselves on our vicar's acumen when a little voice said, 'And what about me?' We all turned to look at Peggy who sat, wide-eyed and rather cross, waiting to hear her fate. There was an awkward pause.

'There's no one at home,' said Mrs Pringle, 'that I do know. Mr Pratt's off doing his annual training with the Terriers.'

'Would you sleep in my house?' I asked her, 'I've got a nice teddy-bear in the spare room.'

This inducement seemed to be successful, for she agreed at once. Mrs Partridge hurried back to tell Mrs Pratt what had been planned, while the vicar sped at an amazing pace back to Bunce's tea-shop, to see if he knew where beds might be engaged for the night.

The coach buzzed with conversation as we waited for the vicar's return.

'Real wonderful, the vicar's been, I reckons.'

'Got a good headpiece on him . . . and kind with it, proper good-hearted!'

'I feels sorry for that little Robin. Must be painful, that. Poor little toad!'

Peggy elected to sit by me and Miss Clare obligingly took herself and her parcel containing the new winter cardigan to Peggy's vacated seat. In a few minutes a sad little group emerged from the chemist's shop. Robin had a large pad of cottonwool over one eye, securely clamped down with an eye-shade. Mrs Pratt was drying her tears as bravely as she could, while Mrs Partridge held Robin by one hand, and Mrs Pratt's shopping bag in the other. They approached the coach and made their fare-wells.

'You be a good girl now, Peg,' adjured her tearful mother, 'and do as Miss Read tells you. And if you'd be so kind as to keep a night-light burning, Miss, I'd be real grateful – she gets a bit fussed-up like if she wakes up in the dark. High strung, you know.'

I assured her that Peggy should have all she wanted, and amid sympathetic cries and encouragement the three made their farewells and departed in the direction of Bunce's.

In record time, the vicar reappeared. Mr Bunce's own sister had obliged with most suitable accommodation and had offered to accompany the Fairacre party to the hospital, in the kindest manner, said the vicar.

The driver set off at once and the great coach made short work of the miles between Barrisford and Fairacre.

Nine o'clock was striking from St Patrick's church as we clambered out and within half an hour, Peggy Pratt was sitting up in the spare bed, drinking hot milk and crunching ginger-nuts. A candle was alight on the chest of drawers, its flame shrinking and stretching in the draught from the open door.

'I likes this nightie,' said the child, looking admiringly at a silk vest of mine that was doing duty as nightgown for my small guest. There had been no tears and no pining for the distant mother and little brother left behind at Barrisford. I hoped that she would fall asleep quickly before she had time to feel homesick.

'I shall leave the door open,' I told her, tucking in the moth-eaten teddy beside her, 'in case you want me. And in the morning we'll have some boiled eggs for breakfast that Miss Clare's chickens laid yesterday.' I took her mug and plate and went to the door.

She wriggled down among the pillows, smiled enchantingly, sighed, and closed her eyes. She was asleep, I think, before I had reached the foot of the stairs.

23. Sports Day

'Mallets,' shouted Mr Willet, above the wind, looking with marked disfavour at the one in his hand, 'ain't what they used to be!'

He was standing on a school chair in Mr Roberts' field, driving chestnut stakes into the ground, so that we could rope off the track for the school sports which were to be held the next afternoon. His scanty hair was blown up into a fine cockscomb, and the rooks in the elms nearby were hurling themselves into the arms of the wind from the tossing branches.

A little knot of children, ostensibly helpers, watched his efforts. Eric had managed to get the rope into a tangle of gargantuan proportions, and the hope of ever finding an end among the intricacies on the grass at his feet, was fast waning.

'You ain't half slummered it up,' said Ernest admiringly, stirring the mess with his foot.

A despairing shout went up from John Burton who was counting sacks lent by Mr Roberts for the sack race. A malicious gust of wind had caught up half a dozen sacks and was whirling them towards the road. There was a stampede of squealing, breathless children after them.

The vicar's tent was being erected, slowly and hazardously in the shelter of the hawthorn hedge. Here lemonade and biscuits were to be sold. John Burton had executed a bold notice saying:

LIGHT REFRESHMENTS
(IN AID OF SCHOOL FUNDS)

and this was to be pinned on the tent just before the parents and friends arrived.

Samson, the house cow, had been moved to the next field, but showed a keen interest in the evening's proceedings, with her head protruding over the hedge and her eyes rolling. There were far more helpers offering her quite unnecessary meals than those who deigned to assist Mr Willet and me in our preparations.

Mr Willet drove in the last stake and looked at his watch. He held it at arm's length about a yard away from his stomach, and scrutinized it from under his lashes, frowning hard as he did so. His second chin settled on the stud which hung in the neck-band of his collarless shirt.

'Nearly seven,' he grunted. 'Better get a move on, miss. It's choir practice tonight and I reckons Mr Annett will be along pretty soon.'

He pocketed the watch and looked about him.

'Pity them moles saw fit to make their hills just where you're running tomorrow.' He turned to Eric and Ernest who were sitting on the pile of rope playing with plantains, one trying to knock the head off the other's, with much ferocity and inaccuracy.

'Here!' he bellowed, against the wind.

They looked up like startled fawns.

'You go and git spades and hit them molehills flat, else you'll be sprawling tomorrow. And let's have a hand at that 'orrible 'eap you made of that rope!'

Miraculously he found an end and handed it to me. Grumbling and grunting, puffing out his stained and ragged moustache, he slowly backed away from me; his tough old hands working and weaving among the tangle as though they had an independent life of their own, so swiftly and surely they moved.

I tied my end to the first stake, and though Mr Willet surveyed it with some contempt he said nothing, but worked down the line, leaning against the wind and brushing stray children out of his way without glancing at them, until the track was roped off from the rest of the field.

The church clock struck seven and I called the children.

'Best go and have a sluice I suppose,' said Mr Willet, as we battled with the gate, 'I'll see you're all straight tomorrow morning, miss.' He looked up at the weathercock that shuddered in the wind above the spire. 'If you races with this wind behind you tomorrow,' he told the children, 'you'll break some records – mark my words!'

I switched on the electric copper ready for my bath-water, when I returned. In the dining-room stood large jugs of lemonade essence ready for the morrow, but from the sound of the roaring wind outside hot coffee would be more welcome. I sorted out coloured braids for the relay race, and a basket of potatoes for the potato race, and hoped that Mr Willet had looked out sound and hardy flower-pots for the heavy-footed boys who had clamoured to have a flower-pot race included in the programme. They had seen this at Beech Green's Sports Day and had been practising in the evenings for weeks, stumping laboriously along, placing one pot by hand before the other, with their crimson faces bent earthwards and their patched seats presented to the sky.

The kitchen was comfortably steamy when I put the zinc bath on the floor and poured in buckets of rainwater from the pump. As I lay in the silky brown water, too idle to do more than relax and enjoy the heat, I listened to the rose tree which Dr Martin had admired last autumn when he had come to visit Miss Clare here. It beat, in a frenzy of wind, against the window-pane. To drown the noise of its scrabbling thorns, I roused myself to switch on the portable wireless set, which was within arm's reach, on the kitchen chair.

'Strong westerly winds, reaching gale force at times, are

expected in all southern areas of the British Isles,' said a brisk, cheerful voice. Snarling, I switched off, and sank back into the comforting water.

Later, on my way to bed, I looked out of the landing window. Ragged clouds were tearing across the darkening sky, and over in Mr Roberts' field a dim, pale shape flapped against the hedge. Giving up the unequal struggle, the vicar's tent had sunk hopelessly to the ground.

Next morning, however, things looked brighter. The wind, though still strong, seemed less aggressive, and two of Mr Roberts' men erected the tent again. The sound of tent pegs being smitten reached us in school, where the children were much too excited to settle to any serious work.

The boys, as usual, were the more anxious about the afternoon. Fear of not doing well made them quite unbearable. They boasted of their own prowess and belittled that of their neighbours, while the girls looked on philosophically at this display of male exhibitionism.

'Look at John rubbing his legs! Thinks that'll make him run faster. Some hopes!'

'Tones up the muscles; that's what it does. All good runners does that before racing. Pity you don't try it. You was like an ol' snail last night down the rec.'

'Only 'cos I was a bit winded. Been overdoing the training, see!'

'You see ol' Eric, Saturday? Thought he was jumping high when he cleared that titchy little hedge down Bember's Corner. Coo, I've jumped twice that!'

'Me too. Easy, that hedge is. You should see me get over that electric wire Mr Roberts has put up in the heifers' field! Up I goes . . . and whoo . . . I bet it was over four foot I done!'

And so on. It seemed best to let them have their heads for a little while, but in the latter part of the morning they settled down to a history test, although I noticed a certain amount of secret muscle-flexing and leg-massage as the athletes prepared themselves for outstanding displays before the admiring gaze of parents and friends in the afternoon.

When Mrs Crossley arrived with the dinner van, the children

were washing their hands at the stone sink. I heard them cross-questioning her thoroughly.

'And what vegetables, Mrs Crossley?'

'Carrots and peas.'

'They blows you out too much. I shan't have they.'

'What for pudding, Mrs Crossley?'

'Some very nice currant pudding, with custard. You'll like that.'

''Twould have been best to have something lighter like. Fruit and that, wouldn't it, Eric?'

'I dunno. I'm hungry. Reckons I shall have some pudden, races or no races.'

'You hear him? Him what was so sharp on us last night eating sweets? Said us was in training? *Pudden*, he's going to eat! Fat chance we'll have in the relay!'

'We best eat summat,' said John Barton's placid voice, 'or we won't have no strength at all.'

'Well,' said Ernest grudgingly, 'it don't sound the sort of dinner that *real* runners would have, to me, but I s'pose us'll just have to stoke up best we can.'

They re-entered the schoolroom and settled themselves for grace. As far as I could see our athletes forgot their Spartan principles as soon as the food was put before them, and second, and even third, helpings of currant pudding were despatched with the usual Fairacre appetite.

There were plenty of people to watch the sports and patronize the refreshment tent. Miss Clare was in charge of the jugs of lemonade and the six biscuit tins and Mrs Finch-Edwards, looking very handsome in a classic maternity smock of polka-dot navy blue silk, with its inevitable white collar, sat beside her with an Oxo tin full of change.

'Yes, I'm keeping very well,' she responded to my inquiries, 'and I think hubby and I have got absolutely everything now. Even the pram's on order!'

There was a grunt from Mrs Pringle who had just brought in a tray full of glasses.

'Defying Providence!' she boomed. 'Never does to order the pram or cot till the little stranger's in the house. Times without number I've seen things go awry within the last three months. Seems to be the most dangerous time – particularly with the first. Why, there was a young girl over Springbourne Common—'

I broke in before Mrs Pringle could chill our blood further. Mrs Finch-Edwards' normally florid cheeks had blanched.

'That'll do, Mrs Pringle; and we shall need at least four tea-towels.'

'And lucky you'll be to get those, I may say,' said Mrs Pringle viciously, thwarted in the telling of her old-wives' tale. But she departed, nevertheless, and went back across the field to the school, limping ostentatiously to prove what a wronged woman she was.

Miss Gray was trying to keep the mob of children in order near the starting line which, being hand-painted by Ernest in yesterday's strong wind, wavered erratically across the width of the track.

A blackboard had been erected here showing the order of races, but so strong was the wind that, after it had capsized twice, nearly decapitating Eileen Burton on the second occasion, Mr Willet had lashed it to the easel. He looked very spruce this afternoon, in his best blue-serge suit as he stood with the vicar and Mr Roberts.

I had decided to be starter, and Miss Gray had the unenviable job of being judge at the other end. Mrs Roberts offered to help her and the two stood, with their hair blown over their eyes, waiting for the first race to start. It was 'Boys under 8: 50 yards.'

The young competitors crouched fiercely on Ernest's wobbly line, their teeth clenched and their lips compressed. 'On your marks, get set – go!' I shouted; and off they pounded, puny arms working like pistons and heads thrown back. The Sports had begun.

Everything went like clockwork. There were no tears, no accidents and the molehills were miraculously avoided by the children's flying feet. The parents and friends of Fairacre School, ranged on hard forms and chairs along Mr Willet's rope, applauded each event vigorously and made frequent trips, with the thirsty victors and vanquished, to the refreshment tent where trade was gratifyingly brisk. The fact that the tent was warm and peaceful after the tempest that blew outside may have helped sales, for the less warmly clad lingered in here, buying biscuits at four a penny, and filling up the Oxo tin with their offerings.

Mrs Moffat, in a becoming rose-pink suit, brought Linda in, flushed with success after winning the girls' sack race. Miss Clare noticed how much happier Mrs Moffat looked and how well she and Mrs Finch-Edwards agreed.

'If you like to go out for a bit, I'll manage the change,' offered Linda's mother, and Mrs Finch-Edwards, taking Linda by the hand, went out into the boisterous wind to see the Sports, leaving her friend in Miss Clare's company.

Perhaps the highlight of the afternoon was an unrehearsed incident. Mrs Pratt's white goat, attracted by the noise, had broken her collar and pushed through the hedge to see what was going on. Fastidiously, walking with neat, dainty steps, she approached the backs of the spectators and before anyone had noticed her, she picked up the hem of Mrs Partridge's flowered silk frock. Gradually, the goat worked it into her mouth, a sardonic smile curling her lips, tossing her head gently up and down, until at last a sudden tug caused the vicar's wife to look round and the hue and cry began.

Startled, the goat skipped away under the rope and charged down to see its friends, who were waiting, in pairs with their legs tied together, to run in the three-legged race. Squealing with excitement, and weak with laughter, they lumbered off in all directions, the goat prancing among them, bleating. Confusion reigned, some children sprawled on the grass, others attempted to capture the goat, and others rushed yelling to their parents. At last Mr Willet grabbed the animal's horns and slipped a rope noose over her head. Resigning herself to capture, the goat trotted meekly after him to the gate, accompanied by many young admirers.

By half-past four the Sports were over and the parents trickled away from the field with their children, some of them boasting of victory and some explaining volubly just how victory had evaded them.

Mrs Moffat, Mrs Finch-Edwards and Miss Gray had gone

home to the new bungalow to tea, and Miss Clare, Mrs Pringle and I collected the debris together in the shelter of the tent.

'It went very well,' said Miss Clare, mopping up lemonade from the table, while I counted braids and sacks, 'and how fit all the children look! I can see the improvement, in my lifetime, in the physique of the Fairacre children. Better conditions have a lot to do with it, of course, but I think less clothing and daily exercise play a great part. When I think how I was dressed at their age—' She broke off and gazed into the distance, seeing, I guessed, that little girl in high button boots, starched underclothes and stiff serge sailor dress complete with lanyard, whose photograph I had seen in the album at Beech Green.

Mrs Pringle's snort brought us back to earth.

'Never had such rubbishy things as sports in my young days,' she remarked acidly, 'making work for all and sundry, regardless! Never saw a jumping stand, or turned those 'orrible somersaults when I was a girl, and look at me now!'

We looked.

24. END OF TERM

It was the last day of term. Jim Bryant had brought the precious envelope containing our cheques; fantastically large ones this time, as they covered both July and August. Such wealth seemed limitless, but I knew from sad experience, how slowly September would drag its penniless length, before the next cheque came again!

Mr Willet was busy pulling up two roots of groundsel near the door-scraper, and expressed his customary surprise on receiving his cheque. Mrs Pringle was scouring the stone sink in the lobby and took her cheque grudgingly in a gritty hand.

'Little enough for the hours I puts in,' she said glumly, folding it and stuffing it down the front of her bodice. 'Sometimes I wonders if I can face next term, with fires and all. And the next few days will be nothing but scrub, scrub, scrub, with disinfectant, I suppose, all them cruel floorboards. Enough to make my leg flare-up, the very thought of it!'

'Well, give me good notice, Mrs Pringle,' I said briskly, 'when you do decide to give up. Then I can look round for somebody who'd like the job!'

There was an outraged snort from Mrs Pringle as she limped ostentatiously to the cleaning cupboard to put away her rags.

The morning was spent in a happy turmoil of clearing-up. Books were collected and counted, and then stacked in neat piles in the cupboards. Ernest and Eric sat at the long side desk, ripping out the remaining clean sheets of paper from the children's exercise books, to be put away for tests and rough work next term. The inkwells had been collected into their tray, and there was considerable competition among the boys as to who should have the enviable job of washing them, in an old bowl, out in the safety of the playground.

While the hubbub rose joyfully, I made my way painfully round the walls, prising out drawing-pins with my penknife and handing over dusty but cherished pictures to their owners. Through the partition I could hear the infants at their clearing-up labours, and when I reached the door I poked my head in to see how they were getting on.

Joseph Coggs was squatting by the big clay tin, tenderly tucking wet cloths over the clay balls to keep them in good order for next term. Eileen Burton was staggering to the cupboard with a wavering tower of Oxo tins, containing chalks, leant precariously against her stomach, her chin lodged on the top one to steady the pile. Some children were polishing their already emptied desks, others were scrabbling on the floor for rubbish, like old hens in straw, and a group besieged Miss Gray, holding such treasures as beads, coloured paper, plasticine and even used milk straws, all clamouring to know what should be done with them.

I clapped my hands to make myself heard above the din, and when it was a little less hectic I asked if any of them knew of any children likely to start school next term. This would give me some idea of numbers for ordering dinners for the first day.

There was a puzzled silence, and then Joseph said in his hoarse voice: 'My mum's coming up to see you about the twins.'

'How old are they?'

'They's five in November,' said Joseph, after some thought.

'Tell Mummy I should like to see her at any time,' I told him and looked to see if there were going to be any more newcomers, but there was no stir.

I returned to my own room, where the noise was deafening. No one seemed to know of any beginners next term, and it looked as though I should have room for the Coggs twins, although they were slightly under age, for John Burton and Sylvia would be leaving to go to Mr Annett's school at Beech Green, and Cathy would be going to the Grammar School at Caxley.

At last conditions became a little less chaotic. The overflowing waste-paper basket was emptied, the jam jars removed from the window-sills and put away, and the room wore a bleak, purged look, shorn of all its unessentials.

I put my old friend 'Constantinople' up on the blackboard, issued a piece of the rough paper and a pencil to each child, bullied them all into silence, and told them to see how many words they could make from it before Mrs Crossley arrived.

All was peaceful. From the playground came the distant splash of water as John Burton dealt with the inkwells, and nearer still, the clank of paint-boxes being cleaned at the stone sink by Linda Moffat. She pleaded so desperately to perform this filthy task, that I had given way, but now I was a prey to awful fears about the welfare of her crisp, piqué frock, and made haste to go into the lobby and envelop her in Mrs Pringle's sacking apron, much to the young lady's humiliation.

One Saturday previously I had taken several of the children into Caxley to buy Miss Gray's wedding present, for which the whole school had been collecting for weeks. I had managed to assemble all the children together, sending Miss Gray to the Post Office for more savings stamps. This manoeuvre was considered highly daring and the children were in a conspiratorial mood during her short absence, Eric going so far as to keep watch at the lobby door while we made our plans.

It was decided, in hushed whispers, that a piece of china would be appreciated, and the deputation, under my guidance, were given powers to make the final choice, not however, without plenty of advice.

'Something real good! Like you'd want for always!'

'And pretty too. Not some ol' pudden basin, say. A jam dish, more like!'

'Flowers, and that, on it . . . see?'

We promised to do what we could just as Eric thrust an agitated countenance round the door, saying: 'She's coming!'

With many secret giggles and winks they dispersed to their desks and all was unnaturally quiet when Miss Gray entered and handed over the savings stamps.

'What very good children,' she remarked; and then looked amazed at the gale of laughter that this innocent remark had released.

In Johnson's shop at Caxley, the business of choosing the present was undertaken seriously. We surveyed jam dishes, dessert services and fruit bowls, and I had great difficulty in steering them away from several distressing objects highly reminiscent of Mrs Pratt's collection. One particularly loathsome teapot fashioned like a wizened pumpkin exerted such a fascination over the whole party, that I feared Miss Gray might have to cherish it under Mr Annett's roof, but luckily, the man who was attending to us, with most commendable patience, brought out a china biscuit barrel, sprigged with wild flowers. It was useful, it was very pretty and it was exactly the right price. We had returned to Fairacre, after ices all round in a tea-shop, very well content with our purchase.

Excitement ran high, for the presentation was to be made at the end of the afternoon, just before breaking up for seven weeks' holiday. No wonder that eyes were bright, and fidgeting was impossible to control!

The vicar arrived in good time, bringing with him an unexpected end-of-term present for me – a bunch of roses from the climber which Mrs Bradley had admired on the day of the fête. Then the infants came into my room with Miss Gray shepherding them. They squeezed into desks with their big brothers and sisters, and the overflow sat cross-legged in the front, nudging each other excitedly.

The vicar made a model speech wishing Miss Gray much happiness and presented her with a carving set from the managers and other friends of the school. I gave Miss Gray my present next, as I guessed the children would like to see her receive it. As it was table linen they were not particularly impressed, and in any case they were far too anxious to see their own parcel handed over.

Joseph Coggs had been chosen to present the biscuit barrel. He advanced now, from behind my desk, holding the present gingerly in both hands. He fixed his dark eyes on Miss Gray's brogues and said gruffly: 'This is with love from us all.'

An enormous roar broke forth, hastily quelled to silence as Miss Gray undid the paper. Her delight was spontaneous and the children exchanged gratified smirks. She thanked us all with unwonted animation and then, putting her parcels carefully on the piano top, sat herself at the keys to play our last hymn of the term.

The vicar said grace; drawings and other treasures were collected, and with a special farewell to Cathy, John and Sylvia, general goodbyes were said and Fairacre School streamed out into the sunshine, free for seven long weeks.

Jimmy Waites could read now. He had had his tea and was sitting on the rag rug in his mother's kitchen, his fair head bent over a seed catalogue. There were certainly some formidable words in it, which he had had to ask his mother's help for . . . 'Chrysanthemum,' for instance, and 'Heliotrope' but 'Aster' and 'Anchusa' and even 'Sweet Alyssum,' he had worried out for himself, and he glowed with pride in this new accomplishment.

'You've done all right, this first year,' approved Mrs Waites who was pinning up her freshly-washed hair at the kitchen sink. She glanced through the window at Cathy, who was practising hand-stands by the wall, and whose mop of dark hair hung down into the dust of the yard. She noticed with pleasure how shapely and sturdy were her daughter's upthrust legs.

'Do her good to get more exercises and that at the new school,' she said aloud to herself. She let herself think for a brief, happy moment of Cathy's handsome father. Proper well-set-up he'd been, everyone agreed, a lovely dancer, and had played a sound game of football once or twice for Fairacre. If young Cathy took after him she'd be a real good-looking girl.

She leant forward anxiously to peer in the mirror. Now that

her hair was drying, the golden glints that the free shampoo (This Week's Amazing Offer) had promised its users were becoming apparent.

'As long as it don't get *too* bright,' thought Mrs Waite, in some alarm, 'I know it said "Let your husband look at you anew," but there's such a thing as making an exhibition of yourself.'

For a moment she was tempted to rinse her locks again in clear rainwater, but vanity prevailed. Anyway, she comforted herself, her husband would probably not notice anything different, even if she turned out auburn. Sometimes she wondered if those ladies up in London, who wrote the beauty hints, really had first-hand knowledge of husbands' reactions to their earnest advice.

Next door Joseph Coggs was submitting unwillingly to his mother's ministrations with the loathsome hair lotion.

'Prevention is better than cure!' Nurse had said dictatorially to the cowering mother. 'Once a fortnight, Mrs Coggs, or it will be the *cleansing station*!' If she had said the gates of hell, Mrs Coggs could not have been more impressed, and faithfully every other Friday evening, Joseph was greeted on his return from school with a painful dowsing and rubbing with 'the head stuff.'

'You ask Miss Read about the twins?' queried the mother, her fingers working like pistons in and out of the black hair.

'Ah!' jerked out Joseph. 'Her said you was to come and see her any time.'

'All right for her,' grumbled Mrs Coggs. 'Any time, indeed! The only minute I has to spare is while your father's wolfing down his tea afore making off to the "Beetle"!'

She released the child suddenly, and he made off, smoothing his greasy locks flat with his hands.

At the door he paused. 'Say! I give Miss Gray our present s'afternoon, and said a piece Miss Read learnt me!'

'Did you now?' answered his mother somewhat mollified at this honour to the family. 'What you give her then?'

'A biscuit barrel. Oh, and I forgot!' He fished in his pocket and produced sixpence. 'The vicar gave it to me for saying my piece all right.'

His mother's face softened a little.

'Well, that was real kind. You best put it where your father can't see it.' She went to the cupboard to find the evening meal. Once she'd got them all settled, she told herself, she'd slip up and see if Miss Read would have them two terrors after the holidays. Into everything, every blessed minute, and Arthur back at the 'Beetle' more than ever, and another baby on the way she'd bet a pound.

Joseph, lingering in the doorway, sensed the change in the atmosphere, and knew that his few moments of sympathy had flown. Sighing, he slipped into the garden and sought solace by the side of the baby's pram. Kicking and gurgling, his little brother looked up at him and Joseph forgot, in a moment, his unhappiness. With an uprush of joy he remembered his sixpence, his afternoon's triumph, and the fact that for seven long weeks he would be free to enjoy the company of his adored baby.

At that moment the future Mrs Annett was measuring the front bedroom at Beech Green for new curtains, happily unaware of the 'mortal damp' and Mrs Pringle's gloomy forecast of coming events in that ill-fated apartment. She was to be married in ten days' time, from the home of her Caxley friends, owing to the recent death of her mother. She wondered, as she strained upwards to the curtain-pole, if she would ever get all the things done that she wanted to do, in those few days.

Mrs Nairn, in her last fortnight as Mr Annett's housekeeper, was mounted on a chair, adjusting the tape-measure. A cloud of dust blew down from the ledge above the window.

Miss Gray gave a horrified gasp.

'Comes in a day, the dust, don't it,' remarked Mrs Nairn comfortably.

Miss Gray made no answer, contenting herself with the thought that in a week or two's time, under its new mistress's regime, their house would be clean from top to bottom for the first time for many years. What her poor darling had had to suffer, she thought to herself, no one could tell. But at least the future should make amends, and she was determined that her husband should be the happiest man in the kingdom.

*

Meanwhile, Linda Moffat, perched up on the dining-room table, listened to her mother and Mrs Finch-Edwards gossiping, as they adjusted the hem of her bridesmaid's frock.

'Four of them, there will be. Three little nieces and Linda. Wasn't it sweet of her to ask Linda too?'

'Very kind. What's her own frock like?'

Mrs Moffat told her at some length, and Linda lost interest as the technical details of ruching, darts, cut-on-the-cross and other intricacies were bandied between them.

At last the hem was pinned up, Linda was released from her half-made frock, and allowed to play in the garden while the two friends settled in armchairs, Mrs Finch-Edwards with her feet up, in approved style, on a footstool, embroidered by Mrs Moffat in earlier days.

'How will you manage without Miss Gray?' she asked. It was a delicate subject, and she decided that a plain approach might be best. Mrs Moffat seemed eager to be forthcoming.

'As a matter of fact, I thought I'd take in dressmaking in a small way. It might make the beginnings of a little business and then in time—' She faltered and Mrs Finch-Edwards came to the rescue.

'You mean, you still think we might, one day, go into this together?'

'I know with the baby coming and so on, you'll be tied; but it won't be many years before we both have more leisure. What do you think?'

Mrs Finch-Edwards put down the bib she was embroidering, and looked soberly at her friend.

'It would be a beginning. You know it's dress-designing we've both got a flair for. If we could persuade the customers to let us design for them, and we were recommended—'

Mrs Moffat broke in excitedly. 'We could get a team of dressmakers, couldn't we, if the thing worked?'

'I've got a little money coming to me in a few years' time from an aunt of mine in Scotland. It might just about set us up.'

The two women gazed at each other, half-fearful, half-enraptured. Little did they realize, on that summer evening, that the foundations of a flourishing future firm (named after Mrs Finch-Edwards' only daughter) were well and truly laid, and that the little girl, now skipping energetically outside in the garden, would become one of the most glamorous and publicized models in the world of fashion.

It was very peaceful in my garden. I sat shelling some peas which John Pringle had brought me, enjoying the warm evening sun.

In the elms, at the corner of the playground, the rooks cawed intermittently, and from the quiet schoolroom came the distant clank of Mrs Pringle's scrubbing-pail.

'Might as well make a start, first as last,' she had remarked morosely to me as she stumped in, limp accentuated, after she had had her tea. Occasionally, I could hear a snatch of some lugubrious hymn in Mrs Pringle's mooing contralto.

I thought, as the shelled peas mounted higher in the basin, of all the changes that had taken place in this last school year. We had parted with Miss Clare, enjoyed Mrs Finch-Edwards' boisterous session, welcomed Miss Gray, and, a rare thing indeed, seen a wedding planned for one of the staff of Fairacre School.

The three new children, who had entered so timorously on that far September morning, were now part and parcel of Fairacre School. Each had added something to the life of our small school; that little microcosm, working busily, within the larger one of Fairacre village.

I watched the swifts, so soon to go, swoop screaming over the garden, and wondered if Mr Hope, that unhappy poet-schoolmaster, who had lived here once, had sat here, as I was doing now, looking back. He, and, for that matter, all my predecessors, whom I knew so well from the ancient log-book, although I had never seen their faces, must have joined in the hotchpotch of fêtes, sales, outings, festivals, quarrels and friend-ships that make the stuff of life in a village.

The click of the gate roused me. There, entering, were Mrs Cogg and her two little daughters. They gazed about them with apprehension, with monkey eyes as dark and mournful as their brother's.

I put the past from me, and hurried down the path to meet my future pupils.

*

High above, on St Patrick's spire, the setting sun had turned the weathercock into a bird of fire. Phoenix-like, he flamed against the cloudless sky, looking down upon our miniature school world and all the golden fields of Fairacre.

If you have enjoyed

Village School

don't miss

Village Diary

the next novel in
Miss Read's Fairacre series
also available in paperback from Orion.

Price: £6.99
ISBN 0-7528-7743-7

Turn the page to read an extract.

JANUARY

As I have been given a large and magnificent diary for Christmas – seven by ten and nearly two inches thick – I intend to fill it in as long as my ardour lasts. Further than that I will not go. There are quite enough jobs that a schoolmistress just *must* do without making this one a burden.

Unfortunately, the thing is so colossal that I shan't be able to carry it with me, as the adorable Miss Gwendolen Fairfax did hers, so that she 'always had something sensational to read in the train'.

It was a most surprising present for Amy to have given me. When we first taught together in London, many years ago, we exchanged two hankies each, I remember; and since she cropped up again in my life a year or so ago, it has been bath salts on her side ('To make you realize, dear, that even if you are a school teacher there is no need to let yourself go completely') and two-hankies-as-before on mine.

When Amy handed me this present she remarked earnestly, 'Try to use it, dear. Self-expression is such a wonderful thing, and so vital for a woman whose life is – well, not exactly abnormal, but restricted!' This smacked of Amy's latest psychiatrist to me, but after the first reaction of speechless fury, I agreed civilly and have had over a week savouring this *bon mot* with increasing joy.

Mrs Pringle, the school cleaner, told me yesterday that Miss Parr's old house at the end of the village has now been turned into three flats. The workmen have been there now for months; they arrived soon after her death, but I hadn't realized that that was what they were doing. A nephew of Miss Parr's now owns it, and has the ground floor. A retired couple from Caxley evidently move into the top floor this week, and a widower, I understand, has the middle flat.

'A very nice man too,' Mrs Pringle boomed menacingly at me. 'Been a schoolmaster at a real posh school where the boys have to pay fees and get the cane for nothing. Not in his prime, of course, but as Mrs Willet said to me at choir practice, there's many would jump at him.' Mrs Pringle eyed me speculatively, and I can see that the village is already visualizing a decorous wooing, culminating in a quiet wedding at Fairacre Church, with my pupils forming a guard of honour from the south door, with the aged couple hobbling down the path between them.

I said that I hoped that now that the poor man had retired, he would be allowed to rest in peace, and went out to clean the car. This is my latest and most extravagant acquisition – a small second-hand Austin, in which I hope to be able to have wonderful touring holidays, as well as driving to Caxley on any day of the week, instead of relying on the local bus on Tuesdays, Thursdays and Saturdays as heretofore. So far I have not been out on my own as I am still having lessons from an imperturbable instructor in Caxley, who thrives on clashing gears, stalling engines and a beginner's unfortunate confusion of brake and accelerator. Miss Clare, that noble woman, who taught the infants at Fairacre for many years, says that she will come out with me 'at *any* time, dear, whether you feel confident or not. I am quite sure that you can master anything.' Am touched, but also alarmed, at such faith in my powers, and can only hope that she never meets my driving instructor.

Miss Clare spent the evening with me recently and our conversation turned, as it so often does, to life in Fairacre in the early years of this century, when Miss Clare was a young and inexperienced pupil-teacher at this village school. I love to hear her reminiscing, for she has a tolerant and dispassionate outlook on life, born of inner wisdom and years of close contact with the people here. For Miss Clare, 'To know is to forgive,' and I have never yet heard of her acting in anger or in fear, or meting out to a child any punishment that was hastily or maliciously devised.

Her attitude to those who were in authority over her is as wide and kindly as it always was to the small charges that she taught for forty years.

We were talking of Miss Parr, who had died recently. She had been a manager of Fairacre School since the reign of King Edward the Seventh, and was a stickler for etiquette. It appears that one day she met Mrs Willet, now our caretaker's wife, but then a child of six, in the lane, and was shocked to find the little girl omitted to curtsy to her. At once she took the child to its mother, and demanded instant punishment.

'But surely—' I began to protest. Miss Clare looked calmly at me.

'My dear,' she said gently, 'it was quite understandable. It was customary then for our children to curtsy to the gentry, and Miss Parr was doing her duty, as she understood it, by correcting the child. No one then questioned her action. "Other days, other ways" you know. It's only that now, sometimes, looking back – I wonder—' She put down a green pullover she was knitting and stared meditatively at the fire.

'When you say that no one questioned the actions of his superiors, do you mean that they were automatically considered right or that verbal protestations were never made, or what?' I asked her.

'We recognized injustice, dear,' answered Miss Clare equably, 'as clearly as you do. But we bore more in silence, for we had so much more to lose by rebellion. Jobs were hard to come by, in those days, and no work meant no food. It was as simple as that.

'A sharp retort might mean instant dismissal, and perhaps no reference, which might mean months, or even years, without a suitable post. No wonder that my poor mother's favourite maxim was "Civility costs nothing." She knew, only too well, that civility meant more than that to people like us. It was a vital necessity to a wage-earner when we were young.'

'Was she ever bitter?'

'I don't think so. She was a happy, even-tempered woman, and believed that if we did our best in that station of life to which we had been called, then we should do well. After all, we all knew our place then. It made for security. And here, in Fairacre, the gentry on the whole were kindly and generous to those they employed. You might call it a benevolent despotism, my dear – and, you know, there are far worse forms of government than that!'

Miss Clare's eyes twinkled as she resumed her work and the room was filled again with the measured clicking of her knitting needles.

Tuesday was a beast of a day; foggy and cold, with the elm trees dripping into the playground. Two workmen arrived from Caxley to see to the school skylight over my desk: it must be the tenth time, at least, that it has received attention since I came here just over six years ago. Usually, it is Mr Rogers, from the forge, who has the job of clambering over the roof, but the managers decided to try the Caxley firm this time, hoping, I imagine, that it might be better done by them. The village, of course, is up in arms at this invasion of foreigners, and Mr Rogers wears a martyred expression when he stands at the door of his smithy. I am confident that he will soon be in a position to smile again, as the skylight has defied all comers for seventy-odd years – so the school log-books say – and I doubt whether any workmen, even if hailing from the great Caxley itself, will vanquish it.

One man, in Mrs Pringle's hearing, said loudly that 'it was a proper bodged-up job,' so that, of course, will inflame passions further. Mrs Pringle, who was scrubbing out the school dustbins at the time, drew in her breath for so long, with such violence, that I thought she would burst; but only her corsets creaked under the strain.

Tea, at Miss Clare's, was the bright spot of the day. We had a lardy cake which was wonderfully hot and indigestible, and conversation which was soothing, until I was putting on my coat when Miss Clare shattered me by asking if I had yet met a very nice man, a retired schoolmaster, who had come to live in Miss Parr's old house.

I am beginning to feel very, very sorry for this unfortunate man, and have half a mind to ring him up anonymously, advising his early removal from Fairacre if he wishes to have an undisturbed retirement.

The last day of the holidays has arrived, and, as usual, half the jobs I intended doing have been left undone. No marmalade made, no paint washed down, only the most urgent mending done, and school starts tomorrow.

It all looks unbelievably clean over there. I staggered back with the fish tank and Roman hyacinths, all of which have sheltered under my school-house roof for the past fortnight. Miss Gray – Mrs Annett, I mean – will have a smaller class this term, only sixteen on roll, while mine will be twenty-three strong.

The stoves are miracles of jetty brilliance. Mrs Pringle must have used pounds of blacklead and enough energy to move a mountain to have produced such lustre. Woe betide any careless tipper-on of coke for the next few days!

Term has begun. Everyone is back with the exception of Eileen Burton, who has, according to the note brought by a neighbouring child, 'a sore throat and a hard, tight chest.' Can only hope these afflictions are not infectious.

The workmen have found it necessary to remove the whole frame of the skylight, so that, having had a clear two weeks to do the job undisturbed, they now tell me that we must endure a flapping and smelly tarpaulin over the hole in the roof, while a new window-frame is made in Caxley. Straight speaking, though giving me some relief, dints their armour not at all as blame attaches, as usual, to other members of the firm 'higher-up and back in Caxley, Miss', so that I can see a very uncomfortable few days ahead.

The children appeared to have forgotten the very elements of education. Five-times table eluded them altogether, and my request to write 'January' on their own, met with tearful mystification. Having walked round the class and seen such efforts as 'Jamwy,' 'Ganeree' and 'Jennery' I wrote it on the blackboard with dreadful threats of no-play-for-a-week for those who did not master its intricacies immediately.

The vicar called, just before we went home, in his habitual winter garb of cloak, biretta and leopard-skin gloves. Surely they can't stand another winter? I only wish I had such a serene outlook as Mr Partridge's. He greeted us all as though he loved every hair of our heads, as truly I believe he does. I see that he has 'Jesu, Lover of my Soul' on the hymn list this week, but haven't the heart to tell him that I think it painfully lugubrious and quite unsuitable for the children to learn.

I invited him over to the school-house to tea and ushered him into the dining-room, where the clothes-horse stood round the fire bearing various intimate articles of apparel and a row of dingy polishing rags which added the final touch of squalor. Not that he, dear man, would have worried, even had he noticed the things – but that clothes-horse was whisked neatly into the kitchen in record time!

I have just returned from a day out with Amy. She rang me up last night to say that there was a wonderful film on, which I must see. It would *broaden* me. It was about Real life. I said that I'd looked through the *Caxley Chronicle* this week, but I thought that both cinemas were showing Westerns.

'Caxley?' screamed Amy down the wire. Did I think of nothing but Caxley and Fairacre? When she thought of what promise I had shown as a girl, it quite upset her to see how I'd gone off! No, the film she had in mind was to be shown in a London suburb – the cinema specialized in revivals, and this was a quite wonderful chance to see this unique masterpiece. She would pick me up at 10.30, give me lunch, and bring me back to the wilds again.

I mentally pulled my forelock and said that that would be lovely.

Amy's car is magnificent and has a fluid fly-wheel, which as a gear-crashing learner, filled me with horrid envy. We soared up the hills, passing everything in sight, while Amy told me that life, even for a happily married woman, was not always rosy. James, although utterly devoted of course, was at a dangerous age. Not that he was inattentive; only last week he gave her these gloves – she raised a gargantuan fur-clad paw; and the week before that these ear-rings – I bent forward to admire a cluster of turquoises – and this brooch was his Christmas present, and was fantastically expensive – but she found she was beginning to suspect the *reason* for so many costly presents, especially when he had been away from home, on business, so frequently lately.

I said: 'Why don't you ask him if there is anyone else?' Amy said that was so like me – it wasn't surprising that I stayed single when I was so – well, so *unwomanly* and *unsubtle*. No, she could handle this thing quite skilfully, she thought, and in any case it was her duty to stick by dear James through thick and thin. Unworthy thoughts crossed my mind as to whether she'd stick so nobly if James suddenly became penniless.

We arrived in the West End; Amy had no difficulty in finding a car park with an obsequious attendant who directed our footsteps to the hotel where Amy had booked a table. I was much impressed by the opulence of this establishment and said so. Amy shrugged nonchalantly: 'Not a bad little dump,' then, scanning the menu, 'James brings me here when he wants to be quick. The food is *just* eatable.'

We ordered ham and tongue, with salad, which Amy insisted on having mixed at our table, supervising the rubbing of the bowl with garlic (which I detest, but could see I must endure), the exact number of drops of oil, etc., and expressing horror that the whole was not being turned with wooden implements.

I would much rather have had my salad fresh and been allowed to ask for Heinz mayonnaise, in constant use at home, but realized that Amy was enjoying every minute of this worldly-woman-taking-out-country-mouse act, and would not have spoiled it for her for worlds.

Over lunch, Amy continued to tell me about James's generosity, and disclosed the monthly allowance which he gives her. This, she said, she just manages on. As the sum exceeds easily my own modest monthly cheque as a headmistress, I felt inclined to remind her of our early days together, teaching in a large junior school not many miles from this very hotel, when we thrived cheerfully on a salary of just over thirteen pounds a month, and visited the theatre, the cinema, went skating and dancing, dressed attractively and, best of all, were as merry as grigs all the time. As Amy's guest, however, I was bound to keep these memories to myself. As I watched her picking over her salad discontentedly I remembered vividly a meal we had had together in those far-off days. It must have been towards the end of the month for I know we spent a long and hilarious time working out from the menu which would fill us up more for eightpence – baked beans and two sausages, or spaghetti on toast.

The cinema was rather hard to find, in an obscure cul-de-sac, and the film which Amy had particularly come to see had just begun. It was so old, that it seemed to be raining all the time, and even the bedroom scenes – which were far too frequent for my peace of mind – were seen through a downpour. The women's hair styles were unbelievable, and quite succeeded in distracting my grasshopper mind from the plot; either puffed-out at the sides, like the chorus in *The Mikado*, or cut in a thick fringe just across the eyebrows, giving the most brutish aspect to the ladies of the cast. Waist lines were low and busts incredibly high evidently when this film first saw the light.

The supporting film was of later vintage, but, if anything, heavier going. Played by Irish actors, in Irish countryside in Irish weather, and spoken in such a clotted hotchpotch of Irish idiom as to be barely intelligible, it dealt with the flight of a young man from the cruel English. Bogs, mist, mountains, girls with shawls over their heads and bare feet splashing through puddles, open coffins surrounded with candles and keening, wrinkled old women, all flickered before us for an hour and a half – and then the poor dear was shot in the end!

We emerged into the grey London twilight with our eyes swollen. Drawn together by our emotional afternoon we had tea in a much more relaxed mood than lunch, and drove back in a pleasantly nostalgic atmosphere of ancient memories shared.

It was good of Amy to take me out. A day away from Fairacre in the middle of January is a real tonic. But I was sorry to see her so unhappy. I hope that I am not so wrong-headed as to blame Amy's recent affluence for her present malaise. As anyone of sense knows, money is a blessing and I dearly wish I had more – a lot more. I should have flowers in the classroom, and my house, all the year round, buy a hundred or so books, which have been on my list for years, and spend every school holiday travelling abroad – just for a start. I think the truth of the matter is that Amy feels useless, and has too little to do.

She used to be a first-class teacher and was able to draw wonderful pictures on the blackboard, that were the envy of us all, I remember.

School has now started with a vengeance, and I have heard all Mrs Annett's infants' class read – that is, those that can. She has done wonders since she came a year ago. The marriage seems ideal and Mr Annett has lost his nervous, drawn look and put on quite a stone in weight. He brings her over from their school-house at Beech Green each morning, and then returns to his duties there as headmaster. I was glad that the managers persuaded her to continue teaching. She intended to resign last September, but we had no applicants for the post, and as the Annetts had had a good deal of expense in refurnishing she decided to work for a little longer. The children adore her and her methods are more modern than Miss Clare's were. She has a nice practical grasp of infant-work problems too, as an incident this morning proved. I was sending off for more wooden beads for number work. 'Make them send square ones,' she said. I looked surprised. 'They don't roll away,' she added. Now, that's what I call intelligent! Square they shall be!

Joseph Coggs appeared yesterday morning with a brown-paper carrier bag. Inside was a tortoise, very muddy, and as cold and heavy as a stone. It was impossible to tell if it were dead or only hibernating.

'My mum told me to throw an old saucepan on the rubbish heap at the bottom of our place,' he told me, 'and this 'ere was buried under some old muck there.' He was very excited about his find and we have put the pathetic reptile in a box of leaves and earth out in the lobby – but I doubt if it will ever wake again. The children, I was amused to hear, were hushing each other as they undressed.

'Shut up hollering, you,' said Eric in a bellow that nearly raised our tarpaulin, 'that poor snail of Joe's don't get no rest!'

The weather is bitterly cold, with a cruel east wind, which flaps our accursed tarpaulin villainously. (The frame 'has been a bit held-up like, miss. Funny, really.') Scotland has had heavy snow, and I expect that Fairacre will too before long.

The vicar called in just before the children went home to check up numbers for our trip to the Caxley pantomime on Saturday. Two buses have been hired as mothers and friends will come too, as well as the school managers who generously pay the school-children's expenses. It is the highlight of dark January.

Mr Annett called to collect his wife – she won't be coming with us to the pantomime – and the vicar remarked to me on their happiness, adding that, to his mind, a marriage contracted in maturer years often turned out best, and had I met that very pleasant fellow – a retired schoolmaster, he believed – who had come to live at Miss Parr's?

An almost irresistible urge to push the dear vicar headlong over the low school wall, against which he was leaning, was controlled with difficulty, and I was surprised to hear myself replying politely that I had not had that pleasure yet. Truly, civilization is a wonderful thing.

I met Mr Bennett as I walked down to the Post Office the other evening. He is the owner of Tyler's Row, four thatched cottages at the end of our village. The Coggs live in one, the Waites next door to them, an old couple – very sweet and as deaf as posts – in the next, and a tight-lipped, taciturn woman, called Mrs Fowler lives in the last.

Mr Bennett had been to collect the rent from his property.

Each tenant pays three shillings a week and parts with it with the greatest reluctance.

'I gets to hate coming for it,' admitted poor Mr Bennett. He is beginning to look his seventy years now, but his figure is as upright and trim as it was when he was a proud soldier in the Royal Horse Artillery, and his waxed moustache ends still stand at a jaunty angle. He has his Old Age Pension and lives with a sister at Beech Green, who is ailing and as poor as he is.

'Every door's the same,' went on the old soldier. ' "Can't you set our roof to rights? Can't you put us a new sink in? Come and look at the damp in our back scullery. 'Tis shameful." And what can I do with twelve bob a week coming in? That's if I'm lucky. Arthur Coggs owes me for three months now. He's got four times the money coming in that I have, but he's always got some sad story to spin.'

The old man took out a pipe and rammed the tobacco in with a trembling finger.

'I shall have to give this up, I s'pose, the way things are. I went to get an estimate from the thatcher over at Springbourne about Tyler's Row roofs. Guess how much?'

I said I imagined it would cost about a hundred pounds to put it in repair.

'A hundred?' Mr Bennett laughed sardonically. '*Two* hundred and fifty, my dear. There's nothing for it, it seems, but to sell 'em for about a hundred and fifty while I can. Mrs Fowler would probably buy 'em. She's making a tidy packet at the moment. Pays me three bob, my dear, and has a lodger in that back bedroom who pays her three pound!'

'But can she?' I asked, 'Didn't you have a clause about subletting?'

'No. I didn't. When Mrs Fowler first come begging, all pitiful as a widder-woman, to have my cottage, I was that sorry for her I let her have the key that day. Now the boot's on the other foot. She earns six pounds a week up the engineering works in Caxley, gets three off her lodger, and greets me with a face like a vinegar bottle. "Proper hovel," she called my cottage, just now, "I sees you don't give me notice though, my dear," I says to her, "and, what's more, that's a real smart TV set you got on the dresser there." Ah! She didn't like that!'

The old man chuckled at the thought of his flash of wit, and blew out an impudent dart of smoke from under the twirling moustaches.

'I've just met Mrs Partridge,' he added. 'She asked me if I'd like to give something towards the Church Roof Fund. I give her a shilling, and then I couldn't help saying: "If I was you, Ma'am, I'd call along Tyler's Row for donations. There's something in the nature of forty or fifty pounds going in there each week. You should get a mite from that quarter."'

He leant forward and spoke in a conspiratorial whisper.

'And you know what she said to me? "Mr Bennett, I'm afraid

their hearts don't match their pay packets!" Ah, she sees it all – she and the vicar! Times is topsy-turvy. There's new poor and new rich today, but one and all has got to face responsibility, as I see it. You can't take out of the kitty and not put in, can you, Miss?'

The bus to Beech Green and Caxley drew up with a horrible squeaking of brakes. The driver, a local boy, from whom no secrets are hid, shouted cheerfully to Mr Bennett above the din.

'Been to collect them rents again? Some people has it easy, my eye!'

The old soldier cast me a quizzical glance, compounded of despair and amusement, mounted the steep step, and vanished among the country passengers.

I have been inflicted with a sudden and maddening crop of chilblains and can scarcely hobble around the house. No shoes are big enough to hold my poor, swollen, tormented toes and I am shuffling about in a pair of disreputable slippers which had been put aside for the next jumble sale, but were gratefully resurrected. A very demoralizing state of affairs, and can only put it down to the unwelcome appearance of snow.

The pantomime was an enormous success. Both buses were full, and Cathy Waites, looking very spruce in her new Grammar School uniform, sat by me and told me all about the joys of hockey. 'I'm right-half,' she told me, eyes sparkling, 'and you have to have plenty of wind, because if you're right-half you have to mark the opposing left-wing, and she's usually the fastest runner on the field.' There was a great deal more to the same effect, and in answer to my query about her prowess in more academic subjects, she said: 'Oh, all right,' rather vaguely, and went on to tell me of the intricacies of bullying-off.

Jimmy, her little brother, who sat by his mother opposite, was eating a large apple as he entered the bus, and in the six miles to Caxley consumed, with the greatest relish, a banana, a slab of pink and white nougat, a liquorice pipe, a bar of chocolate cream, and a few assorted toffees. This performance was only typical of many of his companions.

Joseph Coggs sat by me when we settled in the Corn Exchange. The pantomime was 'Dick Whittington,' and he was overawed by the cat, whose costume and make-up were remarkably realistic.

'How does he breeve?' he asked, in a penetrating whisper.

I whispered back. 'Through the holes in the mask.'

'But he don't have no nose,' objected Joseph.

'Yes he does. It's under the mask.'

'Well, if it's under the mask, how does he breeve?'

We were back where we started, and I tried a different approach.

'Do you think he's holding his breath all this time, Joseph?'

'Yes, he must be.'

'Then how can he talk to Dick?'

Still not persuaded of the cat's 'breeving,' or half-believing it to be a real cat all the time, Joseph subsided. He loved every minute of the show – which was an extraordinarily good amateur performance – and nearly rolled out of his seat with excitement, when I pointed out Linda Moffat to him on the stage. She was a dazzling fairy queen, in a creation of her clever mother's making, and her dancing was a pleasure to watch. I was glad that Mrs Moffat, with her friend Mrs Finch-Edwards, had been able to come with us this afternoon to witness Linda's success.

Several of the cast were known personally to the Fairacre children and storms of clapping greeted the appearance of anyone remotely known.

'Look,' said Eric, on my other side, clutching me painfully, 'there's the girl what drives the oil-van Tuesdays.' And he nearly burst his palms with rapturous greeting.

When we emerged, dazzled with glory, into the winter twilight, the snow was falling fast. Queen Victoria on her lofty pedestal wore a white mantle and a snow-topped crown. The lane to Fairacre was unbelievably lovely, the banks smooth as linen sheets, the overhanging beech trees already bearing a weight of snow along their elephant-grey branches, while the prickly hawthorn hedges clutched white handfuls in their skinny fingers.

St Patrick's clock chimed half-past five when we stepped out at Fairacre, after our lovely afternoon. Our footsteps were muffled, but our voices rang out as clear as the bells above, in the cold air.

Mrs Pringle asked me as we got off the bus if I had ever tried Typhoon tea? I successfully curbed an insane desire to ask her if it brewed storms in tea-cups? I enjoyed this *bon mot* all through my own tea-time.

A most peculiar thing happened today. A very loud knocking came at the door of my classroom, while we were chanting the pence table to 100, in a delightful sing-song that would make an ultra-modern inspector's hair curl – and when I opened it, a strange young man tried to push in. I manoeuvred him back into the lobby, shut the classroom door behind me, and asked what he wanted. He was respectably dressed, but unshaven. He said could he come in as he liked children? Thinking he was an eccentric tramp on his way from the Caxley workhouse to the next, I told him that he'd better be getting along, and shooed him kindly into the playground.

An hour later Mrs Annett came in from P.T. lesson, somewhat perturbed, because the wretched creature had hung over the school wall throughout the lesson making inane remarks. At this, I went out to send him off less kindly. By now, he had entered my garden and was drawing patterns on the snowy lawn with a stick.

When I asked him what he was supposed to be doing, he flummoxed me by whipping out a red, penny note-book and saying he'd come to read the gas meter. As we have no gas in this area, this was so patently silly that I made up my mind at once to get the police to cope with the fellow.

As I opened my front door he tried to come in with me, whining: 'I'm so hungry – so hungry,' and grinning vacantly at the same time. By now I was positive I had a madman on my hands, and very devoutly wished that I had not seen a gripping film about Jack the Ripper in Caxley recently, the horrider parts of which returned to me with unpleasant clarity.

'Go to the back porch,' I ordered him, in a stern school-marmish voice, 'and I will give you some food.' Luckily he went, and I sped inside, locked front and back doors, and rang Caxley police station in record time.

A reassuring country voice answered me, and I began to feel much better as I described the man, until the voice said, in a leisurely manner: 'That'd be the chap that ran off from Abbot-sleigh yesterday' – our local mental home.

'Heavens—!' I began, squeaking breathlessly.

'He wouldn't hurt a fly, miss,' went on the unhurried burr, 'he'll be scared stiff of you. Just keep him there if you can and we'll send a car out – it'll be with you in a quarter of an hour.'

I didn't know that I cared to be told that the man would be scared stiff of me, but I cared even less for the suggestion that I cherished him under my roof. Nor did I like the thought of the forty children, of tender years, for whom I was responsible, not to mention Mrs Annett, whose husband I should never dare to face, if aught befell her. All this I babbled over the telephone, adding: 'I'm just going to give him a drink and some bread and cheese, in the back porch, so please try and get here while he's still eating.'

'Car's gone out already. Never you fear, miss. Treat him like one of your kids,' said my calm friend, and rang off. I handed a pint of cider, half a loaf, and a craggy piece of hard cheese through the kitchen window, and with subtle cunning of which I was inordinately proud, supplied him with a small, very blunt tea-knife which should slow up his progress considerably. I couldn't make up my mind whether to dash back to the school and warn Mrs Annett, or whether to hang on in the house until the police car came. In the end I stayed in the kitchen, watching the meal vanish all too swiftly and edging my mind away from that pursuing film.

After the longest ten minutes of my life, the car drew up. Two enormous, cheerful policemen came to the back porch, and asked the man to come for a ride with them.

He went, without a backward glance, still clutching the plate and mug. Once inside the car he finished his cider, and I emerged from the front door and collected his utensils, wishing him a heartfelt good-bye into the bargain.

The policeman said: 'Thank you, miss, thank you!' and drove off, still beaming.

When I caught sight of myself in the mirror in the lobby I was not surprised. The most scared schoolmistress in the United Kingdom crawled thankfully back to her noisy class, and never breathed a word of reproach to the dear souls.

I really believe that my chilblains have finally gone, and wish I knew. what had cured them – if anything particular, apart from Time-the-great-healer, I mean.

The various suggestions for their rout have ranged from (1) calcium tablets (Mr Annett); (2) painting with iodine (Mrs Annett) which I tried, but found tickly to do and so drying that the poor toes started to crack as well as itch; (3) treating with the liquid obtained from putting salt in a hollow dug in a turnip (Mr Willet, the caretaker); and (4) thrashing with a sprig of holly until the chilblains bleed freely (Mrs Pringle). Needless to say I did *not* attempt the last sadistic assault on my suffering extremities.

I am very worried about Joseph Coggs. His mother was taken to hospital last week with some internal trouble connected with the recent baby. Mrs Pringle, who usually describes any ills of the flesh in the most revolting detail, has seen fit on this occasion to observe an austere reserve about Mrs Coggs' symptoms, taking up the attitude that there are some things that the great army of married women must keep from their less fortunate spinster sisters. The twins, who usually adorn the front desk in Mrs Annett's room, and a toddler brother, have been sent to Mrs Coggs' sister in Caxley; but as she has no room for Joe he is living a hand-to-mouth existence with his father (who is completely useless) and with Mrs Waites, the next-door neighbour, 'Keeping an eye on him.'

It all sounds most unsatisfactory to me. The child is not clean, has not had his clothes changed since his mother's departure, and looks frightened. Mr Willet told me more this morning when he came to fill the two buckets for the school's daily drinking-water from my kitchen pump.

'I don't say nothing about Arthur Coggs' drunkenness,' announced Mr Willet, with heavy self-righteousness. 'Nor don't I say nothing about his hitting of his wife now and again – that's his affair. Nor don't I say nothing about an occasional lift round the ear for his kids – seeing as kids must be brought up respectful – but I *do* say this. That's not right to leave that child alone in that thatched cottage with the candle on, while he spends the evening at the "Beetle and Wedge." Why, my wife and I we hears him roaring along home nigh on eleven most nights.'

'But the candle would have burnt out by then,' I said, horror-struck. 'Joe would be alone in the dark.'

'Well, I don't know as that's not a deal safer,' said Mr Willet, stolidly. 'Better be frightened than frizzled. But don't you upset yourself – Joe's probably asleep by then.'

'I thought Mrs Waites was looking after him.'

'Mrs Waites,' said Mr Willet, with a return to his pontifical manner, 'is well-meaning, but flighty. Never room for more than one thought at a time in her head. Maybe she takes a peep at him, once in a while; maybe she don't.'

Discreet questioning of Joseph, later in the morning, revealed that the state of his home affairs was even worse than suspected. The candle *does* go out, Joseph is too terrified to get out of bed, so wets it, and Arthur Coggs on his return from the pub shows his fatherly disapproval by giving the child what Joe calls 'a good hiding with his belt.' (On seeing my appalled face, Joe added, reassuringly, that 'he didn't use the buckle end.') Joseph's stolid acceptance of this state of things was rather more than I could bear, and I went to Mrs Waites' house during the dinner hour to see what could be done.

She was sensible and helpful, offering to let Joe share her little Jimmy's bed downstairs. This sounded ideal, and I promised to see Arthur Coggs about the scheme after tea. He – great bully that he is – was all smiles and servility, and confessed himself deeply grateful to Mrs Waites, as well he might be.

Luckily, Mrs Waites, who is a confirmed novelette-reader, has just read in this week's number, she told me, a story about a friendless child who later becomes heir to a dukedom and landed estate (no taxes mentioned), and suitably rewards a kindly woman who befriended him in his early years. This has sweetened her approach to young Joe considerably, and though I can't see a dukedom looming up for him, he will doubtless never forget his own neighbour's present kindness. Flighty Mrs Waites may be, but thoroughly sweet-natured, and I can quite see how she has fluttered so many male hearts.

I seem to be more than usually financially embarrassed, and when I had paid the laundry man this morning, found I was left with exactly two shillings and sevenpence. Mrs Pringle brought me my weekly dozen eggs this afternoon, and I had to tip out my threepenny bits which I save in a Coronation mug, and make up the balance.

That's the worst of being paid for December and January just before Christmas! I shall have to take my Post Office Savings Book into Caxley on Saturday morning and withdraw enough to keep me going until the end of the month. It would be more than my reputation's worth to withdraw it here in the village. Mr Lamb, our postmaster, and brother to Mrs Willet, would fear I was either betting or keeping two homes. Meanwhile I must just embezzle the dinner money.

We have had pouring rain all day and – miraculously – the new skylight seems weatherproof.

I gave my class an arithmetic test. Linda Moffat did exceptionally well, and should go on to Caxley High School in two years' time if she keeps on at this rate. She grows prettier daily, and will doubtless become a heart-breaker.

All goes well with Joseph, thank heaven, and the child is cleaner than I've ever seen him. He and Jimmy are great friends and I can see that Mrs Annett is going to have to squash those two young gentlemen before long.

Joe's tortoise seems to have turned round in his box. At my suggestion that perhaps somebody lifted him round, there were hot denials, and I apologized hastily. He certainly looks less dead.

Jim Bryant, our postman, brought our cheques today. He was never more welcome. I gave Mrs Pringle and Mrs Annett theirs, but could not find Mr Willet. However, he had a noisy coughing attack in the lobby this afternoon, which reminded me of his rightful dues.

'There now,' he said, when I gave the cheque to him, 'this is a real surprise!'

Bless him, if anyone ever earned his humble wage it's Mr Willet! He copes with coke, water, dead leaves, dustbins, snow, intruding animals varying from Mr Roberts' cows to black beetles – not to mention the buckets from our primitive lavatories – with unfailing cheerfulness. May he endure for ever!